# A WEDDING PROMISE

The Bajan drums pounded. Isobel thrilled; she was experiencing her body in a way a proper Englishwoman would never dream.

Beckett danced in front of her, his body surprisingly fluid, his strong arms reaching out to touch her. But she sidestepped him and twirled around, just out of his reach. His eyes burned brighter as he watched, and a dangerous smile played upon his lips.

Again he tried to touch her. Again she moved out of range. Isobel relished the power that flowed through her. She twirled again, but abruptly found herself pressed up against his hard body like a wet sheet. It took her breath completely away.

He gripped her arms and held her to him, his eyes traveling over her body. His hips pressed against hers and for an awful moment she worried about such a sensual exchange in public. She closed her eyes.

Beckett pressed harder against her, and she felt her skirts being raised, his hands on the bare skin of her thighs, running up towards— Her eyes flew open, and she saw Beckett's face inches away from her own. Raw desire was painted upon it.

"Shall I make you burn for me, Isobel?" he asked, his voice dangerously quiet. "Shall I worship you with my body, the way I vowed to do at our wedding?" He pulled her closer. "Shall I f

# The MARRIAGE BARGAIN

## MICHELLE McMASTER

LEISURE BOOKS  NEW YORK CITY

A LEISURE BOOK®

August 2000

Published by

Dorchester Publishing Co., Inc.
276 Fifth Avenue
New York, NY 10001

Cover art by John Ennis
www.ennisart.com

ISBN 0-8439-4750-0

Printed in the United States of America.

*For*
*Paulette Phillips*

*My mother*
*My cherished friend*

# ACKNOWLEDGMENTS

I owe a great deal of thanks to a great many people.

First and foremost, to my cousin, critique partner, and best friend, Julianne MacLean; I couldn't have completed this book without you. Also to my sister, Julia Smith, for your valued support and creative input.

To my parents, Paulette and Norm, for always believing in me and encouraging me to pursue my dreams.

Special thanks to my agent, Elaine Koster, for your expert guidance and enthusiasm. Also to my editor, Christopher Keeslar, for your insight and dedication.

Thanks to Charlene Lokey and Andy Wood for their assistance in manuscript preparation. Also to my computer wizard, Mark MacDonald, for working miracles both great and small.

Thanks to my RWA Chapter, Toronto Romance Writers, for all your support and inspiration. Also to Dr. Stephen MacLean for answering my characters' medical questions. Thanks to my cousin, Charles A.J. Doucet for your excellent photographic skill.

And for various other acts of kindness, thanks to: Claire Delacroix, Karyn Monk, Margaret Moore, Brad Smith, Chris Szego, and all of my family and friends.

To all of you, my most heartfelt thanks and gratitude.

# ACKNOWLEDGMENTS

# *Prologue*

*Hertfordshire, England, 1814*

"Ashes to ashes . . . dust to dust," the parson croaked. He raised his hands up to the heavy gray sky that pelted the mourners with icy rain. "Receive these, thy servants, O Lord, Charles and Clarissa. . . ."

Isobel stared down at the twin coffins in the cold ground and felt her heart turn to lead in her breast. A shovelful of dirt landed on top of her father's casket with a thud.

She closed her eyes against the pain, and felt the cold raindrops mix with the tears that trickled down her face.

*Now, she was alone.*

She felt a touch on her arm, and looked up into the dark eyes of Sir Harry Lennox. He smiled down at her, and a chill infused her blood.

He was trying to comfort her, she thought, and

she almost wanted to laugh at the absurdity of that notion.

She had never liked her father's old friend—never trusted him. She thought of the day only a few months ago when she had surprised Sir Harry and her mother in the conservatory; he'd been clutching her mother's arm in a firm grip, and they had been arguing.

Later, her mother had forbidden Isobel to mention a word of it to her father. Her mother's eyes had been haunted, frightened, and she'd desperately crushed Isobel to her breast. She had warned her daughter never to be alone with Sir Harry, but why? Her mother had never spoken of it again.

*What had they argued about that day?*

*And was it just coincidence that Sir Harry had been visiting Hampton Park the very day her parents had been killed by highwaymen?*

Isobel stared helplessly at their coffins, unable to tear her gaze away as each shovelful of dirt covered and hid them from her sight. The finality of it threatened to rip her heart in two.

Sir Harry bent his head down beside her and whispered in a silky voice, "Try not to cry, my dear. You must be brave. You are the mistress of Hampton Park, now, Isobel. You must be mindful of your station."

Making no attempt to hide her hostility, Isobel glared up at the tall, dark-haired man who stood beside her. "I am well aware of my obligations, Sir Harry. My guardian, Mr. Langley, has explained them all to me." She motioned to the man who was heading off to fetch their coach, the man to whom her father had entrusted her care. "With no sons and no other male relations to name as his heir, my father had no choice but to leave Hampton Park to me. I owe it to his and my mother's memory to ensure the estate's protection and prosperity. And I intend to do just that."

"But to do that you will need a *husband*, my dear." Sir Harry reached for her hand. "Have you given any thought to the matter?"

She snatched her hand away.

"No. I have not. My parents have just been buried, sir, and you would have me going to the marriage mart? I will not even consider such a thing until I am out of mourning, in a year's time."

Sir Harry looked pensive. "Of course. But that is not entirely what I had in mind, my dear. You know that I have always been fond of you."

Unable to speak, Isobel simply stared at him in disbelief.

"As your father's oldest and most trusted friend, I must tell you that he and I discussed the idea . . . and he was most pleased by the notion of a match between us."

A sickening stab of fear pierced Isobel's heart. "I do not believe you. He would never have suggested such a thing. Never."

Sir Harry chuckled condescendingly. "My dear, you *are* quite naïve in the ways if the world, aren't you? You've been sheltered here, on this country estate. But it is time for you to grow up, Isobel. It is time to take your place in the world as mistress of Hampton Park . . . and later, as *Lady Lennox*."

Isobel remained silent, fighting against the feelings that swirled within her.

"Your father wanted it to be so, Isobel."

She stepped away from him, seething with anger. "And what of my mother? Did *she* want it, too? I daresay she didn't. She warned me about you, Sir Harry. But she needn't have. I have eyes. I have ears. And I have seen and heard things over the years that told me you were a man to be wary of."

The man was silent, looking down at her with the glittery dark eyes of a snake.

Isobel continued. "I know what you want, Sir Harry. You want Hampton Park. I think you have always wanted it. And now that my parents are dead, you think to take possession of it by making me your bride." She shook her head. "That is never going to happen, I promise you."

He smiled a thin, cold smile.

"You are upset, my dear. Overwhelmed with grief. And I have been too hasty in my proposal. When you are through observing your year of mourning, we shall talk more of it."

"No, we shall not talk more of it. I will *not* marry you, Sir Harry. Not in a year's time, or a hundred years' time."

Sir Harry made to reply, but stopped when he saw Isobel's guardian approaching. She breathed a sigh of relief when Mr. Langley took his place at her side. He and Sir Harry made their bows, then Sir Harry backed away and turned toward his own carriage.

Mr. Langley led Isobel to their carriage then handed her in. She sat forward to look out the window, to reassure herself of Sir Harry's departure.

He walked with long strides toward his carriage, but before he reached it, he looked back over his shoulder and pinned Isobel's gaze with a dark, menacing one of his own.

As her carriage pulled away down the road, Isobel watched her father's friend until she couldn't see him anymore. Horrified, she knew that she hadn't seen the last of Sir Harry Lennox. Of that she was certain.

# Chapter One

*One Year Later*

Isobel stepped back into the shadows, her blood turning to ice water in her veins.

So . . . Sir Harry had come back for her as he'd promised. He had given her a year to mourn, and now he was here at Hampton Park to claim what he thought was his.

Her stomach tightened into a knot of fear and disbelief. She listened intently to the two men arguing in the library, still unwilling to accept what she was hearing.

Did Sir Harry actually think she would willingly marry him?

Isobel's heart hardened with cold anger.

Not as long as there was breath in her body. She would never let Sir Harry take possession of the estate her father had worked so hard to build. And she would never let him take possession of *her*.

"Certainly, it is time for Isobel to marry—" Her guardian's voice floated out of the library to where Isobel listened near the open door.

"It is past time for her to marry. The girl is almost twenty," Sir Harry scoffed. "I'm doing you a favor, Langley, taking the girl off your hands. Of course, I would give you a generous gift to retire on, as well."

*Favor indeed.* Isobel felt her blood heat with anger. Only Sir Harry would have such audacity!

"Isobel's father entrusted me with her care, Sir Harry," her guardian said. "Since her parents' deaths a year ago, she has relied on me to look after her best interests, and it has been an honor to do so." He cleared his throat. "I'm afraid I do not see marriage to you as being in her best interest at all. There are many things to consider—not the least of which is that Isobel is the heiress to a substantial fortune, and you, sir, are deeply in debt."

"Pure speculation, I assure you," Sir Harry said, coldly.

"That is not what my solicitor says."

"Well, your solicitor is misinformed. I have many business interests. I will bring much to the marriage."

"You will bring disaster! Do you think I don't know why you want so badly to marry her, Lennox? What man wouldn't want to marry her? A beautiful young girl with a handsome estate, and enough wealth to turn even the prince regent's head? I know exactly what you're after, and you won't get it! Just because she has no family—"

"You know nothing! A man like you could never understand. I am in *love* with her."

Isobel covered her mouth to keep from making a sound.

*Love? The man didn't know the meaning of the word!*

"Even if that were true," her guardian continued, "it is hardly reason for me to give my consent. You are nothing more than a gold-digger. I would be a fool to agree to such a match."

"Oh, but you're wrong, Langley—about a great many things. You would be a fool *not* to agree."

"Are you threatening me, Sir Harry?"

"Call it what you will. But make no mistake. I shall have Isobel. And I shall have Hampton Park, with or without your consent."

"Over my dead body, Lennox!"

There was a brief silence, then, "If you insist."

Sir Harry's words were followed by the sounds of a scuffle, then an ungodly scream sliced through the night. Isobel tried to stifle her own gasp of horror as she stood immobile, listening helplessly to her guardian's death cries.

She heard the muffled thud of a body falling to the floor. Sir Harry's dark frame appeared in the doorway, silhouetted against the yellow light that spilled out of the library.

"Ahhh." He purred, staring at her with dark, flashing eyes. "*Dessert*."

Isobel turned to flee, but he was quick, his blood evidently still fired by the heady thrill of murder. His iron grip encircled her arm like a shackle, impossible to break.

"Let me go! Let me go—*Murderer!*" she shouted, flailing against him.

"Let you go?" He looked down at her with eyes as black as hell itself. His gaze flicked to the body on the floor. "After all I've done to make you mine?"

"I am *not* yours. I will *never* be yours, do you understand?" Isobel struggled anew.

"I beg to differ, my dear." He pulled her close.

She could feel his breath on her neck. It smelled of brandy.

She turned her face away and saw her guardian's body—the handle of a knife embedded in his chest. A pool of blood stained the Persian rug around him deep crimson. She felt a wave of queasiness and fought hard against it.

"You *will* be mine when you marry me, my sweet."

"Marry you!" Isobel spat, fighting against the hands that imprisoned her. "I would sooner marry the devil himself!"

Sir Harry smiled coldly and pulled her closer. "What a happy coincidence. Mother always said I had the devil in me."

Isobel's gaze returned to the dead man on the floor. Perhaps it was true that the devil himself stood before her now, for what other creature could have murdered her guardian so brutally?

"Killing Edward won't get you what you want, Sir Harry." Isobel stared up at him, refusing to cower. "I shall go to the magistrate. You will hang for murder."

He smiled down at her and chuckled. It was a cold, hollow sound. "You think the magistrate will arrest me, do you? Well, it will be my word against yours. And who do you think they'll believe, hmm? Me, a *baronet*? Or a young girl who is known to be *mentally unstable?*"

"I am not mentally unstable. *You* are!"

He shook his head, sadly. "You see? If you insist on spouting nonsense like that, it will not be difficult to convince them. I assure you, they will believe me. Perhaps I could even convince them that you killed Mr. Langley. That shouldn't be too hard. A lover's quarrel gone wrong, perhaps?"

"They would never believe such a thing."

He smiled darkly. "Won't they? You'd be surprised what people will believe, my dear. I am very well-connected. My business interests have put me in contact with a vast array of influential people, many of whom owe me . . . *favors*, shall we say? I could call on anyone from a pirate to a magistrate, and they would be only too happy to assist me. It would be terribly easy to come up with papers declaring *me* your new guardian, now that Mr. Langley has so conveniently expired."

Isobel struggled anew as fear crept up her spine like a spider. "My *guardian*? No. You can't!"

He jerked her closer to him. "As I said, I can be most persuasive when it comes to getting what I want. And I *always* get what I want."

"Hampton Park will never be yours. And neither will I." Sir Harry tightened his grip, but Isobel ignored the pain. "I would rather die first."

"Silly girl." He stroked her cheek with the back of his hand. Isobel twisted her face away, but he grabbed it roughly and forced her to look at him. "I could make you wish you were dead. *Don't tempt me.*"

"And what will you do?" she demanded. "Tie me to my bed so I can't escape?"

He looked pensive for a moment. "Charming idea. I hadn't thought of that." Then he smiled a dark, horrid smile, and pulled her tight against him. "I must say, the thought of you tied down and helpless fires my passion for you even more."

She spat in his face. "You disgust me!"

He glared down at her, holding her with one strong hand as he wiped his cheek. "You have much to learn, Isobel. And I shall be only too happy to teach you. But why wait for our wedding night to enjoy such delights? We can get started right now. Then you'll have no choice but to marry me. What other man would want you when you're no longer a virgin?"

Isobel flailed against him, but he held her fast. He laughed as she tried to break free.

"You can never escape me, do you hear?" His voice rasped in her ear. "There is nowhere to hide, Isobel. I can find you anywhere. Don't you see? It's useless. Face your fate!"

"That's what I'm doing," she ground out, and brought her knee up hard between his legs.

Instantly, his grip broke and he doubled over in pain, cursing loudly. Isobel spun away from him, but one hand shot out and caught her dressing gown. The delicate fabric ripped, but not fast enough to set Isobel free.

In desperation, she reached for a heavy crystal vase, still full of the white roses her guardian had brought into the house that day. She turned and sent the vase flying at Sir Harry's face. He tried to duck, but the vase caught the side of his head, and he reeled backwards onto the floor.

Without waiting to assess the extent of Sir Harry's injuries, Isobel fled.

She dashed down the hall and cold stone steps of the house, and as she ran into the night she heard Sir Harry's voice on the wind yelling after her.

"I'll find you Isobel! No matter where you go— I'll find you!"

# Chapter Two

Quite entirely against his wishes, Lord Beckett Thornby sailed through the doorway of the Goose and Gunner and landed facedown on the damp cobblestone street.

A moment later, his friend Alfred landed squarely on top of him.

"And don't come back, ye young lords!" the portly owner bellowed from the pub's arched doorway. "I don't care whose sons ye are!"

"Does this mean we are no longer friends?" Beckett punctuated his soft question with a hiccup.

"That's right. That's exactly what it means!" the innkeeper yelled.

Alfred rose to his feet and reached down to pull his friend up.

"I'll send someone 'round tomorrow to pay for the damages." Beckett's head rang like the bells of St. James.

"That's what ye said last time, m'lord, and your notes of credit were refused."

"A mistake, surely." Beckett chuckled.

"It's not me place to say, Lord Thornby, though all o' London knows ye haven't a pot to piss in. And I can't be rebuilding me taproom every time ye challenge Lord Fanshaw to a boxing match. So, I'll thank ye kindly if the next time ye be wantin' a drink, ye take your business elsewhere." The pub-owner wiped his sweat-covered brow and marched back into the Goose and Gunner, slamming the door behind him.

"A fine end to a fine evening," Alfred said sarcastically. "The only thing missing is your bride. Who, I may remind you, we came out to find."

Beckett dusted off his buckskins and regarded his friend with narrowed eyes. "Well, if we had gone to Lady Tippington's assembly as I'd wanted, I might have found the wealthy bride I seek. Instead, you dragged me here."

"Maggie McDuff seemed keen." Alfred gestured toward the tavern. "Had her hands all over you—her lips, as well. And she does pour a grand glass of ale. And there was Hester Scrimshaw, the *amply* endowed washerwoman. At least you could look forward to a lifetime of clean clothes. Of course, you could always go crawling back to Cordelia."

Beckett gave him a look.

Alfred smirked. "Perhaps my Great Aunt Withypoll could find a suitable bride for you."

"Oh, no. Not after the last offering she made to *you*. Lady Hortense Higginbotham? I tell you, I did not know it was possible for a woman to giggle uninterrupted for almost an entire day—without hurting herself."

"Beckett, how cruel!" Alfred admonished.

"Well, I didn't see *you* offering for her hand."

"No. I was afraid if I asked her, she'd just *laugh*."

The men chuckled and thumped each other on the back.

"I suppose we've worn out our welcome, Alfred, old man," Beckett said, looking forlornly back at the inn. "You really must stop getting into rows with that Fanshaw fellow."

"Don't go blaming this on me, Beckett. I distinctly remember you calling him a . . . what was it, now? A 'mutton-headed squeaker.' Oh, and also a 'windy, weasel-gutted jingle-brains'."

"Ah," Beckett replied, "but you're forgetting that he first called you a 'gawky, rattle-pated gollumpus,' which, as you know, is a contradiction in terms. I was merely leaping to your defense, old boy, if not the defense of the King's English."

Beckett and Alfred continued down the dark street, toward the corner of Poole and Lansdowne. They finally reached the intersection, and waited for a coach in the misty lamplight. A fine drizzle dampened their clothes and turned the cobblestones glossy.

Beckett leaned up against the cold lamppost, folding his arms across his gray and black-striped waistcoat. The jacket had disappeared long ago, whether before or during the fisticuffs, he couldn't remember.

He cocked his head—was someone moaning? Certainly he was in his cups, but that had never before affected his hearing. Beckett listened again for the strange sound.

"There it is again!"

"Wha—"

"Shh!" Beckett hissed.

The two men held on to each other unsteadily and listened as the sound seemed to emanate from a pile of rubbish alongside the gutter. It sounded like an animal in distress. Beckett crept toward the source of the sound, and in the dim lamplight, he saw a bedraggled cat hunching over a pile of fish heads in the trash-strewn alley.

Beckett held out his hand to the animal, carefully moving closer to it. But as he neared, the skittish cat sprang away, revealing a sight that made Beckett stumble backward in surprise.

In the misty lamplight, he saw the face of a young woman lying motionless, surrounded by a stinking pile of rubbish that covered her like a vile blanket. Her eyelids were closed and dirt smeared her cheek . . . but even in such a condition, she possessed an ethereal beauty that made his gut tighten to look at.

A small bare foot stuck out from under a ripped sack. Beckett gingerly lifted the sack away, wrinkling his nose at the smell of decaying fish and cabbage that rose from the gutter. The stench made his stomach roil.

The girl's only clothing was a dirty, damp nightdress, which was molded like a second skin to her body beneath. Black grime and dried blood covered the soles of her feet. Her head rested at an awkward angle, and her arms and legs were askew. She looked like a doll that had been thrown away by a careless child.

A surge of protectiveness rushed through his veins, and he fought against it. He didn't want to feel anything for any woman, least of all this mysterious girl. And yet the urge to take her into his arms, to shield her from whatever had brought her here lingered. Unable to stop himself, he reached out to touch her face.

"It looks like some unfortunate trollop has been thrown out for the night," said Alfred. "Cover her back up and let's go."

"What?"

"You heard me." Alfred stepped back and crossed his arms. "Let's go. I'm tired and I'm wet, now leave the wench where she belongs, in the gutter!"

Nausea washed over Beckett in waves as the odor of excrement and rotting meat filled his nostrils. He couldn't believe his friend was immune to the danger this girl was in, foxed as he was or not.

"Alfred, are you blind? She's not from the gutter! Look at her nightdress. Lady Granville has one that is quite similar, if memory serves me right." Beckett fingered the detailed embroidery on the collar.

"And how would you know what Lady Granville's nightdress looks like?

Beckett rolled his eyes heavenward. "Nothing but flim-flam, Alfred, I assure you."

"I'll wager you know more about Lady Granville's nightdress than Lord Granville does, and about what's under it, as well!" Alfred kicked Beckett's shin lightly in admonishment. "But the fact remains that the girl must be a harlot."

"What of it? You should have no prejudice against her if she is, having gotten to know a few quite intimately yourself. It's no reason to leave this poor girl to die."

"Well, what would you have us do, Beckett?"

"We can't leave her here.

"Oh, can't we?" Alfred sighed, folding his arms. "At least try to wake her and see if she's alright. If she is, we'll go on our way."

Beckett nodded. His head was still slightly fuzzy from drinking and being tossed into the street, and the obvious had escaped him. If the girl was fine, they could be good samaritans and help her home. Yes, that was a good plan.

"Miss . . . Miss?" Beckett reached down and

touched her cold, bare arm. There was no reaction from the unconscious girl. He tried again, shaking her shoulder with a little more vigor. "I say, are you alright?"

Still, she did not move.

"Perhaps she's dead, Beckett," Alfred whispered, as if his words might offend her should that be the case.

Beckett grasped a clammy wrist and felt for a pulse. He found a strong heartbeat.

"No, she's quite alive, old man. But she might not survive the night if we leave her here. Help me get her up."

"Oh, why don't we just leave well enough alone? What business is it of ours?"

"Think of what might happen to the girl if we don't take her with us," Beckett insisted.

"Think of what might happen if we *do*. 'Zooks, man—do you really want to be responsible for some wayward girl, whatever her story is? Can't we leave her at one of the hospitals?"

"Alfred, I wouldn't leave one of my worst enemies in one of those hospitals, and you know it. It's too late to call a physician. That will have to wait until morning. Now, you lift her shoulders and I'll take her feet."

Alfred groaned, putting his hands under the girl's arms and lifting her upper body. Beckett took her ankles.

"This is a bad idea, old man."

"You never want to do anything heroic."

"No, I never want to do anything utterly stupid, that's all. I still remember how you insisted it was our duty as officers to save those kittens from Napoleon's guns in Salamanca. It wasn't enough that you'd rescued a convent full of virgins, oh no! You had to save their *cats*, too. I still have the scars from that little escapade. And then there was the cow that we helped to give birth—a very messy episode, as I recall." Alfred shifted the girl's weight and leaned closer. "And need I mention that irate goose who tried to peck us to death when we rescued its eggs from being Wellington's breakfast?"

"Oh, quit complaining. You couldn't turn your back on any of those creatures any more than I could—just as you can't turn your back on this poor girl now. Besides, we're going to be heroes, you mutton head."

Beckett saw the girl's head droop to the side. A mass of damp honey-blond curls fell away from her face and revealed a nasty bruise near her hairline.

The thin nightdress clung wetly to her body, so that it was almost invisible. Beckett wanted to be a gentleman and avert his eyes from this involuntary display of her charms. He wanted to ignore the effect such sweetness was having on his own body. He wanted to tell himself she was just another stray, like the swan he had found walking down the middle of the Strand, or the puppies he had rescued from the pond in Hyde Park. But she wasn't.

Her innocent beauty, her vulnerability overwhelmed him.

Beckett adjusted the weight of her in his arms. Though she was far from heavy, his muscles strained to keep her aloft. The fisticuffs at the inn had exhausted him.

A coach slowed beside the curb and stopped, the black horse stomping its hoof impatiently. Steam blew from its nostrils into the cold, damp night. The two men gingerly placed their silent cargo inside, under the driver's suspicious gaze.

"Take us to Covington Place!" Beckett yelled to the white-haired coachman.

As the vehicle rumbled down the street, Beckett quietly gazed at the girl across from him. He watched her face in the moonlight as her head jiggled against the side of the cab, and he fought the desire to pull her into his arms and cradle her.

What was he doing rescuing this strange girl in the middle of the night? This was no stray kitten he was bringing into his home. She could be anything from an innocent lost lady to a killer, for heaven's sake. And yet, he'd never been able to turn away a creature in need. But would he later regret this penchant for rescuing strays?

He laughed at himself. He already had so many regrets, what was one more?

# *Chapter Three*

As the coach turned onto Curzon Street, Beckett ran his hands over his face, trying to wake himself up. He felt so tired that he was almost nauseous. His head pounded like a drum and his belly burned. Luckily, they wouldn't be returning to the Goose and Gunner anytime soon. The rotgut he drank at that inn would surely kill him one of these days.

The coach came to a jolting halt in front of No. 10 Covington Place, and Beckett felt his stomach lurch like a ship on the high seas. He gazed down at the mysterious girl before him. How was he going to get her inside when all he wanted to do was crawl into his bed and stay there for at least twenty-four hours?

Beckett groaned and opened the door of the coach, stepping out. He reached back in to receive the girl's feet as Alfred lifted her shoulders. Finally, they managed to get her out and entirely into Beckett's sagging arms, and headed up the walk.

The ornately carved door of the townhouse opened silently, as if by magic. Beckett's valet, Hartley, stood behind it as they entered the foyer. Since Beckett could only afford one manservant, the long-suffering Hartley assumed the duties of butler, as well. Sitting on the man's shoulder was Beckett's African gray parrot, Caesar. Both looked at Beckett with interest.

"The lady, sir?" Hartley asked.

"A poor woman in distress. We will be looking after her for a few days. Let's get her upstairs." With a nod to the valet, Beckett commanded him to light their way.

*"Hello. You're a pretty bird,"* said Caesar.

"Hello, Caesar," Beckett replied as they trudged up the staircase. He said to Hartley, "What's he still doing awake?"

*"Still awake,"* said Caesar.

"I put him to bed, sir," Hartley explained, "along with Master Monty, Miss Cleo and the puppies—as you instructed. But Master Caesar simply would not keep quiet. He kept screeching and jabbering until I could take no more. I'm afraid he does that when you are out late at night, sir."

The familiar clicking of twenty toenails accompanied them on the stairs, and Beckett glanced down to see his mongrel, Monty, bounding up beside them onto the landing. "Come to see the new addition, eh, Monty?"

The big brown dog panted up at him in response, his thick, pink tongue hanging out of his mouth.

"What luck, Monty," Alfred whispered. "Your master has found you another playmate!"

"Hartley, we'll need fresh linens and a bath for

30

our wayward miss. She'll sleep in my room tonight," Beckett ordered.

"Your room, my lord?" Hartley asked, an eyebrow raised.

"Yes, my room. And don't look at me like that. I'll sleep next door in the sitting room. I want to keep an ear open if she awakens. She may be frightened by the unfamiliar surroundings."

The servant turned to go, but Beckett swung around and blocked him with the girl's dangling legs. "The girl has nothing to fear. I promise to be a perfect gentleman. But I'm sure she thanks you for your concern." He gave the older man a wicked grin.

Hartley nodded his graying head, fighting a smile of his own. "This must certainly be the most interesting stray you've rescued, my lord. But I'm afraid she smells as bad as the rest of them put together." He chuckled and moved down the dark hall with Caesar still on his shoulder, lighting the sconces as he went.

Beckett looked at the unconscious girl in his arms and took another whiff, turning up his nose. "My word, I think he's right."

Alfred nodded, stifling a yawn. "Why can't you rescue sweet-smelling females?" He turned to go down the hallway toward Beckett's bedchamber, then stopped abruptly. "But who shall bathe her, Beckett?"

"I have no idea . . . but it certainly won't be you."

"Oh, trying to keep her all to yourself, are you?"

Beckett turned from him, adjusting the girl's weight in his arms. Lord, but she was getting heavier by the second.

With Monty at his side, he walked down the short hallway to his bedchamber. Once inside, he carefully laid the girl's limp body on the huge bed, while Alfred followed him and lit the candles.

The girl's hair spread around her shoulders like a halo on the linen-covered pillow. Beckett pulled the covers around her and watched her for a moment. No, she certainly wasn't a trollop, so what was she? *Who* was she?

Hartley hurried into the room carrying linens, towels and blankets, then returned again with a pitcher of warm water. Crossing the room to the washstand, he poured the water into a blue porcelain basin.

"Thank you, Hartley. That is all," Beckett said, and the valet took his leave.

Beckett set the linens on the edge of the bed. "I'm quite sure she won't awaken this evening—we shall try to solve the mystery tomorrow. Now, Alfred, help me get her undressed."

"I didn't think you needed any help undressing a woman, Beckett."

"I don't, you fool! But I'm bloody tired and I want to go to bed, so give me a hand."

"No, Beckett, this was your idea. I'm not interested in playing nursemaid." Alfred folded his arms in front of his chest, and leaned closer to the unconscious girl. "I'll just have a look at her when you've cleaned her up."

"You know, Alfred, sometimes you can be a damned nuisance."

"Poor Beckett. Perhaps it's being such a bloody good Samaritan that's a damned nuisance."

Beckett gave Alfred a warning look, but his friend's words gave him pause. *Gads*, was he doing the right thing? All he knew was that if they had left the girl there in the street, he wouldn't have been able to sleep tonight.

Beckett looked Alfred straight in the eye. "And if that had been me tonight, Alfred, and you didn't know me . . . would you have come to my rescue?"

"Of course not! I would have left you to rot." Alfred rested his fists on his hips and sighed. After a moment he added, "You know what the streets are like these days. You never know who might be lurking 'round a corner, especially in that area."

"But would you have helped this woman if I hadn't forced you to?" Beckett prompted.

"If I say yes, will you be quiet? Let us cease with these hypotheticals. She'll be gone soon, anyway."

Beckett felt his eyes grow heavy as he stared at Alfred. "I wonder who she is, really. . . ."

"You always did love a good mystery, old man." Alfred started for the door. "I'm going downstairs and have myself another drink. Then I am going to sleep in my usual spot: The Blue Room."

"You're leaving me to do this alone?" Beckett grinned at Alfred, then yawned.

Alfred chuckled, saying over his shoulder, "You know, I just thought of something—if you ever call her 'my pet,' it won't be the least bit of a lie. Enjoy bathing her!"

The door closed and Beckett turned his attention to the unconscious girl lying across his bed. His arms and legs felt like lead, and his eyes watered from yawning. Normally he might have been more excited at the prospect of washing a beautiful woman, but he was so tired, he just wanted to go to sleep.

Monty scooted himself closer to the bed and put his chin on it, his big, black nose sniffing energetically at the myriad smells covering the unconscious girl. His tongue snaked out and licked her hand.

"Monty, no!" Beckett whispered, frowning. "I need you to act as chaperon." The dog moved back, but continued to look at the girl as if she were the sweetest-smelling thing he'd ever encountered.

Beckett tapped his chin and surveyed the situation. Perhaps he could just get her out of the damp nightdress and dry her off—instead of giving her a more thorough wash. But beautiful or not, the fact remained that she smelled like the contents of a sewer. He moved closer, and a quick appraisal showed that most of the filth was on her dress.

Beckett lifted up her arm and brought his nose near. Her skin was soft to the touch and her dainty hands and fingers were free of calluses. That lent credence to his earlier assumption. She wasn't a common street-walker, of that he was certain.

Beckett reached down to remove the wet clothes from her clammy body. His gaze fell on the taut nipples straining against the thin fabric. Even in the dim light, he could see their shadow.

*Gadzooks*—he felt like a peeping Tom in his own bloody bedchamber!

Despite the vision before him, his eyelids began to droop as he reached for the lacy collar of her nightdress. Still, he told himself, it wouldn't be the first time he'd undressed a woman with his eyes closed—although on most occasions he'd been kissing her at the same time.

He felt his way to the buttons down the front of her dress. There were so many of them, and the damn things were as tiny as pebbles. They were probably made this way to discourage young women from hasty trysts with lovers. And they were cleverly the size of a woman's fingers, not a man's. This was illogical indeed, he thought groggily, considering it was usually a man's hands that unfastened the tiny buttons—at least here in London. In the country, perhaps it was different. . . .

Finally he was through them all, and he eased the garment from her shoulders. His hands lingered there, and his eyes fluttered open as his forearm brushed against what lay below those creamy shoulders. The softness whispered across his skin like rose petals in the wind.

He was suddenly quite awake.

Beckett bit his lip as he tried not to feast his eyes on her now naked breasts, but he was drawn to them like bees to honey. His hands itched to touch their snow-white delicacy, and his lips ached to kiss the crowns of softest pink.

He shook his head, trying to keep his thoughts in order, and succeeded in peeling the dress off her warm, wet torso and down around her legs.

Now the girl was completely, beautifully naked, lying vulnerable on the bed before him. Almost painfully, Beckett sensed her nakedness in every inch of his body. It called to him like a siren of the sea.

Steadying his breath, he turned and dampened a soft cloth in the basin. He gently dabbed her face with the cloth, careful to keep the pressure light.

He eased the cloth down along her neck and arms, gently washing away the grime that stained her ivory skin. And every time his fingertips brushed the softness of her, he felt an infusion of warmth spill through his veins.

She moaned and turned her head on the pillow.

Beckett froze.

She did not wake up. He grinned in spite of himself, and shook his head. It was terribly wicked, what he was doing . . . terribly wicked, indeed.

Was it his fault that bathing a woman's body could be so damnably diverting?

Gently, he slid the cloth along her stomach, his

35

groin suffusing with heat as he came to that secret place between her thighs. Oh, he had always loved that part of a woman. He had never understood why the women he'd been with had been so shy about that piece of themselves, why they had not been proud to possess such an instrument of exquisite beauty and pleasure. His hands came very close to her there as he smoothed the wash cloth along her hips and down the creamy skin of her thighs, and he found himself biting his lip to keep control. This bath alone was an exquisite torture.

Then he came to her feet, and was sobered by their terrible state. He had to rinse the cloth many times before he'd removed the last of the dried blood and dirt.

Beneath the filth, her feet were soft and dainty, though marred by shallow cuts. As he had suspected, these were not the feet of a guttersnipe.

Questions turned in his head, quelling the desire that had begun to overtake him.

Who was she? Could she be in danger?

He turned to the end of the bed and reached for the blankets Hartley had brought. Finding a soft, thick one of virgin wool, he placed it on the bed beside her.

Beckett slid his arm under her shoulders and lifted her, feeling his fingers brush the round underside of her breast as his hand reached around to grip her.

It sent a tingle through his stomach.

Pulling the blanket about the girl, he looked down at her face, and again felt that overwhelming need to protect her.

Unable to resist any longer, he reached out to touch the perfect beauty of her face.

As if to remind him of the late hour, a huge

yawn came upon him. Reluctantly he lifted his hand from her cheek, and wiped his watering eyes. He checked her pulse, and felt the soft skin of her wrist growing warmer.

Tomorrow he would tell her that a maid had undressed her. Of course, he didn't employ a maid, but that was a minor point easily addressed.

He yawned again and sat down on the other side of the bed. Where was he going to sleep tonight? Had he really intended to sleep in the sitting room, as he'd told Hartley? Alfred was in the Blue Room, and the other rooms weren't prepared. He didn't feel like waking his valet. The sofa in his sitting room would have to suffice.

He crossed the chamber and beckoned to Monty. "Come on, boy."

Panting calmly, the dog showed no signs of movement.

"Monty, come!" Beckett whispered. In response, the dog moved to the foot of the bed and flopped down on the floor.

"So that's the way it is, eh? One pretty face is all it takes to make you forget your master?"

Monty raised his head and looked at Beckett, then laid it down again.

"Alright, have it your way." He took one candle and blew out the others.

It was difficult to simply leave the girl there all alone in his bed. So, watching her through the golden haze of candle-light, Beckett quoted one of Mr. Shakespeare's sonnets. " 'Is it thy will, thy image should keep open my heavy eyelids to the weary night?' " With one last look, Beckett closed the door behind him.

He made his way toward the sitting room sofa, weariness dragging at him like a clinging child. Resting the candle on the table, he struggled to remove his boots, which hit the floor with a dull thud.

He then stretched out on the firm sofa, and let sleep take him where it would.

# Chapter Four

Beckett rolled over, his eyes still closed. He vaguely remembered stumbling into his bed in the dark, wee hours of the morning.

For some reason, he'd fallen asleep on the sofa in the sitting room. Oh, well, he was in his own bed now, and that was all that mattered.

Half-awake, he flung his arm out and it landed on something soft and warm. It felt like a . . .

*Please, please don't let that be what I think it is.*

Beckett opened his eyes.

It *was* what he thought it was. Gingerly, he removed his hand from the girl's naked breast, but it was too late.

The girl opened her eyes, a look of terror in their golden-brown depths. She opened her mouth, and screamed.

Beckett sprang from the bed like a cat. The girl jumped up as well, not realizing her nakedness until she was standing. She screamed again, her face white as she grabbed the blanket and wrapped it hurriedly around herself. She stared at Beckett as if he had struck her.

Monty skittered up, and tail wagging, barked at all the commotion.

"*Who are you?*" she shrieked, grabbing a nearby candlestick. "Stay away from me—or I swear I'll bash your head in!"

"Please refrain, madam! You will ruin my coiffure, not to mention my health."

"I said, stay away!" she yelled, brandishing the candlestick when he took a step closer.

"I'm staying away, see? Far, far away over here. Now, be a good girl and put that thing down."

"Why? So you can ravish me again?" she shrieked incredulously, pulling the blanket closer around her naked body.

"*Ravish* you? No, no—you misunderstand. I can explain everything, but you must be quiet!" He half-shouted, half-whispered his words, not wanting to wake the household.

"I will *not* be quiet until you explain who you are and why you've brought me here! And what have you done with my clothes?"

"Ah, yes. Your clothes—are not here at the moment."

"*Not here?* I suppose they grew tired of my company and simply walked away?"

Beckett tried not to laugh, but the effort seemed to rile the girl's anger even more. She grabbed a little clock and launched it at his head. Beckett ducked, and just missed having his face rearranged by the marble timepiece.

He stood straight again and whistled. He had to admit—he was impressed by her spirit.

"So you intend to keep me prisoner like this?"

she asked heatedly. "Am I to spend the rest of my days naked in your rooms?"

Beckett paused for a moment, regarding her. She looked like a wild angel, golden hair flowing, creamy shoulders bare, with a mouth the color of roses and eyes that flashed like diamonds. "Don't put ideas into my head."

There was a commotion in the hallway. He heard Hartley's voice: "No, no, Lady Thornby, don't go in there!"

The door creaked open. In his strangest nightmare, Beckett could not have imagined what he would see there, standing in the hall behind his worried valet.

His mother and his solicitor.

They stared with pale, bloodless faces at the scene before them. Beckett realized what it must look like, standing there with a beautiful, half-naked woman in his bedchamber. Of course, being bare-chested himself wasn't going to give the correct impression at all.

"Oh, . . ." his mother cried, her hand to her mouth. Her eyes rolled back in her head and she fainted in a heap of ribbons and lace.

Hartley quickly attended Lady Thornby, but Beckett had the brief thought that his mother resembled nothing so much as a fallen souffle that had been dropped to the floor.

Mr. Livingston of Livingston, Farraday & Peel stood frozen with his great mouth agape, and seemed to be transfixed by the tableau before him. Behind him Martha, the portly cook, mimicked Mr. Livingston's expression but covered her mouth with a flour-stained hand.

Alfred suddenly appeared beside Beckett as well, seemingly quite amused by the scene.

Monty skittered around the room, still wagging

41

his tail and barking loudly at the girl in the blanket. She still brandished the heavy candlestick, and sized up the new arrivals as if to choose who first to clobber.

"Monty, quiet!" Beckett shouted.

The dog hushed, but everyone else seemed to take it as a cue to pelt Beckett with questions, though Lady Thornby was still out cold.

"—What is going on, sir?" said Livingston.

"—Oh, m'lord, who is that lady? What shall we do?" said Martha.

"—I demand to know who all of you people are!" shrieked the girl.

"I said, *quiet*, all of you!" Beckett commanded. To his surprise, it worked. "Martha, would you take the young miss into my chamber and try to quiet her nerves?"

"My nerves don't need quieting," the girl retorted, eyeing the cook distrustfully.

"Come on, now, miss," Martha said. "Just do what the master asks."

"He's not *my* master," she said haughtily. "He hasn't even told me who he is."

"Lord Beckett Thornby, at your service," Beckett said, and made a grand, sweeping bow.

"That means nothing to me." The blanket slipped farther down her shoulder, and she fought to pull it up. "How do I even know that you are who you say you are?"

"I can vouch for Lord Thornby's identity, madam," Mr. Livingston said. "I am his solicitor, and have been for many years. He is of the utmost character and breeding, I assure you."

"I don't care if he's the regent himself. He has brought me here against my wishes, and now I want to leave."

"No one is stopping you, Miss . . ." Beckett prodded.

She sidestepped the question. "You know I can't leave. I haven't any clothes—thanks to you, Lord Thornby."

"We shall procure you some clothes, then, posthaste. And then you may do as you wish. But I insist that you at least stay for breakfast. My reputation would be ruined if it became known I didn't properly entertain my guests." Beckett folded his arms in front of his chest and gave a wry smile. "Well? What shall it be, my dear?"

She seemed to weigh her options, and Beckett felt a wash of relief when she nodded her agreement. He nodded to Martha.

"A pot of strong tea for our guest, then, Martha. And whatever else she desires."

Beckett saw the girl look at him, then. It seemed the implication of his last comment was not lost on her.

Still clutching the candlestick, she followed Martha from the room.

"And you thought bringing her home was a good idea," Alfred whispered into Beckett's ear.

"It seems I've made nothing but a mess of this."

"My thoughts exactly."

Beckett patted his thigh to summon Monty, who trotted over to sit obediently beside his master. Beckett crouched down beside his still-unconscious mother.

"Fetch the doctor, Hartley."

"For the lady, sir?"

"No, for me, after Mother comes 'round."

Alfred chuckled.

"I'm glad you find this amusing," Beckett said, glaring at Alfred, and then at his solicitor. "Livingston, what exactly are you doing here, at this hour of the morning?"

"My lord," offered Mr. Livingston. "It is well past noon. I met Lady Thornby as she was coming to your door. It was then that I was able to share with her the good news."

"What good news, Livingston?"

"Why, of your inheritance, my lord."

"I haven't *got* an inheritance, man. That's my whole problem."

"Oh, but you do, sir. Your mother's cousin, the Earl of Ravenwood, has died without any heirs of his body, leaving you the next in line."

Beckett shook his head. "Lord Ravenwood has both a son and a grandson, Livingston. You are terribly misinformed."

"Actually, my lord, I am very well-informed. The earl's son, Lord Haughton, was killed in a boating accident only days before Lord Ravenwood's own death. Unfortunately, Lord Haughton's only son was with him and also perished in the accident."

Mr. Livingston cleared his throat, as if to introduce his next announcement. "I have the honor, my lord, of naming you heir to the sixth earl of Ravenwood."

Beckett looked from Livingston to Alfred and back again. "Is this some kind of joke?"

"I assure you, it is not," Livingston replied.

"Oh . . . I have swooned . . ." Lady Thornby murmured, regaining consciousness.

Beckett crouched down beside her, assisting Hartley as he struggled to raise Lady Thornby to a sitting position.

"Mother, are you alright?" Beckett asked, daintily adjusting her lace cap from where it had fallen over her eye.

He was rewarded with a hearty slap across the cheek. Well, he thought, as he rubbed the stinging flesh, at least his mother was feeling better.

"I am *not* alright, Beckett," Lady Thornby said

haughtily. "Thanks to you and your disgraceful shenanigans."

The portly lady rose to her feet with much grunting and groaning, slapping at the hands of those who tried to help her.

Lady Thornby pointed her finger at her son and brought it and her pinched face slowly in front of his. "I want to know one thing." She paused for effect, her eyes growing as wide as saucers. "*Who* is that *woman*?"

Beckett knew how utterly absurd his reply was going to sound, but he took a deep breath and said it anyway. "I don't know."

"This is no time for your silly games. Explain yourself!"

"It's no game, Mother. Alfred and I found her outside the Goose and Gunner last night and brought her home with us. That's the truth of the matter."

"Oh!" Lady Thornby exclaimed. "Of all the—"

"It's not what you think."

"I saw a half-dressed hussy in your bedchamber—what should I think?" Her lips compressed into a thin line as she waited for a reply.

"The opposite of what you *are* thinking," Beckett said dryly.

Lady Thornby's voice lowered to a harsh whisper. "To let your own servants see you with a—a *trollop* like that! Shameful."

"I told you; she is not a trollop, Mother. The girl was ill. Alfred and I brought her home and we took her straight to bed—I mean, *put* her straight to bed. I went to sleep in my sitting room, but I must have returned to my own bed without realizing."

"Ha! That is not in the least convincing," his mother huffed.

Beckett ignored her remark. "She was unconscious when we found her, so I don't know who she is. But I'm sure of one thing, she's no strumpet. She obviously doesn't live in the street or her feet would not have been cut and bruised so by the cobblestones. And her dress was not in tatters. It looked quite finely made ... merely soiled."

"That only proves that she's new at the profession and she has a good seamstress," Lady Thornby replied peevishly.

"You're wrong, Mother, and I won't apologize for my actions. She most certainly would have died if we had left her in the street. You know I can't abandon a creature in need."

"You want me to believe she's another one of your *strays*?" Lady Thornby shrieked, disbelief in her eyes. "I am getting old, but my brain is far from addled. I saw what I saw. And what's worse, Mr. Livingston saw it as well."

"Well, I'm sure that Mr. Livingston can be trusted to keep this quiet." Beckett gave a meaningful look to the solicitor. "And now that I'm the earl of Ravenwood, what does it matter how many strays I take in—or if they happen to be animal or human?"

"Actually, my lord, you aren't the earl quite yet," Livingston said.

"But you said that I was the heir."

"So you are, my lord, but there is a stipulation in the sixth earl's will, which is quite standard." Livingston cleared his throat and continued. "The will specifies that the heir must be married at the time the will is executed, or the estate will immediately pass to your cousin, Mr. Coles of Dorsetshire. In fact, I have already received a letter from his solicitor. As per the earl's instructions, the will is to be executed tomorrow. Since Mr. Coles is

46

already married, my lord, I would hasten to find yourself a bride."

Lady Thornby grabbed her son's arm. "I'm sure the Honorable Miss Cordelia Haversham will take you back, under the circumstances."

"Mother, I will choose my own bride, if you please," Beckett said stiffly. "Cordelia Haversham is the last woman in the world that I'd marry. And you well know the reason why."

"But that dreadful business is all behind us now," Lady Thornby said, waving her hand in dismissal. "If only I had known that your father had less sense for numbers than a chicken, I could have stopped him from investing in his reckless schemes."

Lady Thornby yanked her son's arm so that his ear was close and whispered loudly, "Now, we need only ensure Mr. Livingston's promise to keep mum about the disgraceful events he witnessed here, and you can ask Cordelia to be your bride. I have always had an affection for her as well you know. She and I are truly kindred spirits. Her mother has been like a sister to me—we are such close friends. And Cordelia would make a wonderful countess!"

"Mother, I would sooner marry that girl in there!" Beckett stood straight and pointed at the closed door of his bedchamber.

"Oh, don't talk flummery, Beckett," Lady Thornby admonished.

"Perhaps it's not flummery," Beckett said, enjoying the look of horror that had crossed his mother's face. "Perhaps I am quite serious about the idea."

"Fuddle-duddle! It is not your place to choose a bride, especially when that bride will be the next countess of Ravenwood."

"But it *is* my place to be led to the altar in a yoke and put to stud, I suppose."

"Beckett . . . remember yourself!" she sputtered.

"I should be so lucky as to forget." Beckett folded his arms across his chest. "It will be up to me to decide, Mother, not you, or the *ton*, or anyone else. But mark me well, whichever bride I choose, it will certainly *not* be the Honorable Miss Cordelia Haversham."

His mother's eyes flashed. "I've always known you'd be a disappointment to me, Beckett. And now, you've ruined the one thing that would have made me happy—to bring Cordelia Haversham into the family where she belongs. But if you're as intent on ruining your life as your father was, well then, I wish you luck."

"Father did the best he could for us, Mother. He was a kind-hearted man who made the mistake of trusting a swindler. I'm sure he didn't mean to leave us penniless."

"Well, you certainly are your father's son, Beckett," Lady Thornby said coldly. "You've done nothing but embarrass me from the time you could crawl. Always courting trouble, with complete disregard for the scandals you caused with your . . . your swans and bags of drowned kittens, and four-legged riffraff!"

She brought her face close to his and whispered in a mocking hiss, "Well, now you're going to create a real sensation, aren't you? Go on, marry that little trollop in there, or any other hussy you like. It's none of my concern."

With a toss of her head Lady Thornby swept down the hall, stopping at the end of it, dramatically. "I will see myself out," she said, chin high, and disappeared down the staircase.

"I don't know why I bother going to the theater," Alfred said. "I see more drama under your roof than I ever do at Drury Lane."

"So do I," Beckett agreed, shaking his head.

Mr. Livingston donned his hat. "I'll be going then as well, my lord. I advise you to find a bride soon, so that we may proceed with the details of the inheritance. Considering the uncertain state of your finances at present, I should think you'll be anxious to take your new title. Until tomorrow, my lord." The solicitor made a quick bow and left.

Moments later, Martha emerged from the bed-chamber and closed the door quietly behind her.

"How is our guest, Martha?" Beckett asked.

"Restin', m'lord. She took some landanum with her tea. She'll sleep for a bit, I expect."

Beckett nodded. "Let's leave her until she awakens. Then she and I shall have a little chat."

The men sauntered down the hallway and entered the drawing room, Monty following. Beckett flopped down on the sofa and looked at his dog, who sat near him, his tongue hanging out of the side of his mouth and dangling in rhythm with his panting breaths. He looked as if he hadn't a care in the world. Beckett reached out a hand and rubbed Monty's head, bringing an expression of pure ecstasy to the mongrel's face.

"It's been quite a day, Alfred. Looks like I've got some searching to do. Fancy a brandy?"

Alfred brought a bottle and two glasses out of one of the cupboards and sat down next to Beckett. He poured the brandy and handed one of the snifters to Beckett. "So, are you going to marry her, then?"

"What, marry the girl?"

Alfred smiled. "It was your idea, man. And, I think, a bloody good one."

"Hmm. This coming from a confirmed bachelor. . . ."

"I'm telling you, Beckett, she's the perfect bride.

Your mother's right about Cordelia—she *would* take you back, and I know you don't want to fall head-over-heels in love with her again. In fact, I remember you swearing you'd never fall in love with any woman again as long as you lived."

"And I never shall," Beckett stated firmly. "Just because I must take a bride doesn't mean I'm going to fall in love with her. In fact, the perfect bride for any man is one that he is *not* in love with. Love just spoils things, in the end."

"Exactly!" Alfred exclaimed, smiling. "Now you're getting it."

"And how does all that fit into your plan, may I ask?"

"Well, for starters, you don't know that girl in there from Eve."

"So?"

"So, if you don't know her, you can't possibly be in love with her, can you?"

"No." Beckett had an image of her naked body beneath his hands as he bathed her. He shook it off.

"Alright," Alfred continued. "Let's review your options. I think I'm right in saying you'd rather have your teeth pulled out by an angry barber than ask Cordelia to take you back. And I think that goes for the other ladies of the *ton*, who, due to your previous lack of funds, have scorned your recent proposals; though they would surely now be yours for the asking."

Beckett sipped his brandy. "You're right about that. I'd sooner wed a goat than take my suit to any of them."

"I am also assuming you've ruled out Martha, your cook, whom—though she is a lovely woman and makes a delicious 'canard l'orange'—I doubt you would want to kiss, let alone take to your bed."

Beckett made a face.

"Right. Which leaves our girl. Her voice and manner show her to be cultured—if you overlook the fact that she tried to brain you with a candlestick. She obviously doesn't have any family, or she would have asked after them. And as for money, she seems woefully without. So you see, she will probably be more than agreeable—and she's here now, which will save you a lot of time. Not to mention that in the light of day, she is quite an eyeful."

Beckett gave his friend a look of warning.

"Oh, come along. You also noticed her charms," Alfred said wryly. "So marry her, inherit the estate, stick her off on one of your properties—as you would do with any wife—then visit her from time to time to make a baby or two, and you and I go traveling about the continent spending your money and having fun!" Alfred downed the last swig of his brandy. "I think it is a marvelous idea."

For some strange reason, Beckett was beginning to agree. "Your reasoning is not without merit. Certainly I never want to fall in love again, with *any* woman. I've learned that lesson. Love is nothing more than a disease that infects your heart and makes you delusional, leaving you wasted and empty when it has run its course."

"You make it sound so dreary." Alfred made a face. "But then again, you'd know. I've certainly never fallen in love."

"It is dreary. It's *worse* than dreary. Love is an illusion, old chum. Cordelia taught me that. I can still see the look in her eyes when I told her my father had lost most of my inheritance in bad investments. She told me everything had changed. I realized then that the only thing that had changed was my eyesight. For the first time, I was seeing things the way they really were."

"Well, you wouldn't have to worry about that with our mystery girl," Alfred argued. "Marry her, and you're the next earl of Ravenwood."

Beckett swished the last of his brandy around in his glass, and then downed it. The fact remained that he had to marry *somebody*, or risk losing his inheritance. There was no doubt—he was attracted to the girl. The golden hair, the challenging eyes, the perfection of a body he shouldn't have seen so intimately, not to mention her spirited nature; she reminded him of a young filly he had tried to tame once in his youth. He hadn't succeeded in breaking the magnificent creature, but he'd certainly enjoyed trying.

The decision was made, then.

"Alright, Alfred. You win. I shall make her my bride." Beckett stood, placing his hands on his hips and bracing his legs apart, ready for battle. "I only hope I can convince her."

As Beckett shook his friend's proferred congratulatory hand, he found himself smiling. It *was* the perfect plan. A marriage of convenience would keep his life just as he liked it. Simple and uncomplicated.

And what could be more simple and uncomplicated than marriage to a beautiful, golden-haired goddess?

# Chapter Five

The pale yellow light of late afternoon crept through the window, filling the bedchamber with a warm, golden glow. Isobel lay on her side in the huge bed, wondering what time it was. She surveyed the room groggily, studying the dark mahogany furniture and the heavy brocade draperies.

There was a distinct smell in this chamber. It smelled faintly of cigar smoke and leather and horse. In short, it smelled like a man.

A knock sounded on the door, startling her. She sat up in bed and brushed the hair away from her face.

Was it Sir Harry, come to take her away? Was she in the house of his minions?

Another knock came, only a little louder.

She grabbed the candlestick and leapt from the bed, looking down to see she was clad in one of the cook's dressing gowns. If it was Sir Harry, he wasn't leaving this house without a nice big hole in his head.

The knob turned slowly, and Isobel watched, readying herself to spring into action. As the door opened, she braced herself for the worst.

Bright blue eyes peered around the door, regarding her inquisitively. It was the man who had lain in bed with her.

He looked to be in his late twenties, tall and sturdy, with a handsome face to match his sparkling eyes. His wavy, tawny-brown hair gave him a mischievous air, and when he looked at her, he smiled.

"I should like to come in for a chat, if you promise not to brain me."

Isobel nodded warily, lowering her weapon. She kept it at her side as she sat on the edge of the bed.

He entered smoothly and brought a chair from his desk, moving it and sitting down at an acceptable distance away from her.

"Feeling better?" he asked, smiling. "You've been resting for a few hours, now."

Isobel felt herself relax a little, and wondered at it. "Yes, thank you."

"I am glad to hear it. I've managed to arrange some clothes for you, so you can leave at any time."

"Thank you . . . that is very kind."

"Not at all. You, of course, are invited to stay for supper before you go. But before you leave, there are a few things I would like to discuss." He languidly crossed his legs and sat back in the chair, a knowing smile curving his mouth.

"You see, my dear, I wish to make you . . . a proposition. I wish to marry you."

The viscount waited for her response. Isobel stared at him silently as a maelstrom of thoughts whirled through her head.

"I beg your pardon?"

"I am Viscount Thornby."

"And . . ."

"Your future husband."

Isobel tried to keep her voice even. "And why should that be, my lord?"

"That is a long story, only some of which you could yet know." Lord Thornby rose and walked around the room, looking at her with disarming blue eyes. "I shall give you the condensed version. You see, last night, my friend Lord Weston and I stumbled upon you unconscious, under a heap of refuse on Poole Street. We decided that we could not leave you there in good conscience, so we brought you home."

He ran a hand through his wavy hair. "We put you to bed and I retired to the adjoining room. Unfortunately, I awoke in the night and through habit made my way back here, unwittingly falling asleep beside you. For which I now offer my deepest apologies."

The man smiled boyishly. "You may remember the fiasco that followed—seeing my mother fainting and screaming in shock, which you, if I may commend you, had the presence of mind not to do. While Martha attended to you, I had the most amazing news from my solicitor. News which also concerns you, my dear."

"Me?" Isobel gasped, her heart racing.

*He'd found her, then. Sir Harry—*

"Yes. You see, it appears that I am the only heir to the sixth earl of Ravenwood. And in order to claim my inheritance, I must have a bride."

Isobel stared at him. "A bride?" *What did any of this have to do with her? Was this man simply playing a cruel game?*

When she didn't reply, Lord Thornby continued. "Yes, my dear, I need a bride. And I feel that you would be perfect." His blue eyes seemed to pin her to the spot, making her his prisoner. His voice became softer. "Considering the circumstances—you and I caught sharing a bed together—I would presume an offer of marriage to be most acceptable to you. In truth, I offer a business arrangement, one that would be very advantageous to both parties. Of course, it would be a marriage of convenience—a union in name only. We would have to make the usual appearances before the *ton*—a few balls, the theater and whatnot, then we could go our separate ways. I would provide a handsome allowance, a nice little property of some sort, and you would, after all, be a countess. That is, assuming that you are not already married."

"No," she said slowly. "I am not married."

"And you have no other family to look after you, or who might object to the match?"

"No." If she had, she wouldn't be in this mess, she thought.

"Good!" he smiled. "It's settled, then. We can be married by special license tomorrow morning—"

"One moment, my lord. I have not yet consented to your proposal."

Lord Thornby paused, piercing her with his dynamic blue eyes. "But I pray that you will."

"You do not even know my name!"

"Details!" he waved a hand in dismissal, then looked alarmed. "You aren't named Hallfrita, are you? I detest that name. Or Egberta? Can you imagine? Egberta, countess of Ravenwood?" He laughed.

In spite of herself, Isobel laughed, too.

"You don't look like an Egberta to me. Or a Euphemia, or a Withypoll for that matter."

"Withypoll?"

"Yes . . . Alfred has a Great Aunt Withypoll. It means 'twig-head.'"

Why was she smiling? Her life had been turned upside down and this man was only making it worse. "No, my name isn't Withypoll. It's Isobel. Isobel Hampton."

"A perfectly good name. You see? Isobel, countess of Ravenwood. It has a ring to it."

"But you don't even know me, my lord."

"Then tell me. How did you come to be in that alley all alone? Where is your family?"

She had never lied to anyone before, never had the need. But she found how quickly one could acquire new skills when it was a matter of survival. She would lie to this man. She would accept his generous offer and gain back her life.

"I have no home, Lord Thornby, nor any family." *That wasn't wholly untrue.* "You see, my guardian—who recently died—had accumulated a vast debt. The barristers sold everything, and they turned me out into the street." Her lies and the truth were all mixing together now like knotted embroidery floss.

"I am terribly sorry to hear that, Miss Hampton. Do not trouble yourself further with those awful memories. You needn't tell me everything now," he assured her. "There will be plenty of time for that, if you consent to marry me."

"But why me, my lord? Surely someone of your rank could have any bride he chose."

"That's true, now that I stand to inherit an earldom. And I choose you, Isobel Hampton."

"But why? I must know."

"I could say all number of things to you, Miss Hampton. I could profess to being overwhelmed by your ethereal beauty. I could confess feelings of undying love for you." Lord Thornby looked away. "I have my reasons for wanting a marriage of this kind, and part of it has to do with love. You see, I have no interest in it. If you agree to this 'marriage bargain,' you must know that love will never have a place in our union. Not now—not ever."

He looked back at her then. "What I propose is not so unusual, after all. Most of the marriages in London fare the same, I'd wager. Hopefully, we will enjoy an amiable friendship. Hopefully, there will be children. I must know as soon as possible if you accept. Because if you don't, I'll need to start looking for another bride before the day is out."

He held her gaze with eyes that glowed like a sultan's jewels. "And I must remind you that although it was an innocent mistake, you have, in fact, been compromised. Of course, the decision is entirely yours."

Isobel twisted her fingers around the candlestick in her hands. The urge to trust him was growing stronger. Something in his voice made her feel strangely comfortable in his presence, though she knew she should be wary.

But if his proposal was serious, it could be the answer to her prayers.

Awful memories spun in her head. Even now, a part of her hoped that what she had seen before her flight from Hampton Park had been some sort of nightmare, but the hard knot of fear in her gut meant it had been all too real.

Yet something had guided her out of that strange hell and led her here . . . some instinct to survive, no matter what the odds. And she was not going to give up now.

Though she felt hesitant, this was a golden opportunity. What other options did she have? She had nowhere to go. Marriage to this stranger would offer her some protection, for the time being. She would be safe. Hampton Park would be safe. And the price would be a loveless marriage. Compared to the alternative—

Isobel cleared her throat. "I accept your proposal, Lord Thornby. I will be your bride. And I understand the terms of our agreement. Completely."

Silently, he reached for her hand, and when he touched his lips to her skin a tingle whispered up her spine. She wanted to lower her eyes to hide her reaction, but found that she couldn't. This man, this stranger with fiery blue eyes, would be her husband.

In name only, though.

"We shall be married tomorrow, then," he said, looking pleased. The man turned to leave, but stopped as he neared the door. "Will you have something to eat?"

She nodded, still feeling rather stunned by the bargain to which she had just agreed. *If Lord Thornby knew the truth—*

"I shall send Martha with a tray. Then you should dress and join me in the salon, if it pleases you. We must discuss some details about tomorrow." He nodded and closed the door behind him.

Isobel looked at a crumpled handkerchief that Martha had given her earlier and smoothed it, fingering the pale-blue stitching of his initials. God in Heaven, had she done the right thing? Was a marriage of convenience to this Lord Thornby the only way to remain safe from the fiend who haunted her nightmares?

Well, soon she would be Lord Thornby's wife. She would spend a few weeks in this man's company, as he'd said, and then they would go their separate ways—as so many other married couples did.

He needn't know about Hampton Park right now. He would inherit substantial property with the earldom. When the time came for her to assume her new residence, she would merely state her preference for her ancestral home.

It was dishonest, what she was doing. It was deceitful. But given the circumstances, it was clearly her only choice.

Another knock sounded at the door, this one lighter than Lord Thornby's had been. The door opened and Martha came bustling in with a large silver tray carrying tea, scones and pastries, and a bowl of fresh strawberries.

"The master said I was to bring ye a breakfast tray, Miss, even though it is almost time for tea," Martha said with a warm smile. She placed the tray over Isobel's lap, then poured some tea. "I hears there's to be a weddin' tomorrow mornin'! And so much to be done before I go home tonight. Cakes and pastries to be made. I'll need eggs and kidneys for the breakfast. And ham . . . Lord Thornby likes ham, so he does. . . ." The cook muttered the last to herself as she waddled out the door.

Isobel raised her cup to her nose and breathed in its warm, earthy scent. Her mother always had said there wasn't a thing in the world that a good cup of tea couldn't cure.

She sipped the drink and took a bite of buttered scone, thinking of her wedding. She would need more than tea to get her through that.

As she devoured the contents of the breakfast tray with unladylike speed, Isobel's thoughts centered around the man who was to become her husband in less than twenty-four hours. Could a man as handsome as Lord Beckett Thornby really be so desperate for a bride that he'd marry a girl he found in a rubbish heap?

Still, Lord Thornby's secrets were none of her concern. Perhaps he wanted to continue with a carefree life, as most noblemen did. Perhaps he had a mistress.

She should consider herself lucky that Lord Thornby had chosen her to be his bride, whatever his reasons.

Suddenly, the memory of waking up next to him sent strange shivers down her back. *She'd been naked in that bed ... and he'd been half-naked, for his part. What exactly had happened between them?*

He'd apologized, but he hadn't explained the full truth of the matter. Who exactly had undressed her? The answer hit her with a horrible certainty. It had been him.

She had assumed that Martha, the cook, had done it. But Martha had said something about getting the wedding preparations done before she went home. She didn't live in the townhouse, so it couldn't have been her.

Isobel felt her blood heat with anger ... and something else she couldn't name. Lord Thornby had taken off her clothes! Had seen her naked body with his own eyes. Had touched her—

They had been in bed together! There had been witnesses. And she had most surely been compromised. She slapped her hand down into the soft bedclothes in frustration. The resulting sound was quite unsatisfying.

Still, if Lord Thornby had wanted to take advantage of her, wouldn't he have done so, and tossed her right back onto the street? He certainly wouldn't have felt obliged to offer for her hand in marriage.

A quick knock sounded at the door and Martha appeared, bringing clothes for Isobel along with warm water for the wash-basin.

Finished with her breakfast, Isobel completed her toilette and donned a plain muslin dress. It had a scoop neck of respectable depth, with a sprigged pattern of clover green. She couldn't help but wonder where the garment had come from. It was certainly not the portly cook's. Perhaps it belonged to one of Lord Thornby's mistresses. Absently, Isobel thought how she missed her own clothes, her own bed, and her own house. If she played her cards right, they would be hers again before long!

Isobel pinned up her long blond curls and arranged them as best she could. The state of her hair was the least of her concerns.

The heavy door creaked as she slowly opened it, and Isobel almost tripped over the dog lying in the doorway. The shaggy brown shepherd bounded to his feet, tail wagging furiously, and turned around to pant up at Isobel.

"I remember you," she said, patting his big furry head. "You certainly gave me a fright when we first met. But now I see you're really a pussycat. Pardon the comparison."

The dog didn't seem to mind. He regarded her through half-lidded eyes, his pink tongue hanging from the side of his mouth.

"Where's your master? Can you take me to him, boy?"

The dog barked, then trotted down the hallway to the top of the staircase. He stopped to look back at Isobel, then headed down.

As Isobel tried to keep up, she heard loud male voices coming from one of the front rooms. Her heart beat a little nervously at the laughter and cursing. Was she confident in the story she had given Lord Thornby earlier? She had better stay true to it.

As the dog led her to a doorway, Isobel heard more of what seemed to be a strange conversation between three people.

"*Caesar want treat. Caesar want treat,*" a strange, high-pitched voice said.

"No, Caesar. No treat," Lord Thornby's voice came in reply.

"*Caesar good boy. Caesar want treat.*"

"I said *no*, Caesar."

*Did Lord Thornby have a child he hadn't mentioned?*

"*Caesar want treat. Caesar want treat. Ahhkk!*"

A loud flapping sound filled the air, and curiosity made Isobel rush around the door. Her eyes widened as she saw a large gray bird sitting on Lord Thornby's head, flapping its wings and screeching like a banshee.

Thornby turned, the bird still on his head. When he saw her, he smiled brightly. A dark-haired man stood beside him and chuckled at the scene.

Isobel covered her mouth as she giggled.

"*Pretty bird. Ahhkk! Pretty bird,*" squawked Caesar.

"That's right, Caesar. She *is* a pretty bird," Lord Thornby said.

Caesar took flight in a flurry of pale gray wings. Isobel squealed in shock as the creature landed on her shoulder and fluffed its feathers.

"Oh!" she squeaked, fearfully looking sideways at the big parrot who was studying her with a yellow eye.

"*Hello. Ahhkk! Hello.*"

"Caesar! Get off Miss Hampton's shoulder at once, you silly bird!" Lord Thornby admonished, coming to her rescue. "My apologies, Miss Hampton," he continued, putting the loudly protesting beast back in its cage. "Caesar becomes excited when he sees new people."

"Oh, no harm done," she replied. "What kind of bird is he?"

"An African Gray parrot. I found him sitting in a tree in Hyde Park one morning. He flew down to see me, and I brought him home to join the menagerie."

"You mean there are more?" Isobel asked.

"Beckett's been taking in stray animals since we were boys," the man next to her fiancé answered.

"Oh, do forgive me, Miss Hampton. Allow me to introduce Lord Weston, who assisted me in bringing you home. Alfred, Miss Isobel Hampton. Soon to be the Viscountess Thornby and countess of Ravenwood."

Lord Weston took her hand and gallantly pressed it to his lips.

"I am honored to make your acquaintance, Miss Hampton, and very pleased to see you recovered from your ordeal."

Isobel smiled gratefully. "I owe you a great debt, Lord Weston. I can only thank you and Lord Thornby again for helping me. I'm afraid most men would have left such a bedraggled creature to her fate."

"Think nothing of it, Miss Hampton. It is the duty of all gentlemen to protect the fairer sex. I am only thankful that we happened along when we did."

He kissed her hand again, and Isobel saw a flirtatious sparkle in Lord Weston's dark brown eyes. She felt like a lamb in a lion's den.

"*Ahem!*" Lord Thornby noisily cleared his throat and glared at Lord Weston, who released her hand and smirked at his friend. Isobel's soon-to-be-husband then turned to her. "I am glad to see that the gown fits you. We borrowed it from

Alfred's sister-in-law until we could properly fit you with your own trousseau."

"You are very generous, my lord—"

"Nonsense, Miss Hampton. I have Madame de Florette coming within the hour. She'll bring a selection of ready-made dresses that she and her seamstresses will alter for you here. They will have to do for the time being, I'm afraid."

"Really, there is no need."

Lord Thornby laughed. "You intend to marry me in that, then?"

Isobel looked down at her plain muslin morning dress. It was totally unsuitable for a wedding. But it wasn't as if this would be a real wedding, anyway. How extravagant could it be with one day's notice?

He approached and held her with those deep blue eyes that seemed as bright as jewels. Why was it so impossible to look away from his gaze? He took her small hand in his and kissed it, saying, "It is my wish that you be beautifully dressed for our wedding, my dear."

Isobel felt tingles skip over her skin at his touch, his words, and the intensity of his eyes. *Her husband.* Tomorrow, this stranger would be her husband. And she would be his wife, for better or for worse.

Thankfully, Martha bustled in with a tray. Isobel sipped the hot lemony tea the cook had brought and felt it calm her as it always did. Perhaps she could get through this after all.

As Beckett had promised, Madame de Florette arrived not thirty minutes later. The diminutive, dark-haired Frenchwoman hurried Isobel into Lord Thornby's chamber and began flinging dresses out of the trunk and onto the bed. Her two assistants stood with needles poised, like soldiers ready for battle.

The women spoke in rapid French as Isobel was fitted for more than twenty dresses. And though Isobel spoke the language fluently, Madame de Florette never asked for Isobel's opinion on any of the gowns—in English or in French. None of the three women seemed even to notice her.

But when Madame de Florette presented the last dress, she gave Isobel a brilliant smile. "Your wedding dress, *ma belle*. I had been making it for Sir Wilfred's daughter, but her wedding is not for a few weeks. I can make her another one. For you, *ma chere*, I'll put more bagatelles, a different trim, and no one will know ze difference!"

Isobel held her arms out as Madame de Florette slipped the dress over her shoulders. The women fluttered around her like sparrows—pinning, stitching bows and trims, and Isobel felt a huge sadness wash thickly over her like a cold ocean wave.

This was her *wedding* dress. So many times as a girl, she had dreamed of her wedding. Of marrying a dashing, gallant god of a man—some handsome hero who had won her heart. She had not dreamed of a marriage of convenience to a man she barely knew. Obviously, such girlish wishes of love no longer had a place in her life.

Now, there was only duty. To her husband. And to Hampton Park. For one thing was certain: If Isobel didn't become Lord Thornby's bride, Hampton Park would be lost forever.

The thought of Sir Harry clouded her vision and made her stomach swirl with loathing. After tomorrow, she would be safe from the foul monster. He would never put his threatening hands on her again. He would never—

"There, *ma petite. C'est fini!*" Madame de Florette said, waving her hand dramatically. Her assistants seemed to agree, cooing in French and making last-minute adjustments to the flounces and bows.

The dress was beautiful, but Isobel felt nothing for it. Still, she forced herself to smile as Madame de Florette attached her veil.

She just wanted the ceremony to be over. Then she would feel safe. And she would be that much closer to starting her new life alone at Hampton Park as the countess of Ravenwood.

The dressmaker and her assistants spent the rest of the day taking measurements, showing her fabrics and patterns, until Isobel's arms ached from being held out straight and her eyes itched with tiredness. Could it be time for supper already?

When Madame de Florette and her girls finally took their leave, Isobel found herself alone in the grand townhouse. It seemed that her husband-to-be and his friend Lord Weston had gone to their club for the evening and were not expected to return for some hours. Isobel took her supper alone, and then retired early, exhausted from the day's preparations.

Isobel was wakened and helped to dress by Martha, who, though she undoubtedly knew how to dress a turkey, proved to be all thumbs with a woman and a wedding gown. Still, together Martha and Isobel managed to secure all the buttons and affix the veil to her hair with some semblance of style.

As Isobel descended the townhouse staircase, Lord Thornby waited for her at the bottom. He leaned against the banister with one foot crossed over the other, looking for all the world as if he were about to go and play at cards. He was impeccably dressed, with his dark blue superfine coat making his eyes glow like sapphires.

Suddenly, her knees seemed made of apple jelly.

As Isobel placed her hand in his, she realized that as his bride, she would have to do whatever this man wanted. Wasn't that what all women had to do when they married? Why should her marriage be any different?

If he wanted to exercise his rights as a husband, she would have to surrender. Still, whatever Lord Thornby would do to her couldn't possibly be as vile as being touched by Sir Harry.

She struggled to shut the images from her mind. Her skin crawled as she felt Sir Harry's hard hands pulling at her bodice, roughly spreading themselves over her body like a greedy horse-buyer.

Well, she would be safe now. No matter if she'd sold herself into a marriage of convenience for protection. Everything had its price.

The carriage ride to the little church in Carberry Lane took only fifteen minutes, and it seemed to take less time than that for Lord Beckett Thornby to slip a ring onto her finger and for the rector to pronounce them man and wife.

Isobel looked up at Beckett's face as he leaned down to kiss her, but her eyes closed as his lips touched hers. She'd been quite unprepared for the warmth of her husband's mouth, for the heady, male scent of his skin, and for the thrill that shot down her spine and the backs of her legs to the tips of her toes.

If her knees had felt like apple jelly before, they were now no more substantial than clotted cream.

He broke the kiss and she looked up into fathomless eyes. Her husband smiled down at her.

The rector spoke again, though what it was exactly that he said, Isobel didn't quite know. She was too busy staring at the man she had just bound herself to for life, as his friend Lord Weston shook his hand and gave him a beaming smile.

This was her husband. . . .

As they descended the church steps, a beautiful woman with rich red hair walked toward the bridal party. The woman's dark green eyes flashed up at her. An unbridled hostility glowed there—and seemed to be directed at Isobel.

Who was this woman? And what did she want with them on their wedding day?

"So, Beckett," the flame-haired woman spat. "*This* is the woman you dared to marry instead of me."

# Chapter Six

Beckett kept his expression impassive. It would do no good to give Cordelia any satisfaction. This was his wedding day. And it might have been hers, too, if she'd been interested in more than just his inheritance. It stung to think of how blind he'd been.

"Miss Haversham. You're looking well," he said, fighting to sound gracious.

"I wish I could say the same for you, Beckett. You seem a trifle out of sorts. Of course, the stress of such hasty wedding plans would give anyone a turn, wouldn't it?"

"Strange how you found out about them so quickly, considering I made them only yesterday."

Cordelia smiled, but there was no warmth in it. "Yes. Thankfully, your mother called upon me and told me of this ridiculous notion. Did you think I was going to let you make both of us the laughingstock of London?"

"Meaning?"

"All of the *ton* knows about this girl you found in the gutter, Beckett," Cordelia said, as though Isobel were not standing right there beside him. "Yet, I want you to know that I'm willing to overlook this bit of madness. You can have the marriage annulled immediately and we will have a proper wedding, not some farcical ceremony in a rundown church in the most unfashionable part of London."

Cordelia adjusted her gloves and looked at Beckett as if all were decided. "I must say, Beckett, I had no idea what lengths you'd go to in order to win me back. Truthfully, I am flattered. But it really was a bit much, don't you think, darling?" She glanced at Isobel. "A fine countess she'd make!"

"Why thank you, Miss Haversham," Isobel said sweetly. "Coming from one of my husband's oldest and dearest friends, your approval means even more to me than you could know."

Cordelia glared and opened her mouth to say something, but Beckett interjected.

"I, too, thank you for the compliment, Miss Haversham. You are right, of course. Isobel is now Viscountess Thornby, and will soon be the countess of Ravenwood. My new wife shall undoubtedly make me the envy of the *ton*." Damn, but he was enjoying this.

"You can't be serious, Beckett," Cordelia snapped, vainly trying to regain her composure. "You and I were to be married. Be assured—I won't be put aside so easily."

"I'm afraid you already have been." Beckett looked over at his true bride. Isobel would make quite a countess indeed. She was beautiful and witty. What more did one need?

Cordelia's green eyes shot sparks at him. "You

can't do this to me, Beckett. You made me promises. And I intend to have what is rightfully mine!"

"Nothing of mine ever was or will be yours, Cordelia. You were quite willing to break our engagement when you found my inheritance to be no more than a few shillings. And your feelings on the matter are worth less than that to me now."

"But surely you knew that I wasn't serious about breaking our engagement, Beckett. A woman never is."

"So I mistook your intentions when you threw the ring in my face?"

"A lovers' quarrel, nothing more. We can put that nonsense behind us. And I will be your wife, as you've always wanted."

"It is strange to think it, Miss Haversham. I did want that once. But I have chosen my bride, and I intend to keep her," he said, glancing down at the woman beside him.

"But—" Cordelia looked disbelievingly at Isobel and then back at Beckett. "But, I *must* be your wife. I must be the countess of Ravenwood!"

"I'm afraid the position has been filled. Good day, Cordelia," Beckett said, touching the brim of his hat and leading Isobel toward their waiting coach.

Beckett handed his new wife into the plush interior and stepped in beside her, settling onto the burgundy velvet seat. He realized that his heart was beating faster than usual, but it was a satisfying feeling. He felt that a chapter of his life finally had been closed. And another one was just beginning.

Beckett glanced at Isobel and smiled. Her engaging brown eyes looked at him curiously as the coach jerked forward.

"My apologies for that dreadful scene, my

dear," he said. "What is it they say—hell hath no
fury like a woman scorned?"

"But I thought it was *she* who had scorned *you*."

"Well, my dear, Cordelia was only interested in
my money, and when it turned out that I had
none—" He laughed, but it was a bitter sound.
"Now that I am to become an earl, she has
changed her mind once again."

"But you have not?"

"What—changed my mind about Miss Haversham? Certainly not," he said stiffly.

"I thought her quite beautiful."

Beckett chuckled cynically. "As beautiful as a
rose. With rather vicious little thorns. And having
got too close before, I'm pleased to say that I've
learned my lesson."

Isobel studied him with intelligent eyes. "And is
that why you have chosen me for a bride, my
lord? Because thorns pricked you last time, and
you've sworn to give up gardening?"

Beckett regarded her silently. It seemed his
wife was more shrewd than he'd thought.

"I was never much for roses," he said, adjusting
his cuffs. "They make me sneeze."

Isobel closed the heavy book and rested it in her
lap. Somehow, reading *The Taming of the Shrew*
again had failed to lighten her mood as it usually
did. Instead, it made her feel like Katharina, suddenly wed to a stranger—her world irrevocably
changed. The play had a happy ending. Would
her marriage turn out as well?

She had spent the afternoon and evening alone.
After the wedding breakfast, Beckett had gone to
complete the business of his inheritance with
Lord Weston in tow. He had assured her that he
would be home by six o'clock. It was now half-
past nine.

Oh, she wanted to kick herself! Not even married a full day, and she was already acting like a shrew. Her husband's affairs were none of her concern. What did it matter when he came home, if at all? For if he did, it would bring up the question of the handling of the wedding night.

Lord Thornby had said the marriage was no more than a business transaction. But would he want a wedding night, with all the trimmings? What man wouldn't?

Perhaps if she retired now to her chamber, he would be reluctant to disturb her when and if he came home. Yes, that was a good plan. And besides that, it was the only plan she could come up with at the moment.

Isobel rose from the library sofa and replaced the heavy volume on the shelf. Just as she opened the door into the hallway, another door opened, and accompanied by a draft of cool night air, her husband walked into the foyer. Isobel stared up into bright blue eyes, and felt a thrill move through her.

"Good evening, Isobel." He took off his hat and passed it to Hartley, who quickly left them alone.

"I was just going up to bed," she blurted.

"To bed. That sounds like a wonderful idea."

"It does?"

"Yes."

"Oh, no. In this case, it doesn't."

"Why not?" He regarded her seriously, but Isobel could have sworn there was the hint of a smile on his lips.

"Because—I am very tired. And . . . I'm not feeling well at all. In fact, I am quite ill." It was true. Her stomach churned dreadfully at the thought of a wedding night. Truly, she felt she must be turning green.

"Really? How unfortunate."

"Yes. I am very, very ill indeed. In fact, I may faint."

"Oh, then I must carry you up to your chamber then, before you do."

"Oh, no! There is no need—*ooh!*"

In one swift motion, Lord Thornby had swept her into his arms and held her as if she weighed no more than a feather.

"Really, I *can* walk." Isobel pushed against his broad chest, but to no avail. Her husband had her in his arms, and she was helpless to escape. And worst of all, the sensation was anything but unpleasant.

Was he holding her tighter?

Whatever he was doing, he was taking his time!

The moments seemed to pass with agonizing slowness as Lord Thornby carried her up the staircase. Funny, but Isobel had never noticed there were so many steps, or that the hallway was so long, or that her husband smelled so alarmingly good.

Then, they were in the Blue Room, and he was carrying her to the huge, soft bed. Isobel's pulse quickened as he gently lay her down. She half-feared, half-hoped he would join her there.

He stood straight, looking down into her eyes. Reaching out a hand, he lifted an errant curl from her forehead, letting his knuckles lightly brush against her skin. "I'll send Martha up with something to help you sleep. And I bid you goodnight."

Isobel stared helplessly as he bent down toward her. She closed her eyes and waited for his lips to claim hers.

He placed a chaste kiss on her forehead.

She opened her eyes to see him quietly leaving the room, and realized there was a knot forming in her heart. He was leaving her alone for the night. Wasn't that what she'd wanted?

But as Isobel lay there alone on the big, empty bed, she realized that it wasn't what she'd wanted at all.

"Good morning, Hartley." Beckett poured himself a cup of hot coffee and took a sip. "Have you seen my wife about? I was told she came down before me."

"Lady Ravenwood is in the garden, my lord."

"And how did she seem? Did she look to be in good health this morning?"

"She seemed in excellent health, my lord."

Beckett popped a strawberry in his mouth. "Good. I am afraid the excitement of yesterday's events made her somewhat ill."

Hartley nodded sagely. "It is often the case with new wives, my lord. These wedding-day illnesses are usually cured the next day—or night."

Beckett chuckled. "I'm sure you're right, Hartley. I'll just go and bring her some breakfast, then." He took a linen napkin and placed a handful of strawberries in it, bundling it up and heading down the hallway.

He opened the French doors and walked out into the bright morning. Quickly, he spied her. She was facing away from him, but he could see her profile in the warm yellow light.

She looked like an angel.

Enthralled, he watched as the sunlight played upon her golden curls, and made them glint as if they were crowned with fairy dust.

Gadzooks, but she was beautiful.

Where Cordelia's beauty was almost blinding, Isobel's was soft as a rose petal. Cordelia's eyes burned with heat, but Isobel's glowed with warmth, like the play of firelight through a whiskey glass. Where Cordelia was statuesque and voluptuous, Isobel was dainty and petite.

And while Cordelia's voice was deep and throaty, Isobel's was soft and sweet. Beckett watched her as she sketched. She seemed so innocent, so unaware of her own loveliness. The realization stirred something within him.

Damn it! He didn't have time for such nonsense. He would *not* start mooning over this woman like a bloody schoolboy! Wasn't that why he'd married Isobel? To keep things simple?

That was why he'd been glad she had feigned illness last night. For he had been so tempted to take her to his bed and touch again the perfection of her body; it had haunted him since the night he'd found her. But he'd wanted to do much more than touch her. He'd wanted to pull her close against his own naked form, and feel her warm skin next to him, her lips on his, and feel her legs wrapped around his waist as he thrust himself into her.

Theirs was the perfect marriage: one of convenience. He would not let his base needs play havoc with his plans. She would want to be gone within a few weeks, anyway. It would be no use discovering any charms of Isobel's that might reduce him again to a blithering idiot. He had played that role once for Cordelia, and found it quite tiresome.

Certainly, he would be polite, and treat Isobel with the utmost respect. He hoped they would even become friends.

And, he thought cynically, friends it would have to be. No one would be allowed to sink his or her claws into him except his parrot.

Isobel sat on the marble bench beside the little pond and watched the fish swim up to the surface, then flip their tails as they headed back down toward the dark, soft bottom. This place was not unlike her own garden at home, except it was not as grand.

She had spent another restless night filled with terrible dreams of Sir Harry and Hampton Park. She'd awakened to find her nightdress soaked through, her hands shaking in terror. Seeking to banish the fears of the night, Isobel had come out to the garden with her pencils and paper to sketch.

A bee buzzed past her on its way to some sweet-smelling roses. She watched the insect fly into the center of a delicate pink blossom, and gather its nectar to bring back to the hive.

She thought of Beckett's talk of roses yesterday in the coach. There were indeed many sharp, wicked-looking thorns adorning the flower's stem, a potent protection from anyone trying to possess its delicate beauty.

The confrontation with Cordelia Haversham had been unsettling. Isobel knew she had no reason to be jealous of Beckett's previous fiancée. After all, this marriage was purely a business arrangement. Hadn't last night's events, or lack thereof, proven that? Yet she couldn't help but be curious about her husband's former love. From what she'd seen, the woman was as spoiled as a wicked child. And though extremely beautiful, her personality was as pleasant as ants at a picnic.

She had been trying to sketch all morning, but the face that flashed before her eyes clouded her vision. Dark, glittering eyes stared up at her from the blank paper and mocked her.

Isobel tried to concentrate on her view of the pink rose and the yellow-striped bee that flew happily around it. Forcing her hand to the paper, she slowly sketched the rose on the blank sheet in front of her. As the picture took shape, the fluid lines and shadows drew her problems into the folds of the petals. Her artwork had always soothed her like a gentle embrace.

Taking a new sheet of paper, Isobel thought of Cordelia, of her rich red hair, porcelain complexion and bright green eyes. Though Isobel had no love for the woman, she would be a superb subject.

She moved the lead quickly this time, her soft lines becoming Cordelia's cheekbone, her regal nose, her coy eyes. Isobel worked methodically, the action blotting out the whirlwind in her mind. Using her fingertip, she smudged some lines to make them softer. Isobel looked down at Cordelia's likeness with a bit of shock.

Revealed were the woman's calculating eyes and cold, thin smile. She was beautiful, yes, but had the cold beauty of a marble statue whose eyes appeared sightless, whose mouth would remain hard and frozen for eternity.

"I didn't know you were an artist," a voice said from behind her, breaking the silence of the garden.

Isobel looked up to see her husband's face shaded by the branches of the oak tree. She felt a thrill of surprise, then self-consciousness. Usually, she didn't show her drawings to anyone. Let alone the subject's former love.

"May I?" Beckett asked, his hand outstretched.

Reluctantly, Isobel gave him the drawing. "I hope it doesn't offend you, my lord."

"Why would it offend me? It is merely a piece of paper." Beckett's voice was unreadable, but she heard something dangerous in it. Abruptly, he held the picture toward Isobel. "You've captured her, my dear."

She retrieved it and stared at him for a moment, taking in his relaxed attire. The white shirt he wore was not buttoned to the top, and showed the soft, cinnamon-colored hair of his chest.

She had never been this close to a man who wasn't fully dressed before. No—she corrected herself. There had been that morning in his bed-chamber. Of course, she had been unconscious for most of that. He'd been entirely without his shirt, but she'd been so concerned with her own state of undress that she hadn't really looked at him very closely.

But this was outside. In daytime. She could see the texture of his skin in the sunlight. Isobel wanted to shake the thoughts from her head. She shouldn't be thinking about his skin, she should be thinking about her own. Isobel forced her eyes back to his roguish expression and took a deep breath.

A faint hint of his cologne drifted toward Isobel on the soft breeze, tantalizing her senses just as it had done yesterday when he'd held her close and carried her upstairs.

"You are looking well this morning, Isobel. I trust you slept well last night."

"Yes, my lord. I slept quite well." It was a lie. She hadn't slept well, at all.

He made a face, waving his hand in annoyance. "And let us dispense with you calling me 'my lord.' We are husband and wife now, Isobel. You are the Viscountess Thornby and the countess of Ravenwood. I insist that you call me by my Christian name."

"Yes, my—Beckett," she replied.

"Yes, my Beckett!" He laughed. "Very well, *my Isobel*."

She couldn't help but laugh with him.

"Well, I am glad that your health has improved since last night. Too much excitement, I expect. You had a very full day, as did I. Alfred took me

to White's after I officially became Lord Ravenwood. We had supper, played at cards, and found
I had all manner of new friends crawling out of
the woodwork to congratulate me. Comes with
being a wealthy earl, I suppose, because none of
them was the least concerned with me when I
was only an impoverished viscount. What did you
do, Isobel?"

"Oh, after supper I retired to the library and
read Mr. Shakespeare's *The Taming of the Shrew*."

"*The Taming of the Shrew?* Is there something I
should know about, Isobel? Am I to play Petruchio to your Katharina?" He pursued. "Or Lucen-
tio to your Bianca?"

She looked up at him. What game was he playing with her? "I cannot say, my lord, for those
that you mention are both pairs of lovers. And as
you have said, ours is a marriage only of convenience."

He regarded her for a moment, then stepped
closer to her, as his penetrating blue eyes held her
gaze. "You are right, of course. That is what we
both wanted. Is it not?"

"Yes. It is what we agreed upon."

"So it is, Isobel. So it is." Beckett's voice seemed
to hold a touch of regret as he looked away. "I
shall be off to the solicitors' again this afternoon.
Don't wait up for me, hmm?"

Isobel watched him walk across the lawn to the
doorway. He glanced back over his shoulder just
as he went inside, and Isobel could have sworn
she'd seen a sorrowful expression on his face.

Slowly, she packed up her drawing leads and
papers, trying to quiet the thudding of her heart.
She wanted nothing more than to retire to her
room where she could be alone.

Doubts swirled in her head, as dark and brittle
as a whirlwind of autumn leaves.

Who was this man that she'd married so hastily? He seemed such a contradiction—one day insisting that he wanted a marriage of convenience, and the next, teasing her about lovers and wedding nights.

But as strange as this marriage was, it was necessary for her survival. She would make sense of it somehow. If Katharina and Petruchio could make their marriage work, then so could she and Beckett.

Surely, most of the women in London would trade their best bonnet for a true marriage with a man who was so attractive. And he was an earl, to boot. A very wealthy earl.

As she entered her room, Isobel found herself remembering the softness of Beckett's lips on hers yesterday in the church, and then last night so chastely upon her forehead. If her husband meant to honor their agreement, she probably had tasted her first and last real kiss yesterday in front of the rector.

She sighed and plopped herself down on the bed, lying upon her back and staring up at the ceiling.

But *did* he intend to honor their arrangement? His words in the garden had been most puzzling. She could have sworn he'd been flirting with her.

If Beckett decided he wanted her in his bed, he should know she would have no right to refuse him. And what was more worrisome, she knew she would have no intention of doing so.

# Chapter Seven

Beckett stood in front of the mirror and arranged his ivory silk neck cloth. Unfortunately, Hartley's talents in this regard were sorely lacking, and Beckett himself had been forced to learn how to tie a proper knot or risk looking like an uncultured oaf. He pulled on the bow to make it puff. There. Much better.

Tonight he and his wife were making their first public appearance since their wedding two days ago. By all accounts, their attendance at the Whitcomb Ball was the talk of London. It seemed everyone wanted a glimpse of the new earl and countess of Ravenwood. Especially of his mysterious bride.

Word was that Cordelia would be there, also, with talons sharpened. According to Alfred, Cordelia had been campaigning to win support from some of the old guard—no doubt trying to discredit Beckett and his new bride. Not that Beckett cared what any of those old crones thought.

But for Isobel, meeting the *ton* tonight would be like battling lions in a Roman coliseum. And unfortunately, these lions were particularly hungry.

Beckett adjusted his cuffs and took one last look in the glass. It would do.

He trotted down the staircase with Monty on his heels, then stood near the bottom to await his wife. He felt the dog's hot breath on his pant leg and moved away. The beast scooted closer, so that he was exactly the same distance from Beckett's leg as he had been before.

"Monty, I've already applied my cologne for the evening, thank you very much. Go on, now," Beckett said, pointing.

Monty looked up at him with happy brown eyes and continued to steam Beckett's trousers.

"Monty, go!" he said firmly.

The dog raised sad eyes to his master and slunk away.

"That's not going to work, my friend. Just lay down there and be good."

Just then, a flapping of feathers whooshed through the air and Caesar flew out of the salon, landing on his favorite perch: Beckett's head.

"Oh, Caesar—get off!" Beckett reached up to disengage the parrot from his head.

"*Get off . . . get off, ahhkk!*" The bird flapped its wings enthusiastically, and flew up just out of Beckett's reach, then landed on his head again. They repeated this process until Beckett finally gave up, and stood with his hands on his hips.

"Caesar, I believe you have ruined my hair."

Light feminine laughter trickled down the staircase.

Beckett looked up to see Isobel standing at the

top, covering her mouth with a dainty gloved hand as she giggled.

"Oh, you think this quite funny, do you?" Beckett asked.

Isobel appeared to be swallowing her smirk as she descended the stairs and stopped at the bottom.

"Hmph." Beckett reached up and successfully grabbed the bird before he could flap his gray wings and escape. "Caesar, I'm afraid that your career as a hat is over. Back in your cage, now."

*"Ahhkk! Bye-bye. Bye-bye,"* the bird squawked as his owner placed him back in his big brass cage.

Beckett returned to Isobel's side. For some reason, she kept putting her hand to her lips and looking at the floor, or the door, or anywhere but directly at him.

"What? What is it?"

She looked up at him. "Your hair."

"Damnation." He crossed over to the glass in the hallway and almost laughed himself when he saw the strange coiffure the bird had wrought on his head. It stuck out in every direction, and one clump of hair in particular made a perfect little triangle on top of his head. He turned back to Isobel, and with as serious a face as he could muster, said, "You mean you don't like it? But it is quite the dash, I hear. Tip-top. Sparkish, what?"

Isobel seemed unconvinced.

Beckett ran his hands through his hair and fluffed it out, then checked in the mirror. It would have to do.

"Hmm, well, it is a good thing Caesar didn't want *your* head as a perch."

It seemed that only then did he notice her gown, a stunning creation of amber silk with a daring neckline. Well, he supposed it was respectable enough for a married woman. "The new maid must be doing a good job, then, Isobel. You look quite ready to take on the *ton*."

But the thought niggled at him that she was *his* married woman, and perhaps he didn't want all of society looking at her breasts as he was doing.

Isobel smiled almost shyly. "Thank you, my— thank you, Beckett."

"Ah, you've remembered my name, I see. Always a good sign on the third day of a new marriage."

She laughed again, and he felt warmed by her eyes, as sweet as cinnamon sugar. He offered his arm and felt her little hand tuck into the crook of his elbow. It was terribly pleasing.

"Now, you know what to do?"

"Yes. If anyone says anything out of turn, I am to bat my eyelashes, laugh, as charmingly as possible, and perhaps sigh rather whimsically."

"Exactly. And if that doesn't win them over, be sure to swoon. Most people love a good swoon."

"Will Miss Haversham be there?"

Beckett nodded. "Like Napoleon, itching for battle. And you must be like Wellington. Stand your ground, and you'll see the enemy run."

"Oh dear," Isobel said, looking worried. "Will there be time to dance, in between dodging enemy volleys?"

Beckett laughed, admiring Isobel's spirit. "I will make certain you do more dancing than dodging, my dear. Now, this is our first ball as the earl and countess of Ravenwood. Let us do nothing more than enjoy ourselves, and make those fools regret not having attended our wedding, hmm?"

Beckett led his wife out the door and helped her into the waiting carriage. As they pulled away down the tree-lined street, he hoped for Isobel's sake that this evening would not be the disaster Cordelia would surely try to make it.

\* \* \*

The carriage rolled into the long torchlit drive of Whitcomb Park and stopped as they waited for a space. Carriages lined the circular drive from end to end. In the flickering light, a steady flow of guests promenaded up the wide staircase and through the main doors.

Isobel had never seen so many fashionable people in one place before. But these were members of the *ton*. They made the fashion. And tonight they were here to see her.

Surely, though, they would see *through* her. Surely they would see that she was not truly the countess of Ravenwood, so much as an actress playing the part. Who was she, really? Certainly she was no longer the innocent girl she'd been at Hampton Park. Now, she was the wife of a virtual stranger . . . and she herself was a stranger in a strange world.

As they waited to pull up beside the steps, Isobel looked across at Beckett, who sat back leisurely as if this were a simple soiree they were attending. The flames from the torches lit the inside of the cab, flickering over his face in the dark.

Beckett was not the first handsome man she had ever seen, certainly not. But for some reason, over the last few days, Isobel found herself stealing glances at him when he wasn't looking. And then she would remember that he'd undressed her that first night and her face would blush with heat.

Since they were man and wife, she told herself, she could have much more to blush about than the fact that he'd undressed her once.

The door opened and a footman appeared, reaching his hand in to help Isobel out of the carriage. She gathered up her skirts and put her hand in the footman's as he helped her to the ground. Beckett quickly followed, offering his arm to Isobel.

"We must keep watch for Alfred," Beckett said. "It's always good to have him around once the quips start flying."

Isobel glanced at her husband, suddenly feeling uncertain. It must have shown on her face, for Beckett clasped her hand in his and smiled down at her reassuringly. Strange how one touch of his hand could calm her inner fears, while at the same time set her heart to racing.

Through the massive front doors, Isobel could see the dancers swirling around the ballroom. Music drifted out to greet them on the soft evening breeze. The orchestra played a sprightly waltz, which rang over the sounds of conversation and pattering feet.

The women all seemed to be floating in concoctions of diaphanous fabric, their jewelry glittering in the light from the hanging candelabras. A heady mixture of flowers, food, and brandy perfumed the air.

Isobel looked down at her gown of amber silk and hoped she looked like a countess. She touched the topaz necklace that her husband had given her, and took a deep breath.

"The earl and countess of Ravenwood," the butler announced, holding his arm out and motioning them ahead.

"My dear, may I present the earl and countess of Whitcomb."

Her husband's hand touched her lower back, steering her toward their hostess and her spouse.

"She's lovely, Beckett." The aged noblewoman smiled, offering her hand to Isobel. "Wherever did you find such a treasure?"

"You know what they say about treasure, countess. One always comes across it buried in the most unusual places."

Their hosts eyed each other, shaking their heads. "Beckett, you are still the charmer, I see." The countess laughed. "I hope you can handle him, my dear."

"I will certainly try, Lady Whitcomb." Isobel smiled and made her curtsies as Beckett made his bows.

They passed through the outer doors and into the ballroom. From behind her, Beckett put his hand on her elbow and leaned around to whisper in her ear. "There—you're through the first assault of this ballroom battle. Stay sharp, Lady Ravenwood. This is where it gets interesting."

Beckett led her through the crowd, introducing her to so many viscounts, marquesses, earls, and even a few dukes, she knew she'd never remember all their names. Finally, he turned away from her to speak to a round little admiral with enough medals on his chest that it was a surprise he didn't topple over.

Isobel felt a man's hand on her arm. Startled, she whirled around to find Alfred close beside her, though she couldn't stop a little squeal from escaping her lips.

"Terribly sorry," Alfred said. "Forgive my appalling manners, Lady Ravenwood. I did not mean to frighten you." Languidly, he brought her hand to his lips and gently kissed it.

"What do you think you're doing?" Beckett asked, turning away from the admiral. "Trying to woo my wife, are you?"

"Why, yes, actually. She *is* the prettiest woman here."

"You'd better watch your tongue, Alfred. If you insist upon shamelessly flirting with my wife in such a manner, I may have to box your ears," Beckett said, but he was smiling at his friend.

"Hah!" Alfred scoffed, good-naturedly. "I'd like to see you try, old man. Until then, I shall admire Lady Ravenwood's stunning beauty to my heart's content."

Isobel blushed as Alfred pressed his lips to her hand.

"Might I ask the lovely creature to dance, Beckett?" Alfred inquired.

"You might."

Alfred performed an elaborate bow for Isobel's benefit, his mischievous dark eyes shining up at her. "Lady Ravenwood, would you do me the honor of accepting my request for a dance?"

"I'm afraid I am not a very good dancer, Alfred," she warned.

"Wonderful. Neither am I!"

But he was a good dancer. He guided her gently and helped to cover up her mistakes as they moved across the ballroom. Isobel swirled around and around, letting the music make her feel light as air.

The room spun around her as Alfred expertly maneuvered them through the crowd. Lord Weston was like the older brother she'd never had, for his embrace was strong, kind and protective. Isobel felt weightless as she danced in the glow of the candlelight, but Alfred's touch didn't make her skin tingle as Beckett's touch did. She glanced over at her husband.

For a moment she forgot everything. For a moment, as she met those intense blue eyes across the room, she felt real, unexpected happiness.

Less than a week ago, she would have thought it impossible to feel anything but fear. Had it all really happened? Right now, in this ballroom, the memory of Sir Harry and her flight from him seemed only a bad dream.

She would not think of it! She couldn't. Not

here. She was safe now, surely. Sir Harry Lennox would never have her or Hampton Park. He would never be able to make her his bride, now that she was another man's wife.

Isobel stole another glance at Beckett and saw his gaze upon her—a penetrating mixture of ice and fire. Yes, she was certainly another man's wife. Instantly, the memory of their wedding-day kiss flooded her senses, a reminder that Sir Harry could never claim her.

Isobel would fulfill her part of the marriage bargain by appearing publicly united with her new husband. Then she would retire to Hampton Park as the true mistress of the estate. And she would rid herself of Lennox once and for all. It was a perfect arrangement.

At least that's what she kept telling herself.

# Chapter Eight

"So. You actually had the audacity to attend Lady Whitcomb's ball. How very provincial."

Isobel turned around slowly, as befitting a countess, and met the icy green eyes of Cordelia Haversham.

Where was Beckett? He was nowhere in sight. She would have to do battle with this harpy alone.

"My husband, the earl of Ravenwood and I, were specifically invited by Lady Whitcomb. I am sorry if our presence distresses you, Miss Haversham."

"Distresses me?" Cordelia gave a brittle laugh that was quite unattractive. "Oh, I assure you, I am not in the least bit distressed. It is you, my dear, who should be distressed."

"Miss Haversham, I wonder, are you planning to use the word 'distressed' with such constancy during our discourse? Because if you are, and you surely have a preference for the word, I will leave off using it. I have found that it is quite tiresome to use the same word so very much during genteel conversation."

Cordelia's eyes blazed. "You have *quite* the nerve!"

"I am sure you think so."

Cordelia's eyes narrowed. "You are deceiving yourself if you think he married you for any other reason than to get back at me. You are a joke, my dear. A little trollop from the gutter, masquerading in a countess's clothing. Everyone knows who you really are."

"Oh—Lady Ravenwood, you mean? Why, thank you for reminding me, Miss Haversham. I can hardly get used to the idea myself. And considering that you yourself might have been Beckett's countess, it really is so very kind of you to point out my good fortune."

If steam had risen from Cordelia's ears, Isobel would not have been the least bit surprised. As it was, the woman's face contorted into a strange configuration and turned a very unbecoming color.

"My word," Isobel intoned. "Are you ill, Miss Haversham? You look as if you've swallowed a large fruit."

Cordelia seethed. "If there *were* any large fruit near at hand, I would most likely stuff it down your throat!"

"There is a pineapple across the room, there," Isobel said, pointing, "and I would dearly love to see you attempt it. Shall we give everyone a good show?"

"Do you think me stupid enough to cause a scene? There's no use in trying to make *me* look a fool."

"Oh, you don't need my help, Miss Haversham. You're doing quite well on your own."

Cordelia looked around quickly and grabbed Isobel's arm, jerking her close. Her voice was a harsh whisper in Isobel's ear as she said, "Look, you little harlot. You may be the countess of Ravenwood but who knows—you might get sick. You might die. People have accidents." The woman pulled her closer, so that they were nose to nose. "I had Beckett wrapped around my little finger before, and I can do it again. I could have any man in this room, but I want Beckett and I want the Ravenwood estate. *No one* casts me off, do you hear?"

Isobel yanked her arm back and met Cordelia's venomous eyes. "If you'll be so kind as to remember, Miss Haversham, it was *you* who put Beckett aside when you learned that he had no fortune."

"Well, now he has one, doesn't he? That was the only reason I broke the engagement." Cordelia made a face. "And don't try telling me that you married him for love. I know very well why you married Beckett, and so does everyone else in this room."

"For his fortune and title?" Isobel asked. "Those were *your* reasons. Not mine."

Cordelia stood back and glared at Isobel. "Whatever the reason, be warned. I shall not rest until *I* am the countess of Ravenwood."

"Then you shall not rest, shall you, Miss Haversham? Do enjoy the rest of the evening. I must return to my *husband*."

Isobel turned slowly, as she had before, and walked away as if she hadn't a care in the world. She heard Cordelia behind her, snorting and stomping like a badly behaved horse. It made her smile.

Moving through the crowd, Isobel saw Beckett

near the refreshment table. As she drew close to him he handed her a glass. She brought it to her lips and tasted the raspberry punch, its welcome sweetness filling her mouth.

"Are you enjoying the evening, Isobel?" her husband asked, catching her eye meaningfully.

She met his gaze and smiled. "Yes, I think so. Though I was unable to use your advice about swooning while conversing with Miss Haversham."

"Cordelia? What did she say? What did *you* say?"

"Well, at one point she looked unwell and I remarked that she resembled someone who had swallowed an oversized fruit. To which she replied that if there was one available, she would take great pleasure in stuffing it down my throat. I pointed out the pineapple, but she abandoned the notion."

Beckett stared at her, seemingly dumbfounded. Then his face lit up, and he doubled over with boisterous laughter. "A pineapple! A *pineapple?*" Eventually, he regained control of himself and regarded Isobel with laughing eyes. "My dear, I knew you would make a name for yourself, but I had no idea that name would be the countess of Pineapple."

Isobel smirked and surrendered to her own laughter. "Do you think that it shall get around?"

"I wouldn't completely rule it out. We shall have to check the Times tomorrow morning."

"Oh dear. I shall cause a scandal."

"I don't care if you do, Isobel. And neither should you. I shall be quite happy being husband to the Lady of Large Fruit."

"Of large *what?*" Alfred said, popping up beside Beckett. "I say, is that any way to speak to your wife?"

Beckett bowed over Isobel's hand. "They are

beginning another waltz, my lady. Would you do me the honor?"

Isobel felt a little thrill at the warmth of his hand. "I would be most pleased."

Beckett led her onto the dance floor and curved one arm around her waist, his hand flat against the small of her back. She looked up into his face and saw that the laughter was gone from his expression. He stared down at her with glowing blue eyes, and all at once Isobel knew why moths flew into the flame.

Isobel felt herself becoming terribly warm all over, but was it from the dancing, or his nearness? The memory of his lips on hers kept returning, and suddenly, unexpectedly, she wanted him to kiss her.

"What are you thinking?" he asked, his voice like velvet.

Isobel lowered her gaze to his chest. *Oh, please don't let me blush.*

"You're flushed, Isobel. Is it from your thoughts, or is it from the dancing?"

"I'm sure it is from neither."

"Are you, now? Well, I am not so convinced. Let us do an experiment, then. What would you say, Isobel, if I pulled you close and kissed you here in front of this whole room?"

Isobel's head jerked up as she met his twinkling eyes. "You wouldn't." A thrill swept through her body, and hot tingles spilled down her back.

"You see, I was right. You blushed because of your thoughts. Of course, this time I planted the seeds. I would dearly like to know what you were thinking before that made you blush so sweetly."

Feeling suddenly daring, as she had with Cordelia, Isobel answered. "If you *must* know, I was thinking about when you kissed me on our wedding day." She paused and looked up at him.

"I imagine you must be quite shocked by my forwardness. I admit, I am feeling very bold tonight. This being a countess must be going to my head."

"Well, then, it agrees with you. I like a woman who can speak plainly." He brought his face closer to hers and they stopped swirling. "And I like a woman who thinks about kissing. Especially about kissing *me*."

Isobel stared transfixed. Was he really going to kiss her in front of all these people?

"Perhaps we should take a turn out in the gardens. It is a lovely night."

Isobel nodded silently. Beckett was her husband, now. If he wanted to kiss her senseless up against a tree, that was his right. And suddenly she knew that if he wanted to do more, she would not protest!

Beckett was so unlike Sir Harry. Certainly, he was handsome—but at first glance, some would say that Sir Harry was handsome, as well. But Sir Harry was so menacing, so dangerous that to her he appeared as attractive as a warthog.

Beckett led her out onto the balcony. He smiled at the other guests and as they walked, he lifted her hand to his lips and kissed it. They made their way down the steps and headed toward one of the torchlit paths on the grounds.

Oh, why was her heart pounding, so?

Beckett looked down at her and placed his hand over hers in the crook of his arm. "One of the benefits of marriage is being able to enjoy a walk in the gardens like this without causing a scandal. I daresay these gardens are as big as Vauxhall. And just as private."

They walked farther, and Isobel became aware of a number of couples embracing in the shadows. The muffled sound of their giggles and laughter floated on the still night air and seemed to tease her with forbidden promise.

97

Beckett stepped off the path and led her into the trees. He turned her around to face him, and she could just make his features out in the dim torchlight that spilled from the pathway.

Beckett lowered his mouth and captured her quivering lips with his own. His hands moved around to Isobel's back and pulled her close as his warm tongue delved into her mouth and sent hot sparks shooting down her spine.

Beckett's powerful arms encircled her and brought her hips tight against his own. Isobel clung to him, not knowing whether it was uncertainty or pleasure that made her do so.

"Oh—" she whispered. "I fear I may faint."

"Too much for you, is it?" Her husband breathed in her ear, teasing it with his tongue. "And this is just the beginning, Isobel."

"You mean it gets worse?"

"*Much* worse."

"How much?"

Beckett smiled and slid her dress down off of her shoulder. Isobel gasped in shock as the cool night air touched the bare skin of the top of her breast. Certainly, this must be terribly wicked. Even if he was her husband!

"Well, this is one of the ways," he growled, lowering his head to her breast and brushing his lips against it.

"Oh . . . Oh my. My goodness."

"Your goodness is right," he said, briefly lifting his head and flashing her a wicked grin.

The mixture of the cool air and his hot breath on her skin threatened to drive her mad as he continued his torment. Her knees felt as if they would buckle.

He lifted his head again and stepped back, drawing her gown back into place.

"Why are you stopping?"

He chuckled. "Well, I must stop now, or not at all. And I do not want to take your virginity in Lord and Lady Whitcomb's garden."

"Oh."

"Unless you have a preference for gardens, of course."

"No. No preference. I mean, I'm sure I have no preference at all . . . where to do such a thing." Goodness, had those words really come out of her mouth?

Beckett's eyes sparkled with amusement. "Well, we shall have to do something about that, now, shan't we?" He looked her up and down, and smoothed away some of the wayward curls around her face. "Your face is a trifle flushed, Isobel. And we have been gone a decidedly decadent amount of time. Everyone will know what we have been doing, I think."

"They will?" she said, alarmed.

"Well, anyone who was paying mind. And it will only serve to intrigue the *ton* down to the soles of their shoes." He smiled.

Beckett led her back to the path and they moved toward the huge manor house.

"I'm not sure I should want to intrigue the *ton*. Or their shoes," remarked Isobel.

Beckett laughed. "Too late, my dear. You did that when you walked in the door."

They walked up the steps and across the terrace, re-entering the ballroom. A few curious couples noticed their arrival, and began commenting behind their fans. Isobel could almost hear the gossip-mill turning now.

"I must find Alfred. He's in the card room, I think," Beckett said. "Wait for me here, will you? I see Lady Whitcomb just over there. I'm sure she will keep you company until I return. I'll be back directly."

Isobel nodded and watched her husband round the corner and disappear into the hallway. She glanced around and took a step toward Lady Whitcomb.

She was totally unprepared for the sickeningly familiar grip that suddenly caught her wrist, but even as she turned to face him, she knew whose it was.

As icy fear squeezed her heart, Isobel looked into the glittery dark eyes that had haunted her dreams since that terrible night at Hampton Park.

It seemed a lifetime ago, and yet all too fresh in her mind. What had been happening at Hampton Park in her absence? Had Sir Harry Lennox installed himself as master of the estate, as he'd promised he would? And now he was here, like a wolf at the door. . . .

Sir Harry smiled, snakelike. He pulled her close and brought his mouth to her ear.

"I've missed you," he whispered.

# Chapter Nine

"Come with me out into the garden, Isobel," Sir Harry ordered in a calm voice that gave Isobel chills. "Don't make a scene. We have much to discuss, my precious. Very much indeed."

Isobel glanced around, but there was no one near. No one who could help her. *Oh, where was Beckett?*

As if reading her thoughts, Sir Harry said, "Your dear husband is searching out that dreary friend of his. Good of him, really. Giving us this time to be alone."

"What do you want?" she spat.

Sir Harry dug his iron-hard fingers into her flesh and she struggled not to wince. She would give him no satisfaction. He couldn't hurt her now and she wanted to tell him so.

"What do I *want*? Why, only what's mine of course. You remember what's mine, don't you, Isobel?"

Quickly he walked her down a deserted pathway, dragging her deep into the trees. He spun her around and held her in front of him.

"Foolish, foolish girl," he said, almost sympathetically, lifting her chin with his fingertips. "Whatever am I to do with you?"

"I'm sure I don't know what you mean. I am the countess of Ravenwood, now—and under my husband's protection."

"Yes, I know about your farce of a marriage to that fop."

"It is not a farce!"

"Does he know who you are? From what I can tell, he knows nothing about Hampton Park or your deceased guardian, Mr. Langley. It was wise of you not to tell him, Isobel. Very wise, indeed."

Something in the tone of his voice made her very, very frightened. She tried to keep her expression even as he reached up and stroked the side of her face.

"I saw you out here with him . . . saw his hands touching your naked skin. I heard you sighing and gasping like a little trollop. *Naughty girl*," Sir Harry said, bringing his face inches away from hers. "I advise you not to make a sound, or I will be forced to hurt you. And I would rather save your punishment for later."

Suddenly, the scene of her guardian's murder flashed into her mind. She pushed it away, refusing to let the terror overtake her. She would not show fear to this man. For that was what he wanted—what he needed to feel powerful.

"You hold no power over me," she insisted, meeting his cold, dark eyes.

"Oh, my dear, sweet Isobel. I shall have both you and Hampton Park before the season is out."

"And how do you propose that? As Lord Ravenwood's wife, my husband now has claim to my property."

"Hmm. Well, if you were his wife, yes. But if you were no longer his wife, what then?"

"What do you mean?" she whispered, a little vein of fear snaking its way around her heart.

Sir Harry smiled nonchalantly. "Would he care to tarnish his name by staying married to a murderess?"

Isobel was dumbstruck. "What are you saying?"

"Do you know Lord Palmerston, the chief justice of the King's Bench? He's an old friend of mine. I explained it all to him, you see. After you are quietly arrested for the rather grisly slaying of your late guardian, I'm certain Lord Ravenwood will arrange for a divorce with great haste. And Palmerston has agreed to hand you over to me. For a price, of course. So you see, Isobel, you *will* be mine, after all."

Isobel tried to swallow her fear.

Sir Harry reached up to stroke her face again. Isobel jerked away. His hand shot up to grab her jaw, and he cruelly snapped her head back to face him. "You have been missing for over fifteen minutes, now, Isobel. You were seen coming out here with me. How will you explain that, eh? Do you think your new husband will believe you? Or will he believe *me* when I tell him I'm your lover and I've just enjoyed your favors?"

"No!" She bucked and struggled against him, but he held her fast.

"*Yes*, Isobel. Keep this up. You'll only look exactly as you should from a little tryst in the garden."

She squealed with outrage and flailed at him, clipping his chin with her fist.

Quickly, Sir Harry blocked the next strike and pinned her arms to her sides. He smiled dangerously. "You'll pay for that later, my dear, along with your other transgressions."

With all her might, she pulled against his grip, unbalancing him. She brought her heel down sharply on top of his foot, and he groaned in pain, momentarily releasing his hold on her arms.

Fleeing, Isobel ran down the dark path as if wolves were chasing her. She heard Sir Harry curse from the darkness behind her.

She reached the terrace steps and looked quickly over her shoulder. In the distance, she saw Sir Harry emerge from the darkened path. With a trembling hand, she smoothed her hair and tried to steady her breathing. She ascended the stairs with as much grace as she could muster. Coming around the corner and through the French doors, she almost slammed into her husband.

"Oh! I—"

Beckett paused and took quick stock of her appearance. "Where have you been, Isobel? I've been searching everywhere for you."

"I needed a bit of air." She pointed feebly toward the gardens. "I felt quite ill."

"You're as white as a sheet." He put a hand on her forehead. "And you're cold as ice."

She glanced behind her and felt her heart leap into her throat as Sir Harry entered the ballroom. His dark, menacing eyes locked onto hers as he strode toward her.

There was no other choice. Isobel let her knees go weak and gave a piteous little moan as she collapsed into Beckett's arms.

"Oh!" she heard someone exclaim beside her.

"My word, is the lady alright?" another asked.

She felt herself being hoisted into Beckett's arms, and let her body flop like a rag doll's.

Where *was* Sir Harry?

"Make way!" Beckett shouted as he moved through the crowd. "Lady Ravenwood has been taken ill. Alfred, run ahead and see that the coach is not blocked in. Hurry, man!"

In moments they were outside. Beckett carried her into the carriage and laid her down on the seat. He draped a cloak over her and took her hand in his, slapping it lightly.

"Isobel. Isobel, can you hear me?"

She waited a few moments, then slowly opened her eyes. There. She was safe, now. Safe with Beckett—for the time being. Immediately, he came to her side and helped her sit up.

"Oh, dear . . . I must have fainted." Her shaky voice sounded surprisingly genuine, even to her own ears.

"You most certainly did. You finally took my advice about swooning, I see." Beckett took her hand in his. "How are you feeling?"

"I'll be fine. Too much excitement, I expect." *That was an understatement if ever there was one.*

"It was the dancing, no doubt," Alfred remarked. He sat across from them in the carriage, looking quite concerned. "They say too much waltzing can cause terrible health problems. And you, my dear Lady Ravenwood, seem to be living proof."

"I am sure it was not the dancing that made me ill, Lord Weston." *It was coming face to face with my enemy that has made me so.*

Though she had feigned the swoon in order to escape the ballroom, there was no doubt that she now felt as ill as she'd claimed. She could still feel the touch of Sir Harry's hands on her skin. It made her want to retch.

Soon they were pulling up in front of the townhouse at Covington Place. With his arm around her, Beckett helped Isobel up the walk and into the foyer.

"I should like to retire, now, I think," she said, desperately wanting to be alone to sort out her thoughts.

"Of course," Beckett said. "Shall we fetch Doctor Pembleton?"

"Oh, no," Isobel protested. "It is not necessary. I need to rest, that is all."

Beckett hesitated. "But surely, a doctor must be called."

"No, no, I am feeling much better, now. Only tired. A good night's rest will cure me."

"If you are certain, my dear."

"Yes, I just need to go to my chamber."

Beckett supported her arm as they mounted the stairs. "Hartley," he said over his shoulder. "Will you bring Lady Ravenwood a tonic to help her sleep?"

"Certainly, my lord," the butler replied from the bottom of the stairs. Beckett and Isobel continued up.

After what seemed like an eternity, Isobel was finally alone in her room. She had ignored the sleeping tonic, dismissed the maid, and lay on the bed still dressed in her ballgown. She stared up at the ceiling, vainly trying to calm the waves of fear that washed through her. The nightmare was upon her again, her enemy nipping at her heels like a hound from hell.

Sir Harry had found her. It was all over.

The reality of that thought made her eyes well with heavy tears. She closed them, feeling helpless as a rabbit in a trap.

Surely, it was only a matter of time before Beckett abandoned her and washed his hands of his mysterious bride. What reason would he have to stand beside her? They had married for convenience, not love, and it was hardly convenient to be married to a woman accused of murder. No matter the brief flirtation they'd shared in the garden.

Sir Harry could be a very persuasive, charming man. After all, her poor father had considered the despicable villain a friend. She had no doubt that Sir Harry could make Beckett believe whatever he chose to tell him.

What had ever made her hope to escape Sir Harry and his hateful plan? She'd been like a little mouse trying to outrun a tom cat—blindly running for her life, and all the time within sight of the amused and capable predator.

She had to take action. She couldn't just sit here and wait for Sir Harry's men to come for her. Beckett might very well do as her enemy had predicted. She couldn't blame him if he did. Worse, her very presence here might be endangering the man who had saved her life.

She had to leave. She must run again. But she would wait until dawn. The London streets were dangerous at night, as she had learned before.

Isobel turned onto her side and stared into the darkness of her chamber, knowing that sleep would be impossible for more reasons than one. Memories teased and swirled around her . . . of Beckett's hard body pressed against hers, creating those intoxicating sensations that she'd never felt before. Sensations she would never feel again.

Banishing such pointless thoughts, she waited for the dawn to light her escape.

# Chapter Ten

Beckett closed the ledger and pushed it across the oak desk. Well, it was official.

He was terribly, terribly rich.

Beckett hated to admit it, but he didn't feel much different from the impoverished viscount that he'd been. He wasn't different—except that he now had bags of money and vast amounts of land.

Besides the Ravenwood estate in Kent, he now held property in Cumberland and Lancashire, as well as a large sugar plantation in Barbados. According to the ledgers, this plantation had enabled the previous earl to almost double the family fortune.

He would settle some property upon his mother, as well as a generous allowance and a fashionable London residence in which she could again hold court. That ought to put him back in her good graces for awhile, at least.

He poured himself another cup of tea from the

silver service and opened the second ledger. But as he tried to concentrate on the figures, his mind returned to Isobel once again.

He would have to arrange for her settlement with the solicitors and install her in her own residence, as they'd agreed. But at some time, he supposed, there would have to be an heir.

Though he had never really discussed it with her, he'd assumed Isobel would understand her duties as his wife included producing an heir. They didn't have to live together to do that. They didn't have to be in love. They could stick to their agreement. Like many other men of his rank, he could visit his wife wherever she chose to live until she was with child. *His* child.

Happily, she had not been averse to his advances last night in the Whitcomb garden. She'd been like a quivering little flower in his arms. And he had wanted to coax her open like a new bud, soft and fragile. It had taken a good deal of his strength not to lay her down in the grass and take her right then and there. Just thinking about it brought a wicked smile to his lips.

She had done battle with Cordelia and survived. Isobel had a sharp wit that he found refreshing, and an uncommon beauty that made him want to protect and ravish her at the same time. Well, she was his wife. Why shouldn't he feel that way? Better that than being married to someone he despised.

Though it *was* terribly bad form to become sentimental about one's wife. That was the very reason he'd married Isobel in the first place, he reminded himself. He'd wanted a business arrangement, and that's what this was. The need to have sexual relations with her, no matter how enjoyable, was purely part of their duty to the estate and family.

He would make sure that while he was kissing Isobel, and stroking her, and mounting her, and burying his face in her neck as he exploded within her—that it was purely business.

Unable to fix his attention on the figures before him, Beckett closed the ledger and looked at the clock. Quarter-past-ten.

He had thought it best to let Isobel sleep late this morning. But he was curious as to her health after last night's excitement. If she was recovered, perhaps they could conclude their *business* tonight.

Beckett found Hartley in the salon. "Has Lady Ravenwood arisen yet?"

"She has, my lord. The countess went outside to draw in the garden earlier this morning. She must still be there, as I have not seen her since."

"Is she feeling better?"

"She looked well, my lord."

Beckett nodded. "Thank you, Hartley."

He stepped through the French doors that led out into the garden and glanced about the grounds. Isobel was nowhere in sight. He could only presume she was behind the bushes on the other side of the fish pond.

He walked across the garden, a smile stealing across his lips. How much better she would feel when he made love to her. He would do so tonight.

He stopped, wondering if she'd heard his approach, then peered around the bushes.

No Isobel.

Only Monty. Beckett's big brown dog jumped to attention and barked happily when he saw his master. Beckett smiled and patted the dog's head. "Did Isobel bring you out, boy?" Now, where was she?

He turned around and looked toward the wrought-iron fence.

Not there, either.

He and Monty walked around the oak tree. "Isobel?"

The garden answered with silence. Perhaps she had gone in again.

Beckett walked back to the house with Monty beside him and went inside. "Isobel?" he called. He trotted up the stairs and nearly bumped into Isobel's new maid.

"Oh, Katie, is Lady Ravenwood in her chamber? I should like to speak with her."

The dark-haired girl shook her head. "No, m'lord. I haven't seen m'lady since early this morning."

Beckett's brow furrowed. Obviously, this was one of the irritating aspects of marriage. He guessed that most of the husbands in London spent the better part of the day trying to find where their wives had got to. Oh, why couldn't women sit still? Bother!

Beckett hastily checked the upstairs, then descended to the first floor and took a quick look in all of the downstairs rooms.

No Isobel anywhere.

"Perhaps she has taken a walk, my lord," Hartley offered. "The park, perhaps?"

"It may be possible," Beckett replied, running his hand through his hair. "Though I'd have thought she would have more sense than to go to Hyde Park alone. If she does not return soon, we shall go and look for her. She may have become lost."

The door-knocker sounded, and the two men looked at each other with knowing expressions.

"That must be Lady Ravenwood, now." Beckett smiled as Hartley went to answer the door. "Doesn't know that she needn't knock at her own door, I suppose."

Hartley opened the door, but instead of Isobel standing there, three gentlemen stared back.

**111**

"May I help you?" Hartley asked.

"I should like to know if Lady Ravenwood is at home, if you please," the white-haired man said.

"She is not at home," Beckett said, quickly coming up beside his butler. "I am her husband."

"Then you are most unfortunate, sir," the man replied.

"And who are you sir, to speak so?" Beckett felt a strange mixture of irritation and foreboding swell in his gut.

The older gentleman paused for effect, staring at Beckett with unamused eyes. "I am Lord Palmerston, chief justice of the King's Bench."

"And what could you possibly want with my wife?"

Lord Palmerston pulled a sheet of paper from his coat pocket.

"I am here to arrest her, sir."

"On what charge?" Beckett demanded, snatching the paper away.

Looking quite bored with the matter, the old man straightened his cuffs.

"Murder."

Beckett blinked, finding it hard to believe his ears. "I beg your pardon?"

"She is accused of the murder of Mr. Edward Langley, her late guardian," Palmerston said with obvious satisfaction. "Well, where is your wife, Lord Ravenwood? The constables will take her into custody until trial."

"*Until trial*? Who is Edward Langley? And why would you think that Lady Ravenwood could be guilty of the crime?"

"We have witnesses, sir, who claim to have seen the former Miss Isobel Hampton stab her guardian at Hampton Park, a week ago."

*Hampton Park?*

"You must be mistaken, Lord Palmerston. I

know nothing of Hampton Park. My wife is from . . ." Good God, where *was* she from?

"I assure you," Lord Palmerston said, "she is Isobel Hampton, late of Hampton Park, and soon to be of Newgate Prison."

"She is not here." Beckett folded his arms. "She has gone to visit a family friend in Chilton."

"In Chilton." Lord Palmerston did not look pleased at this news. "And what would be the name of this 'friend?'"

"Lady Withypoll Weston." Alfred's Great Aunt would be thrilled to have visitors from London. He wished these thick-headed oafs a heap of luck with the eccentric old woman.

"Well, I shall send constables to fetch her then," Palmerston said, clearly perturbed that his quarry was not immediately available.

"You must know these charges are pure flummery."

"That remains to be seen. You sound very confident about the character of a woman you've known only a week, Ravenwood."

At the man's cheeky words, Beckett felt uncertainty slowly spreading through his gut, dark and bitter as cold coffee. Alfred's warnings about taking Isobel home that night echoed in his head. Who *was* this mysterious girl he had married?

Beckett didn't know the answer.

"I shall ask you to leave now, Palmerston." Beckett stood back so Hartley could close the door.

Lord Palmerston opened his mouth to say something, but before he could, Beckett's valet slammed the door in his face.

Beckett patted the servant's shoulder. "Good job, Hartley."

"Shall we go and look for Lady Ravenwood, my lord?"

"Yes, but first you must have a message sent to

Lord Weston. We shall need his help." Beckett hastily donned his jacket. "If any of us find Lady Ravenwood, we must take her back to Lord Weston's townhouse. Not here, is that understood? I'm sure Palmerston will have someone watching this place."

"Thank goodness Lady Ravenwood went out for a walk when she did."

"Yes, very convenient of her to disappear just before a magistrate came to arrest her for murder, wasn't it?"

"You don't think . . ." the servant began, aghast.

"I have no idea what to think, Hartley." Beckett ran his hand through his hair. "But we'd better find her before they do. I'd like to ask my *wife* a few questions of my own."

It was hopeless. She was totally lost.

Street after busy street seemed to be populated with the same people, the same carriages nearly running her over, the same hawkers yelling at her to try their sweetbreads and pastries.

Isobel brushed aside a curl from her face and tried to look like she knew where she was going. All the while, she kept her eyes alert for Sir Harry. She didn't bother looking for Beckett. There was no chance that he would pursue her. Surely Sir Harry's cronies had come by now, and her husband had surely been soured to her by their lies.

Sometimes, Isobel would spot Sir Harry moving in the crowd ahead of her. A piercing fear would rip through her gut like a pistol ball. Then she'd see that it wasn't him at all, but the whisper of terror would stay with her. It was a terrible feeling to live in fear.

"Ow!" Isobel stumbled on a loose cobblestone and lost her shoe. Quickly, she placed it back on her foot before a hungry-looking dog could snatch it out of her hands. "Go away! Shoo!"

The dog snarled at her, then ran off after some other prize.

Isobel resumed walking, wondering where on earth she was going to spend the night. Perhaps a church would offer her shelter. At least she looked like a proper young lady, although walking the streets of London by herself, even in daylight, was anything but proper.

Her feet began to ache. Her shoes were not designed for anything more strenuous than sitting down with needlepoint in her lap. How long had she been walking? And how much farther would she have to go before she could stop?

She had no money and nothing of value to trade or pawn . . . except for herself.

Certainly, she could have taken the topaz jewelry that Beckett had given her to wear to the ball. Or she could have ripped the expensive lace and pearl trimmings from some of her dresses and sold them to a dressmaker.

She'd learned, it was hard to know what to pack when you were fleeing for your life. Wasn't that how she'd ended up in the alley in nothing but her nightdress—without even shoes to cover her feet?

She looked down at the leather slippers that peeked out from under the hem of her skirt. Well, this time she had shoes, at least. And they would have to do.

Taking the topaz earrings, or the expensive trimmings that Beckett had given her would have been theft. And though money would have been helpful, she could not steal from the man who had come to her rescue.

Somehow, she would manage.

Isobel looked at the wide, busy street ahead of

her, hoping she could manage to get across it without getting herself killed.

A carriage charged in front of her, practically spinning her around like a child's top. When the dust settled, she turned to cross again, but stopped when a huge white stallion blocked her way. Could these Londoners be any more rude? Looking up, she shielded her eyes from the midday sun to see the rider.

*Beckett.*

His blazing blue eyes flashed as he swung a leg over the saddle and jumped to the ground.

Isobel turned to run, but he was immediately upon her, strong hands grabbing her arms and jerking her out of the middle of the street.

"And just where do you think you're going, my charming little countess?" he asked, his face towering above her, blocking out the sun.

"I—I went for a walk and I became lost." She tried to free herself from his grip, but his powerful hands held her prisoner.

"Lost? You managed to get yourself halfway across the city! Very conveniently, I might add. You had some callers this morning. Lord Palmerston and his constables."

Isobel felt the blood drain from her face. "Lord Palmerston—"

"He came to arrest you for murder." Beckett pulled her close, and Isobel stared helplessly up into eyes as hard and shiny as sapphires. "For *murder*, Isobel! Why would anyone suspect you of such a thing? And why didn't you tell me about Hampton Park?"

As he said the name of her home, Isobel jerked backward, struggling to break her husband's hold.

Beckett mercilessly tightened his grip. "What are you hiding?"

*Would he turn her over to Palmerston, as Sir*

*Harry had claimed?* She squirmed and wrenched free, darting into the busy street.

"Isobel!" Beckett shouted from close behind her. "Isobel, come back!"

Fear pulsed through her blood as she dashed between carriages and horses, but it wasn't from the danger of the street traffic. It was her husband she feared.

It was all over, now. She had lied to the man who had saved her life. And now, he too, would abandon her.

She was almost across the street. Was he still behind her? She dared a quick look over her shoulder and didn't see him.

As she turned her head to look forward, she saw the strangest sight. It seemed to be happening so slowly, yet she knew that the curricle bearing down on her was travelling terribly fast—so fast that she couldn't get out of the way in time.

She was going to die. Merciful heavens, she was going to die!

Suddenly she was flying. The ground came up to meet her and she hit it with a breathtaking thud. A heavy weight pressed down on her and she tried vainly to get a breath, but the wind was knocked out of her.

Strong hands yanked her up and thumped her back. In a moment, her lungs found the breath they'd been struggling for, and she closed her eyes in relief.

"That was bloody stupid!"

Her eyes flew open and she saw Beckett looking down at her, fuming. She fought against his grip but knew it was fruitless.

"Let me go, you great oaf!"

"*Oaf*? Oaf, you say? Well, if that's the thanks I get for saving your life, I should have let the blasted curricle run you down." Beckett grabbed her shoulders and pulled her closer.

"Call me 'touched-in-the-head,' but I have a strange aversion to becoming a widower in the same week that I was married. And I do not like to be lied to by my wife, do you understand?"

He released her and stepped away, folding his arms across his chest. "To say I am curious to hear what possible explanation there could be for all this—starting with why you ran away this morning—is putting it mildly. Promise me you will never do anything so foolish as that again."

Momentarily silenced by his words, Isobel nodded. A faint glimmer of hope shone in her heart. Would he stand by her, then?

"Good. Obeying your husband. Very good. Yet, I think you need more improvement in that regard." He put his hand around her shoulder and steered her down the street. "I am taking you to Alfred's townhouse."

"Lord Weston? But—"

"They will be waiting for you at Covington Place, Isobel. I told them you've gone visiting Alfred's Great Aunt Withypoll in Chilton, but I don't think they quite believed me. So we will stay at Alfred's until we sort out what to do. And I would like a quiet place in which to hear your answers to this murder charge."

Isobel stopped and looked up at him.

His eyes were guarded. "Just because I didn't wring your lovely little neck doesn't mean you are forgiven."

The ride to Alfred's townhouse in Mayfair was terribly quiet. Isobel stared out the window of the hired coach and tried to collect her thoughts. So much had happened today, it was difficult to make sense of it all. So instead, she watched the city go by as the coach wheels rolled toward Lord Weston's home in Upper Stanbury Street.

What would Beckett do to her? Would he wash his hands of her, and turn her over to her enemies? Many men in his position would, she knew.

But surely, Beckett was not a cruel man. He was angry with her, and would probably be even more so before she was through explaining the truth of the matter. But would he have come looking for her if he didn't care?

She looked at him as if he had spoken, but it was only her thoughts that made her do so.

He must have felt the weight of her stare, because he glanced at her with eyes that seemed to pierce straight through her. Then he looked away.

His indifference felt like a slap, but Isobel was grateful. It made very clear how things stood.

Certainly Beckett cared about her, just as he cared about Monty and Caesar and the other animals he'd rescued. She was simply another stray, a wayward creature he'd found on the street.

Yet, Beckett was her husband. She was his property in the eyes of the law, and therefore her life was very much in his hands. Sir Harry's threat echoed in her ears. Would Beckett believe her story after he realized she'd been lying to him about everything? If he didn't, what would her fate be then?

Oh, this would not do. She had to get her head on straight before they reached Lord Weston's. She wanted to be calm when she told Beckett her story. She needed to be calm, because the truth would bring the horror of that night back to torment her.

In far too short a time, the coach stopped in front of a fashionable townhouse. Isobel felt her stomach tighten in apprehension as Beckett got out of the cab and handed her down onto the cobblestone street.

He looked at her silently before mounting the steps to the great oak door. Before Beckett could knock, it opened, and a gray-haired butler ushered them in.

Beckett addressed the man. "Crandall, will you tell Lord Weston—"

"That you are here, yes, yes," Lord Weston finished, bounding down the staircase. He took Isobel's hand in his and kissed it. "Are you alright, my dear lady? We have been looking for you all day. Beckett, is she alright?"

"Yes, Alfred, she is in perfectly good health." Beckett looked impatient.

Isobel felt another wave of fear sweep through her stomach. She didn't think she could bear the ugly scene that was surely only minutes away. But she would have to, just as she had borne everything else.

"But we have need of a place to stay," Beckett continued. "May we presume on your hospitality—"

"Well, of course you shall stay here. Now what's this about Hartley wanting to stash Isobel out of Lord Palmerston's clutches? It sounds positively fugitive. Has your man gone daft?"

Beckett glanced at Isobel and hesitated before answering. "May we use your library, Alfred? I hate to be a boor, but I need to speak with my wife. *Alone.*"

Isobel tried to calm her beating heart. It felt as if a bird were trapped inside, beating its wings furiously to escape.

Alfred guided them down the hall to the huge book-lined library. "I shall have Crandall bring some tea."

"Thank you, old man. My wife is in need of

some, I expect." Beckett opened a cupboard and brought out a decanter and crystal glass. "But I think I shall have something stronger."

Alfred nodded, smiling. He turned to Isobel. "The tea will be along directly."

"Thank you, Lord Weston," Isobel said quietly.

He bowed and left them alone.

*It would be over soon.* Her husband would finally know the truth. That alone would be a relief.

Beckett lifted the glass of brandy to his lips and downed a mouthful.

"Shall we begin?" he asked, his eyebrows raised in question. "And I warn you, my good humor is back at my townhouse. I believe I left it in the front hall when Hartley opened the door for Palmerston. Let us start with Hampton Park."

Isobel met his eyes and took a deep breath. "It is my home. In Hertfordshire."

"Go on."

"You're wondering about my parents, I suppose? They died in a carriage accident a little over a year ago. I was left in the care of Mr. Edward Langley, my guardian. He was a very kind man." Isobel felt the lump forming in her throat. She stared at her hands.

"He was murdered?"

"Yes."

"But not by you?"

She looked up at him, stung by the question, but not surprised. In her mind's eye she could see the fondness that had always swept over Edward Langley's face at the sight of her, and her heart knotted painfully in her breast. She forced herself to go on. "I was there. I saw it happen. I saw—"

A knock sounded at the door and Isobel turned her head away as Crandall brought in the tray.

"Tea, m'lord."

Isobel wiped at her watering eyes and glanced up at the butler who quietly set the tea service down on the table before her. Crandall gracefully gave her a handkerchief, and exited the room on silent feet.

"Continue, my dear."

She looked up to see Beckett scrutinizing her with a guarded expression.

"I—I'd heard an argument. So I came downstairs to see what was happening. I hid behind the door, but when I heard him . . . stab Mr. Langley, I screamed, and he came after me."

"Who came after you?"

Her voice shook with loathing. "Sir Harry Lennox."

"Lennox? Who in blazes is that? And what reason would he have to kill your guardian?"

"Because he—he wants Hampton Park. Sir Harry had wanted to strike a bargain with Mr. Langley to buy my hand in marriage. But Langley would have none of it. That's why he killed him."

"And you didn't wish to marry this man?"

Isobel looked at Beckett as if he had lost all sense. Once again, his actions had removed hope that someone might understand. But what had she really expected? This man did not know her. He knew nothing except that he'd found her collapsed in the street.

Isobel shut her eyes tight. It was no use.

"I take that to mean you wanted little to do with this Lennox." A twinge of sarcasm darkened his voice.

Her eyes flew open and she stared at Beckett, incredulous. Didn't he know how difficult this was for her? Perhaps he did, and this was her punishment for her lies.

"He was a friend of my father's," she continued.

"Though if my father tolerated him, he could not have known his true nature. Sir Harry Lennox is a blackguard . . . and a murderer. He wanted to be master of Hampton Park. But to get it, he needed to claim me first."

"So you ran. And that's how you came to be on the street the night that I found you."

Isobel nodded, inhaling deeply to steady herself. "Sir Harry saw me in the shadows. He came after me. He caught me easily, and he tried to—it was indecent. I managed to break free of him. Then I ran and ran until I couldn't anymore. The next thing I remember is waking in your bed."

"Ah." Beckett nodded, one eyebrow cocked. "And this Palmerston fellow. What sort of evidence could he have against you, eh?"

"Whatever Sir Harry gave him. He's a very persuasive man." Isobel searched Beckett's eyes, but they gave away nothing. He just stared at her with his arms folded across his chest, seemingly waiting for her to continue. Isobel wiped her moist palms on her skirt and forced herself to keep going. "Sir Harry found me at the Whitcomb ball. He took me out into the garden—"

Beckett set the glass down on the desk and took a step toward her. "To the garden? You went with him?"

"Not willingly! Have you heard nothing I've said? When he had me alone, he threatened me. He told me he would have no trouble convincing you that we were lovers—so that you would abandon me."

"And how do I know you aren't lovers?" Beckett asked half-jokingly. But there was an edge to his voice.

"With him? With Sir Harry Lennox? How *dare* you say such a thing!"

123

"You'll have to forgive me. I have not had much practice in accusing a wife of being unfaithful. Is there a trick to it I don't know?"

Before she knew what she was about, she struck him. All the anguish and desperation of the past weeks erupted from her heart and found its target in the man before her. Isobel beat her fists against his chest and flailed in his arms as Beckett struggled to hold her.

"Isobel!"

She thrashed and pounded against him. "Get your hands off me!"

"Isobel, stop it!" Beckett shouted, quickly winning the battle and holding her immobile.

"Let me go, sir," she said, panting helplessly against the power of his embrace.

"I will not."

"Why? Surely you don't want to keep a murderess as a wife?"

Beckett held her in front of him. "I don't believe you are a murderess, Isobel."

She stared up into his eyes, unwilling to hope. "You don't?"

"No." Beckett's grip relaxed and he touched his hand gently to the side of Isobel's face. "I am your husband. And I will protect you."

At those words Isobel's heart swelled painfully. She closed her eyes against the burning tears. A strong hand curled gently around her neck and Beckett pulled her head against his chest.

"Thank you," she whispered, not knowing what else to say.

"You needn't thank me. Isn't it my duty, Isobel? I swore to honor and protect you all the days of your life. And all the days of mine, for that matter." He pulled away and looked down at her. She saw the wariness in his eyes. "Yet you should have told me before."

"I was afraid."

"Yes, I can imagine you were." Beckett turned away from her. "This changes things, Isobel. I will have to take you away from London, certainly— someplace where you'll be safe from both Lennox and Lord Palmerston's arrest warrant. Until we can get these charges dropped and find some evidence against Lennox . . ."

"What if we can't?"

Beckett turned to face her. "Then I suppose we shall have to live abroad."

Isobel studied him for a moment, still mystified by her husband's decision to stand by her. "Why are you doing this? Most men in your position would think twice about giving up so much . . . especially to protect a woman who was a wife in name, alone."

Beckett returned nonchalantly to his glass and downed the rest of the brandy.

"I am not most men."

"You'll go to Barbados, then?" Alfred asked.
Beckett nodded, his mouth full. He, Alfred and Isobel sat at the long dining room table, break-fasting on braised ham, poached eggs, toast with blueberry compote, and fresh strawberries with cream. There was nothing like an adventure to stir up a man's appetite.

"Barbados?" Isobel set down her teacup and looked at Beckett, her soft brown eyes wide with shock. "Well, that's not a very civilized place, is it?"

"How civilized is it here in London with Sir Harry Lennox running around? I don't think it's safe to stay in England at all, not with Lord Palmerston looking for you." Beckett swallowed a bit of coffee. "I was planning to go to Barbados next month at any rate to visit the Ravenwood sugar plantation there. We could leave as soon as possible. Lord Palmerston thinks you've gone to Chilton. I'll have it put 'round that I've gone off to Ireland, or someplace that will take them awhile to get to. Before they can get back to London, we'll be aboard a ship bound for the islands."

"A capital idea, Beckett. I'll go along with you," Alfred said. "Make sure you don't get into trouble."

"Oh, no you won't, Alfred. I need you to stay here and find proof of Isobel's innocence. And Sir Harry's guilt."

Alfred brightened at that. "Even better! I adore a good mystery. You know, if I didn't have to be a lord of the realm, I always thought I should make a dandy Bow Street runner."

"But Lord Weston," Isobel began. "Surely it isn't safe to start poking about on your own. And I do not like to think of what might happen if Sir Harry gets wind of your plan. He is a dangerous man."

"As am I, dear lady." Alfred smiled and kissed her hand.

Isobel looked imploringly at Beckett. "But there must be another way."

"Lord Palmerston's men will be back from Chilton in a few days," explained Beckett. "We must be safely on our way before they return to London."

"But what if Alfred doesn't find any proof?"

"Of course I will, dear lady," Alfred assured her. "I possess a wealth of skills. Isn't that right, Beckett?"

"Very true, though I doubt most of them have any relevance here." Beckett saw the worried look in Isobel's eyes, and took her hand. "Isobel, you must obey me in this. We will be on the next ship bound for Barbados. It is the only choice we have. Besides, I believe the challenge of this situation is part of my earthly trials."

Isobel smiled slightly.

"As for Alfred, he and I have been getting in and out of trouble together since we met at Oxford. And we always get out, don't we Alfred?"

"Yes, but I do admit, this raises the challenge to new heights."

Beckett laughed. "Alfred, please try to contain your confidence in our plan."

"It is a forgone conclusion. Good will inevitably triumph over evil, and history proves my theory. At least I think it does. It should, or we'd all be in a terrible state. Why, just look at—"

"Oh, enough, Alfred! If I wanted a history lesson, I'd open a book." He looked back at his bride, who seemed unaccustomed to making light of serious topics.

"Of course, we'll be leaving London as quietly as possible. And we'll book passage under assumed names. Alfred, I'll need you to spread the word that I've gone off to Dublin. I shall have to return to the house briefly to have a trunk packed for my 'trip to Ireland.' That will include a few dresses for you, Isobel. But we must both travel lightly. You won't be needing ball gowns where we're going."

Isobel smiled soberly. "You can be assured that fashionable dress is the furthest thing from my mind."

Beckett turned to his friend. "Now remember, Alfred, I shan't tell the new house staff anything. Sir Harry may find some way to get information out of them, and if he thinks they know anything he's more likely to use stronger methods. The less they know, the better. I shall have to tell Hartley, though, as you may need his assistance in your investigation. We'll spend at least a month or so in Barbados. When we return, hopefully you'll have gathered enough evidence to refute this ludicrous murder charge against Isobel. And do me a favor, Alfred—look in on the pets from time to time, will you? I don't want Hartley to get over-run. And Alfred. Be careful."

Alfred chuckled and slapped him on the shoulder. "Don't worry about me, old man. You know it is Sir Harry Lennox who should be careful."

# *Chapter Eleven*

Isobel inhaled the strong, clean smell of the sea. Overhead, the gulls' cries made an eerie music.

How on earth had fate brought her to this place? Here she stood at the Portsmouth dock, about to journey to a tropical island with a man who had found her in an alley. Good Lord, what strange twists and turns life could take.

They boarded the ship, and Beckett introduced her to the captain, using their assumed names. They were travelling as Mr. and Mrs. Cox, well-to-do merchants from London. She had still been trying to get used to being called the countess of Ravenwood, and now she had another name to answer to.

At last, the ropes that moored them to the wharf were cast off and the ship was moving through the gray-blue waters. Isobel stood beside Beckett at the starboard side and waved goodbye to Alfred, who bid farewell from the dock.

So much of this plan rested on her husband's friend's shoulders. But Alfred, who appeared so light-hearted and genteel, had a mind as strong and sharp as a sword. Her husband had sworn to it. Isobel would depend upon that sword to fight the battle for her here in England, while she was spirited safely away. It seemed strange that she no longer had to defend herself, and that others were willing to stand by her. But it felt good.

The ship's captain, Mayfield, took them on a brief tour of the craft and Isobel was glad for the distraction.

She found herself fascinated with the rhythm of the huge vessel. Its sailors all seemed to work together effortlessly, as if they could hear each other without speaking. From time to time, the bosun would call out orders, and the sailors would respond with feline agility and grace. They flew up and down the rigging as if it were more natural to them than walking upright.

But more striking than the rhythm of the crew was something entirely different: a large black-and-white cat. She supposed that cats were not uncommon upon seagoing vessels, what with the mice, but this cat in particular seemed strange; it surveyed the crew as if it were his own. She wondered if perhaps the animal was friendly.

As she stood there, wondering at the beast, it met her eyes. The cat stared at her intently from across the deck, and Isobel felt strangely unnerved. She glanced away. Had that been intelligence in its eyes? Obviously, her misadventures had to be taking their toll on her, if she were imagining such things.

When she looked back, the cat was gone. She returned her attention to Captain Mayfield.

At last the captain returned to his duties, leaving Beckett and Isobel standing together on deck.

130

She looked up at her husband as he surveyed the ship. An uncomfortable silence thickened the air between them.

She wondered what would happen, now. Although he had assured her of his protection, she had sensed Beckett distancing himself from her since she'd explained Edward Langley's death.

He hadn't mentioned her guardian's name since then, or the other sordid circumstances leading to this impromptu journey. And yet the silent questions stood between them like a wall. The jesting and flirting they had enjoyed at the Whitcomb ball were gone.

Certainly, he had not kissed her since.

The wind lifted Beckett's hair with invisible fingers, taunting Isobel to reach out and do the same. But she knew that was impossible now. He had stood by her out of duty, not because of any feeling he had for her. It would do no good to become sentimental about a relationship that would never be.

As the ship left Portsmouth harbor, they were shown to their quarters. Their cabin was spacious enough to accommodate them both, though of course, it held only one bed. And though they had already shared a bed inadvertently, it would be very different indeed to sleep next to him tonight, now that they were man and wife.

Dinner was brought to their door and they ate it without ceremony. Then Beckett produced a deck of cards, and enticed her to play *ecarte*. With the maelstrom of thoughts that swam in her head, she welcomed the diversion.

They played countless games, until Isobel found her eyes watering as she tried fruitlessly to ward off the heaviness of sleep.

"You look tired, my dear." Beckett put down his cards. "It has been a long day. Shall we go to bed?"

Isobel looked up at him, her blood suddenly racing. *"To bed?"*

"Yes. I am tired as well." Beckett stood up, his expression remote. "I suppose it is a good thing that we are married, isn't it—seeing as there is only one bed? We can sleep in it together with a clear conscience."

Isobel stared at the bunk they were to share as if it were engulfed in flames. They had not shared a normal-sized bed as man and wife, and this one looked unable to accommodate two. Surely he would make some alternate arrangement.

She looked back at Beckett who was now pulling off his shirt. Though she tried to tear her gaze away, she couldn't help but stare as he pulled the white shirt up over his head. The lamplight gave his skin a golden glow, and accentuated the powerful muscles of his arms and stomach. The sight of his body astounded her, sent waves of heat washing through her in a most distracting fashion.

"Come here," he said.

Unable or unwilling to refuse, Isobel obeyed. He raised his hands toward her slowly, cupping her shoulders in a warm, solid grip. *What was he doing?* Their agreement was one of conven—

He turned her around, sliding his hands slowly down to the little cluster of buttons that fastened the upper part of her dress. He began to undo them.

"I thought you might need help, without a maid to undress you." He eased the garment apart and slid his hands in, easing the dress down just over her chemise. Then he twisted her around again, and after an excruciatingly long moment, released her. "I think you can manage the rest."

Confused, Isobel searched his eyes. He seemed to be holding something back, just behind the impenetrable walls of his stormy-blue eyes.

132

*What did he want from her?*

She turned around and searched for her night-dress, and finally found it. She hesitated for a long moment, but there was nowhere to hide in such limited space. Reluctantly, Isobel faced the fact that she would have to disrobe in front of her husband. As she squirmed out of her clothes, she felt her face flush with heat.

As fast as she could, Isobel shimmied out of her dress and chemise and threw the night rail over her head. She glanced over her shoulder and saw that Beckett had climbed into bed. At least he'd had the decency to face the wall as she approached. Gingerly, she turned down the lamp. Feeling much braver in the dark, Isobel pulled back the covers and slipped between them as if this were the most normal thing in the world. Then she lay on her back near the edge of the bed and waited.

And waited.

She listened to Beckett breathing.

Her whole body seemed to be acutely aware of the hard warm masculine presence next to her. It was to be expected, she thought, having never slept next to a man before. But she would not let *him* know. Not after he'd made this whole business so embarrassing for her. . . .

She heard her husband's breathing take on a new tone. It was lower, deeper, and calmer.

Devil take him, he was snoring! Her husband, whose very presence made her tingle with awareness of this, their first night together in bed, was snoring.

Well, if that didn't just take the flip. The lumping dandy-prat was asleep!

# Chapter Twelve

Beckett looked out over the railing, marvelling at the beauty of the ever-changing sea. It calmed him to watch the movement of the gray-blue water, whose only constant was its never-ceasing movement. Like life itself, it made no promises to anyone.

He turned his head and saw Isobel approaching. The sight of her, as ethereal as an angel, sent a wash of heat through his body.

*Damn and blast!*

She was his wife, a complete mystery who had been implicated in horrible goings-on, yet here he was mooning over her as if he were a youth and she a beautiful chorus girl.

She came to stand close by, favoring him with a smile and the sparkle of her warm brown eyes. Then she looked out over the beckoning sea, and let her arm brush against his as she leaned on the railing.

Beckett regarded her, so calm and composed beside him. At first glance she would seem the embodiment of innocence and purity, but was she indeed the innocent victim she appeared to be? There were certainly some claims that should make him question such a notion.

And yet, Beckett felt his gut tighten at even the notion of abandoning her. He could never fully dampen the flame of passion that she stirred in him, or fight the powerful conviction that because he had found her, she now belonged totally to him.

He would protect her.

Or die trying.

"There is something you never told me, Beckett." Isobel's voice came softly as the breeze itself.

He looked down at her. Against his will he reached for a golden tendril that floated in the wind. Then his hand cupped her face, and he brushed his thumb against her delicate skin.

"Told you *what*, Isobel?" he whispered.

"*Why?*" She looked up at him beseechingly, searching his face for the answer she sought. "Why did you bring me home that night?"

He saw something in her eyes that made a knot form in his heart.

*Why had he helped her?* He had asked himself the same question as he'd undressed and bathed her that night, and as he'd ducked from the clock she'd thrown at him, as he'd stood next to her at the altar and taken her as his wife.

And still the answer eluded him.

Was it her beauty that had captured him and taken him prisoner? It was more than his habit of helping strays, he knew.

He curved his arm around her narrow waist and pulled her close. He felt his passion flare as their bodies touched, and fought to control it. "Do I have to give you a reason?"

She nodded.

"Then perhaps it was because I wanted to hold you in my arms and do *this*." He covered her mouth with his own, and felt her lips tremble as he kissed her. He felt his own desire building, and imagined what would happen if he let it run unchecked. He could take her down to their cabin right now. She was his wife. He had every right. And somehow he knew she would not protest.

He kissed her hungrily, as if she were the only nourishment his body would ever, *could* ever need.

Oh, how he wanted her beneath him, naked and open and weak with desire—desire for *him*.

It frightened him how much he wanted it.

She stirred dangerous feelings in him, powerful feelings—and if he fed them with the taste of her in his arms, shaking with desire as he loved her, he might lose himself.

He broke the kiss, but still held her close.

"There, Isobel." He brushed away a silken curl from her cheek. "That is the only answer I can give you."

She studied him for a moment with eyes that seemed to see far too much for his liking.

"Your answer only raises more questions, Beckett. For both of us."

An uneasy silence remained between Beckett and Isobel for the remainder of the voyage.

As husband and wife, they maintained a cordial atmosphere that Isobel considered might be quite common to any marriage. But beneath that calm veneer lurked the shadows of the past, like a great sea-monster that swims below a ship—far too deep to be seen—and yet still posing a dangerous threat.

Every night Isobel found herself hoping that Beckett would reach out and pull her close, kiss her as he had on the deck, and touch her in a way she could only imagine.

But he didn't.

He only snored loudly enough to wake the whole ship, and probably most of London, though they were halfway to Barbados. Beckett's snoring only served to keep Isobel awake and thinking. And her thoughts were always of him.

To keep her mind off her husband during the day, Isobel observed ship-board life on deck, recording all she saw in her sketch-book.

She drew everyone—including Captain Mayfield and the large sailor with the black-and-white cat she'd seen curled on top of his shoulders. She'd had to make her observations from afar, as the beast seemed always to disappear when she approached.

On a particularly breezy afternoon, while she was drawing a sailor who worked up in the rigging, the cat appeared beside her and sat still. It seemed to study what she was doing as it sat there, silent yet imposing.

Isobel reached out to stroke his soft, furry head in greeting. The cat's green eyes narrowed to slits, and he purred in pleasure. Reluctantly taking her hand away, Isobel flipped to the next blank sheet of paper and began to render the feline's image.

The cat was huge—not fat by any means, but with muscular shoulders and haunches. No doubt, he was well fed by keeping rats and mice out of the galley.

Isobel noticed that one of his black patches covered the side of his head and his left eye, looking remarkably like a pirate's lopsided kerchief and eye patch.

As she drew, Captain Mayfield came to stand in front of her, but at his approach, the cat rose, stretched, and walked away.

"Oh, but I wasn't finished," Isobel called out, but the cat simply walked haughtily across the deck and disappeared from sight.

Mayfield chuckled. "I suppose I didn't mention that this ship has two captains, did I?"

Isobel shook her head. "Two captains? I've never heard of that. Who is the other?"

"You just met him."

Isobel put her pencil down and paused. "Just met . . . ?"

"That cat is more than he seems, my lady. He's Captain Black." Mayfield sat down beside her, resting his elbows on his knees, and gazing at her slyly. "I first met him on one of my journeys in the Caribbean, which is swamped with pirates, as you must well know."

Isobel smiled at the gray-haired man beside her. He was going to tell her a sea-faring yarn, she supposed. He was just having fun with a land-lubber. She would play along with the old soul.

"We were off the coast of Jamaica," the captain began, "carrying a heavy cargo of coffee beans, when we were attacked by a rather notorious pirate ship, the 'Midnight Star.' Its captain was named Worthington, a shrewd but fair man who was more famous for his cat companion. Legend has it that the beast was the ship's previous master, a man named Black, who had been transformed into the guise of a cat during an obeah ceremony in Jamaica."

Isobel was delighted. This was just the thing to get her mind off her woes. "Obeah? What on earth is that?"

"The religion of the Haitians. It's also known as voodoo," Captain Mayfield explained. "Their ceremonies are filled with chanting, wild dancing, and other practices that are too indelicate to mention."

"And they used it to put a spell on Captain Black? But how?"

"Apparently this man Worthington had planned to mutiny against his captain and take over the ship himself. While in Jamaica, he discovered the powers of obeah and arranged to do away with his rival."

Silly or not, the tale was suitably unnerving. Isobel admired the old captain's story-telling ability.

"And there were witnesses, members of the pirate crew that saw their captain changed into a cat during one of those frightening ceremonies."

"But how did Captain Black arrive on board your ship?"

"It was during the battle with the 'Midnight Star,' when the pirate ship caught fire. We searched for survivors after she sank, but found no one. Except for a mysterious cat who appeared on our ship, as if out of thin air. The crew was naturally suspicious, but unwilling to dispose of the creature—they believe that he possesses mystical powers."

The cat suddenly appeared again, as if he'd heard them talking. He leaped up onto the railing and landed solidly, turning to arrange himself into a comfortable position.

Captain Mayfield smiled and regarded the cat, who looked back at him through half-lidded eyes.

"Though we found no other survivors, there are rumors that Worthington is still alive, and even now searches the seas for his cat companion. As you can see, we gave Captain Black a position on our ship as chief mouse-catcher, one that he performs exceedingly well."

Isobel giggled and regarded him with a wary smile. He'd almost had her believing the incredible tale. "Hmm . . . you wouldn't be teasing me now, would you, Captain Mayfield?"

"That is Captain Black before you, Madam! In flesh and blood. He tries to steer the ship, you know—among other things."

Isobel laughed, and Captain Mayfield leaned toward her in a conspiratorial way.

"And sometimes, I let him," he whispered, then turned and walked back to his post.

Isobel smiled and looked at the cat, still sitting on the narrow railing in front of her. "So, are you really a pirate, then?"

The cat returned her gaze, then answered with a long "meow."

"Perhaps you are," Isobel mused. She watched Captain Black walk down the long railing and leap to the deck. He strolled away from her, doubtless to resume his mouse-catching duties below.

An eerie moan broke the dark silence of the cabin. Beckett jumped up and hit his head on the low ceiling above him. He was momentarily stunned, but quickly became alert as another hair-raising wail cut through the darkness from beside him.

*Isobel.*

He could hear and feel her thrashing around on the bed next to him, her breathing shallow and strained. He reached out to touch her and heard her whimpering.

"Isobel, you're dreaming." He managed to grab hold of her and pull her into his arms, stroking her damp forehead as she struggled in her sleep. He touched her face and felt her cheek hot and damp with tears. Her whole body was covered in perspiration, soaking her linen nightdress.

She stiffened and seemed to awaken. Beckett loosened his hold on her, suddenly aware of how intimately he held her.

"Are you alright?"

"Yes, I think so," Isobel whispered, her voice slightly shaky.

"You were having a bad dream. Lie down and try to go back to sleep." He tried to settle her back under the covers.

"No—" She sprang up and clutched at his hand. "I don't want to go to sleep. I don't want to have that dream again."

Beckett propped himself up on one elbow and turned the covers back gently. "Come, now. Lie down here with me. There's no one to trouble you here."

She remained where she was. While he waited for her to make up her mind, Beckett lay back down, and soon began drifting toward sleep.

It was with a bit of shock that he felt her snuggling up against him. For a moment, half-asleep, he forgot entirely where he was, why he was there, and who the lovely creature beside him could be. He simply enjoyed it.

She exhaled slowly, then moved closer to him. Her rose-water scent reached out to him, teasing his senses.

"Thank you, Beckett," she whispered.

Then it came back to him. He was Beckett. The earl of Ravenwood. And the woman beside him in bed was his wife.

Beckett watched the moonlight that spilled through the window play on Isobel's hair, like silvery fingers dancing across a river of gold. Before he knew what he was about, he stroked it. He felt Isobel go still in his arms at his touch, but he continued caressing her soft curls. The texture of the silken strands running through his fingers sent a shock of heat through him.

He thought of Cordelia then. Of how he'd never done anything like this to her, and even if they had married, probably never would have. This was too affectionate, too warm. He saw now that she'd borne his touch as a means to an ends—to acquiring his title and fortune. She would surely have done the same with any prospective husband.

But he had fancied himself in love with Cordelia. And it had all been an illusion. Hadn't it?

The Whitcomb ball had seen his new wife in a battle *royale* with his former intended. Why would Cordelia have bothered to challenge Isobel if she'd indeed felt nothing for him? He'd always found it difficult to understand her. Now that he had some distance, Cordelia was no easier to comprehend.

But still, he couldn't imagine his previous fiancée curled up in his arms as Isobel was now. Seeking solace from her nightmares in the safety of his arms. Letting him stroke her hair. Again, he basked in the warmth of his desire for the woman whose body curled next to his.

A surge of gratitude and something else unfamiliar welled up inside his chest, and he hugged Isobel closer.

Isobel opened her eyes slowly, peering at the dim morning light through squinting eyes. She had done it. She had fallen asleep and not dreamt the awful nightmare again. As she became more fully awake, she remembered what had made her tranquil sleep possible.

Beckett's arm lay curled around her waist, a bit of her nightdress bunched loosely in his fist. A breath caught in her throat at the sweet heaviness of the embrace that surrounded her so possessively.

It was unusual for married couples to sleep together in the same bed, she knew. Civilized society insisted on separate chambers for husband and wife. But, oh, how wonderful it would be to wake like this every morning.

Her eyes opened wide and her breathing quickened as the arm around her waist tightened and drew her closer.

Beckett's deep, steady breathing told her that he was still asleep. Her back was pressed against the hard wall of his chest as he held her firmly to him.

Then Isobel felt something else hard, pressing gently against her buttocks. It couldn't be his knee. . . .

It was . . . it was . . . Good Lord, it was his—

She knew she should try to get up, but it clearly seemed impossible without waking him. And surely this situation would embarrass him as much as her. No, she would have to endure this wicked intimacy until she could unlock his arm from her waist and move safely across the bed.

Gingerly, Isobel closed her hand around Beckett's wrist and tried to lift his arm. This was going to be more difficult than she'd thought. Although he was asleep, Beckett's muscles were anything but relaxed. The arm around her waist hugged her to him as if she were a doll.

Isobel closed her eyes as his hips pressed against her bottom. She clamped her lips together to keep from making a sound as he ground himself against her.

Exquisite sensations swept through her body, making the tips of her breasts hard and sensitive. Heat seared between her legs, unnerving her with its intensity.

*This was dreadful. Wasn't it?*

Abruptly, Beckett released his hold on her waist and turned over. The continuous sound of his rhythmic breathing, deep and even, travelled through the cabin.

Isobel lay in stunned silence, feeling an absurd

sense of disappointment. He was still asleep. Thank the Lord.

She pulled back the covers and tiptoed across the room to the screen in the corner. Isobel pulled off her night dress, wet a cloth, and rubbed it over her hot skin, trying desperately to slow her racing pulse.

Isobel donned her underclothes and stockings, followed by a somber fawn-brown day dress. She hoped it would set the mood for the rest of the day. She picked up her paper and leads, but paused a moment before leaving.

Beckett was still asleep. Taking advantage of the moment, she watched him in the pale morning light.

An uneasiness crept into Isobel's heart, like a soft-footed cat bent on mischief. She had been fooling herself to think she could make this marriage purely one of convenience. Their arrangement was doomed to be a dismal failure. Like it or not, Beckett stirred feelings in her. And like unruly children, each day she found them harder to control.

# Chapter Thirteen

Isobel watched as a dark shape grew along the horizon. She had dreamed with such longing of land beneath her feet again.

As they neared the island, she was entranced by the clear, turquoise waters. The sun shone high in the sky, and made the water sparkle as though covered in twinkling jewels.

The heat grew a little more intense as the ship neared the island. The wind had been constant out on the open water, and the temperature on deck had been warm but bearable. Now, she felt the sun beating down on her and she shaded herself with a parasol.

Isobel looked over the side of the boat into the depths of the blue-green ocean, and was startled as she saw a large, dark shape swimming through the water far below.

"Captain Mayfield, what is that down there?" Isobel said, with some fear.

The captain looked over, but the shadow was no longer in sight.

"Most likely a dolphin, Mrs. Cox. Though to an untrained eye, a shark can easily appear to be a dolphin."

Isobel nodded, remembering the stories he'd told her during their voyage about life in the tropics. Aside from the assortment of poisonous plants and insects, and the wild animals, there was also the native religion of obeah to send shivers down her spine.

"I needn't remind you that this isn't England," Captain Mayfield teased. "But many Europeans enjoy living on these islands and have done so for years with no harm coming to them."

Isobel smiled and tried to reassure herself. After all, they had come here out of necessity— not to establish a home in a strange land.

"Still, be sure your husband teaches you how to shoot a pistol." Captain Mayfield turned and walked along the deck to join his first mate.

Isobel looked across the water to the island. The captain was poking fun at her, she reminded herself. However, learning to shoot might be a good idea.

Beckett appeared beside her, a look of quiet anticipation on his face as he surveyed the approaching shoreline. "I hope you won't find life here on the island too uncomfortable, my dear. My experience in Wellington's army has prepared me for almost any kind of accommodation, no matter how rough. But a lady might find such a wild land to be quite an adjustment. He held his hand out to her. Taking a deep breath, she placed her hand in the warm, solid strength of his.

Beckett smiled at her as the wind whipped his tawny hair. The effect was stunning. The sunlight lit his eyes and hair, and as he stared at her, Isobel was unable to look away.

"I have been well prepared by Captain Mayfield for the way of life here in the tropics," Isobel said, meeting Beckett's eyes. "Perhaps I might even teach you a thing or two."

"I look forward to being your pupil." He gave her a playful look.

Isobel turned toward the dock as the ship approached. She did not want to think about what he might want her to teach.

She stared at the long wooden dock and watched the men, both Europeans dressed as they might be in London and native workers loading various cargo.

The ship docked smoothly, its sailors all working in tandem to tie the lines. Some of their cargo was unloaded at once before the passengers began to disembark.

Isobel lifted Captain Black into her arms to say her goodbyes. She'd become fond of the surly animal during the journey, as had Beckett, with his natural affinity for animals. She smiled as she thought of the lovely sketches she had made of both Beckett and the cat. Would she stare wistfully at them in years to come, when she and her husband were finally able to live out their separate lives?

Captain Mayfield approached from across the deck.

"My dear Mrs. Cox," the captain began. "It seems that Captain Black has grown tired of a seafaring life and now seeks employment on land. Could you perhaps find a suitable position for him at your new residence?"

Isobel looked at Captain Mayfield and then Beckett, who grinned and said, "My wife and I would like nothing more."

147

Isobel stroked the cat's soft fur. "But Captain Mayfield, how can you be sure that Captain Black has given up the sea?"

"Oh, I am quite sure of it." The old man nodded. "You see, I just left him in my cabin, having locked the door but a moment ago. And now, here he is in your arms."

Everyone looked at Captain Black for some explanation, but the cat merely blinked at them.

"Apparently, he has grown quite attached to you, my dear. Considering his experience with obeah, he will no doubt be adept at protecting you from any island mischief." Mayfield cocked an eyebrow at Isobel in confirmation.

Isobel nuzzled the cat before the captain gently placed him inside a carrying basket.

"Now, you must promise to stay in your basket, Captain Black. *Please*." Mayfield shook his finger at the cat inside and then fastened the lid.

Beckett shook hands with the man. "Thank you for delivering us so expertly, Captain."

"It has been a pleasure, sir."

Guided by Beckett, Isobel made her way down the boarding plank and onto the dock. She turned to wave, but Captain Mayfield was gone, doubtless seeing to some part of the ship's business.

"We'll miss Captain Mayfield, won't we, Captain Black?" she said to the meowing creature in the basket, as she followed Beckett down the length of the dock.

Beckett looked back at her over his shoulder. "Quite an elaborate story just to get rid of a cat. I suppose he wouldn't have known we'd be happy to adopt the creature. I must say, I miss being away from Monty and Caesar. Captain Black shall be good company for us."

148

One of the men from Ravenwood's Barbados property stood beside the waiting coach, hat in hand.

"Lord Ravenwood," he said, bowing, "Hal Cobb, sir, at your service."

"Mr. Cobb, may I present my wife, Lady Ravenwood." Beckett took her hand and brought her a step forward.

"M'lady."

Isobel fanned herself as the man made his bows to her. "I am pleased to make your acquaintance, Mr. Cobb. Tell me, is it always this hot on the island?"

"Oh, no, m'lady. It's usually much hotter."

Isobel glanced at Beckett and saw him grin.

"I told you Barbados was not for the faint of heart," was all he said.

"So you did." She purposely closed her fan. "I shall have no trouble at all, then."

Beckett chuckled and handed her up into the carriage. Soon they rolled into motion and started down the rough dirt road.

Her fan did not stay closed for long. Much to her dismay, Isobel's entire body quickly developed a sheen of perspiration. As soon as she discreetly wiped some away from her forehead, it was instantly replaced. Her light muslin dress stuck to her like glue and most likely showed off far too much of her body. Isobel fanned herself energetically. It gave some relief.

She noticed that Beckett was also covered in sweat, and wiping at his forehead from time to time with a handkerchief. At last, he caught her staring at him.

She quickly looked out the window. Captain Black meowed loudly and scrambled about inside his carrier like he was possessed.

As they traveled down the road, Isobel tried to focus on the beautiful countryside to take her mind off the heat. They left St. Michael and Bridgetown, and entered the district of St. James, which would be her home for the next while.

Outside, all around them bloomed flowers in colors Isobel had never seen before, with trees and various plants in such strange sizes and shapes, she wondered at nature's handiwork.

Questions and observations tumbled out of her like rambunctious children.

"—What is that tree?"

"—That flower, do you know what is it called?"

"—What an odd looking fruit! Surely no one eats such a thing."

Beckett patiently pointed out banana and fig trees, but he was silently chuckling at her, she was quite sure. He also identified mangoes, sugar apples and hog plums—all hanging in the thick boughs like richly colored jewels. The smell of their sweet scents on the breeze made Isobel long to stop and pick some of the succulent fruit.

The sky above them was a bright, warm blue— the same color as Beckett's eyes, Isobel noticed. Huge puffy clouds decorated the expanse of sky like dollops of clotted cream. This mysterious place was like a spell cast to invade all the senses at once. The sights, sounds and smells were almost impossible to resist. She turned and saw that Beckett's gaze was fixed firmly on her, but as usual it was unreadable.

"Such untamed splendor often has an intense effect on the human heart, does it not?" he asked quietly.

"I do not know, as I have had no experience in such matters."

"I daresay that during our time on Barbados,

you shall experience a great many things to remedy such a misfortune."

Isobel opened her mouth to reply, but squealed as something quite large flew by the window. "Oh my! Whatever was that?"

She leaned closer to the window and almost bumped heads with Beckett as he did the same. They laughed, and Beckett pointed through the open window to the treetops.

"You see up there, in the tree? Those are wild macaws. A macaw is a rather colorful type of parrot."

Isobel located the beautiful birds sitting high in the branches overhead.

"Oh, Beckett. It's as though someone has painted them by hand! But Caesar is not colored so."

"He would surely have something quite nasty to say on the subject." Beckett chuckled, sitting back. "We can count our blessings that it's Captain Black we have with us instead."

The carriage turned down a long drive. In the distance, Isobel could see Ravenwood Hall. It was surrounded by a magnificent lawn and exotic gardens, with palm trees standing tall overhead. Behind it, the vast sugar fields stretched out of sight.

They pulled up in front of the large, two-story house, which was surrounded by a verandah on both levels. Constructed of an unusual pink-colored stone, the house was offset by bright white shutters that flanked its long windows. Though the architecture copied the English style, the house seemed far more exotic than anything found in the British Isles.

The house staff of Ravenwood Hall stood at attention outside before the steps, waiting to greet the new earl and countess. Beckett handed

Isobel out of the carriage as Mr. Cobb prepared to introduce them to the staff.

Various male and female servants peered at them curiously, all seeming to be native islanders. There was a mature butler with a white beard, beside him a substantial woman whom Isobel took to be the housekeeper, and a few young girls who made up the rest of the household staff.

Mr. Cobb introduced the butler first. "This is Isaac."

The man made his bows, and spoke in a raspy voice. "It is a pleasure to welcome the new lord and lady to Ravenwood."

"It is a pleasure to be here, Isaac," Beckett replied.

"This is Josephine," Mr. Cobb said. "The housekeeper of Ravenwood Hall."

Beckett nodded at the woman. Her high cheekbones and intimidating stare made Isobel feel as if she herself should be making a curtsy to Josephine, not the other way around.

"Welcome, m'lord," she said in a voice as dark and rich as coffee. She curtsied with a regal air, just as Isobel had imagined she would.

"Thank you, Josephine. I am sure our stay here will be very enjoyable now that we are in your capable hands."

The woman nodded silently.

"May I introduce my wife, Lady Ravenwood. And this is her cat, Captain Black."

Isobel smiled as Josephine looked suspiciously at the meowing basket she held.

"You 'ave Captain Black in dat basket?" Josephine raised her eyebrows.

Surprised, Isobel nodded.

"Captain Black is famous in dese islands," she whispered to Isobel, then let out a booming laugh as she pointed towards the door. "Come inside, now, come inside!"

Isobel looked to Beckett for direction. He responded by putting her hand through his arm, and leading her through the doorway.

The interior of the house was stylish but not ornate. It had been decorated in vibrant colors too outrageous for London, but perfectly suitable for this island manor house. There were the usual comforts of home—a salon, a dining room, a small library. In each room, lovely arrangements of native flowers and plants made the house look and smell like a garden.

"We should like some tea in the salon please, Josephine," Beckett said.

Josephine smiled and nodded. "Yes, m'lord."

"Well, what do you think of your new home, Isobel?"

She turned to look at Beckett as she lifted Captain Black out of the basket, and felt a wave of mixed feelings wash over her. The house was lovely. Barbados was a paradise on Earth. Beckett was a kind and dutiful husband. But the circumstances that had brought her here cast a dark shadow over the island's beauty, and over their marriage of convenience as well.

"I think it very beautiful, Beckett. Very beautiful, indeed."

"That does not sound very convincing. Come, let there be no more secrets between us, Lady Ravenwood. We have surely had enough of those."

Beckett's words stung.

"I meant what I said. This island, this home is indeed beautiful. I was only saddened by the memory of what brought us here in the first place. And you are right, Beckett. Secrets have no place in a marriage. Even a marriage such as ours. And yet I find it strange to hear you say such a thing, when you yourself do not practice what you preach."

Beckett's eyes blazed for a moment. Then a barrier went up, cloaking their fire from view.

"You see? Even now you keep your feelings hidden from me."

"Perhaps it is for your own good, my dear." He stepped toward her, letting the fire in his eyes blaze freely once more.

"So you are a hypocrite, then. You are allowed to keep secrets from me, and yet you are unable to forgive me for keeping those I did from you—even though I felt my life depended on it."

"I am doing my best to be a dutiful husband, Isobel."

"Oh, yes. You are very *dutiful* indeed. A perfect gentleman, in fact. You treat me more like a sister than a wife."

Beckett stepped closer and pulled her up in front of him. "And what would you have me do, little wife? Hmm? What would you have me do?"

Isobel opened her mouth to reply, but Beckett silenced her with his lips. His arms went around her, pulling her hard against his strong, muscled body. He parted her lips with his tongue, deepening the kiss until Isobel felt her legs would no longer hold her upright. She grabbed onto him for balance.

He broke the kiss, looking down at her with an intensity that threatened to ignite her like kindling where she stood.

Then, without so much as a glance over his shoulder, he turned and hurried from the room.

# *Chapter Fourteen*

Alone in his new bed, Beckett was unable to sleep. His mind kept settling on Isobel. Every time he closed his eyes, it seemed he saw her with her hair spread out on a pillow, her body riding the waves of pleasure as he filled her with his own.

He flipped over onto his side, punched the pillow to make it comfortable—though it was not in the least bit uncomfortable at all—and closed his eyes again.

There she was, on her side with her back pressed against him, gasping as he entered her. His hands roamed over her breasts as he thrust into her . . . teased their hard peaks. . . . reached down to stroke between her thighs as she moaned and—

*Damnation!* This would not do at all. Not at all. But the insistent hardness of his manhood would not go away.

He flipped over again onto his other side, determined to purge his mind of these tempting, vexing thoughts. But then the memory of kissing her so passionately in the salon jumped into his brain, along with the silken texture of her skin, the smell of her hair, and the maddening pleasure of her kiss.

It was no use. He was fighting a losing battle with his base desires. Determined to clear his mind, Beckett rose and lit a candle, electing to read Milton's *Paradise Lost*. Perhaps that distraction would cleanse the impure thoughts from his head.

He read a few pages, and then felt his mind drift back to the woman who had been nothing but trouble since he'd found her that night in the rubbish heap.

*Isobel*.

The woman who plagued his thoughts day and night. The woman who ignited his desires and made them burn with blazing heat. The woman who had lied to him about everything in her past.

*His wife*.

Devil take it, he was trying to keep their agreement. And she did nothing but upset his plans at every turn. Didn't she know that it was all he could do to keep his hands from touching her, his lips from kissing her, and his body from taking her?

If he did that now, he might lose himself in her. And he could not risk that. He *would not* risk that. For the truth of the matter was that Beckett was harboring a secret.

He had a bad heart.

It was *bad* because it was always getting him into trouble, developing feelings for women who would only hurt him.

And he couldn't let Isobel know the truth, for if

he let her into his heart now, he knew he'd never get her out.

After a breakfast of pastries and delicious exotic fruit, Beckett decided to take Isobel on a small tour of the St. James district. After he swung himself up onto his mount, and she onto hers, they set off down the grassy tree-lined road.

He glanced over his shoulder to see her riding behind him, the wind playing with the curly tendrils of her hair. Isobel had forgone a bonnet today, telling him that she preferred going without. To tell the truth, he preferred it also. The sight of her hair, arranged simply and much looser than she'd worn it in London, made him long to see it flowing wild and free about her shoulders.

Beckett slowed his stallion and let Isobel's mare walk beside him. The two horses greeted each other, their noses nuzzling slightly whenever they could.

"They seem quite fond of each other, do they not?" he asked.

"They do, indeed." Isobel smiled.

They stopped and let the horses communicate in their secret way. "Do you think? . . ." Isobel began.

"What?"

"It sounds silly, but . . . do you think these two could be in love?"

Beckett watched the horses' heads rub against each other and listened to their quiet whickering.

"Isobel, I would daresay that these beasts are irrefutably, indisputably, and most conclusively, in love."

Isobel smiled and the sight was so radiant it threatened to blind him.

"Then they are fortunate creatures."

"Some might disagree with you, there."

"Like who?"

"Romeo and Juliet. Hamlet and Ophelia. Othello and Desdemona. Love didn't make them very happy, did it?"

"No. But it made Beatrice and Benedick happy. Not to mention Orsino and Viola, Orlando and Rosalind, and Titania and Oberon. So there."

Beckett found himself smiling. "It seems you are having the better of this argument, madam. Shall we let the lovers alone then, and go exploring on foot? Mr. Cobb told me there were some very interesting caves down there by the beach. What do you say? Are you game for a little adventure?"

"There are very few things that could frighten me from it."

"Then follow me."

Beckett dismounted and tied his horse to a bush. He reached up to help Isobel down from her mare, then tied it next to his. Taking Isobel's hand, he led her through the tall grasses toward the full sound of crashing waves.

They came around a bend to see the white sandy beach that stretched from the nearby cove as far as the eye could see. The turquoise water caressed the sand in frothy waves.

Beckett stopped near a jagged rock formation, resting his boot on the bottom of it. Above, a huge cave towered majestically over the rocks and beach below.

Isobel joined him. Before them, the entrance of the cave gaped like an enormous mouth.

"Might you be brave enough to go in there with me, my dear?" he said, flashing her a challenging look.

Isobel met his gaze evenly. "Of course. After all, someone has to protect you. Lead the way."

Beckett started up over the rocky terrain to the entrance. He glanced back over his shoulder to make sure she was following, and was surprised to see her only a few steps behind him. She was a brave little thing, wasn't she? Brave enough to challenge and escape a murderer. Brave enough to marry a stranger who might have turned out to be no better. She obviously felt she could take care of herself.

As they reached the cave mouth, he noticed that the air coming from the opening smelled rather earthy and pungent. It was strong but somehow pleasant.

"I should warn you, Isobel," Beckett said as he helped her over the rocks. "From what I know of them, caverns can be treacherous places. So watch your footing and your head. Stay close to me and don't make any noise."

"Why should we not make noise? There is no one in there, surely."

Beckett shrugged innocently. "For all we know, this is a pirate lair. They could be in there right now burying their treasure."

Isobel put her hands on her hips, looking unamused at his teasing, yet cautious just the same.

Beckett laughed at her expression. "I thought you said you weren't afraid."

"And so I am not. I am sure that I am not."

"You are *quite* sure that you're *not*, then?"

Isobel huffed in exasperation and stepped away from him.

Beckett chuckled, then began searching the ground. "Cobb said that he left a torch here. He told me these caves are sometimes used by the natives in those rituals they have. Perhaps we'll find a few skeletons. What do you think? Ah!" Beckett picked up a well-used torch and reached into his pocket for a match to light it. The acrid smell of the burning torch mixed with the cave's unusual odor, but again, Beckett found it invigorating.

"Shall we?" he held his hand out in invitation.

Isobel took a deep breath and lay her hand in his. For an odd moment, Beckett found himself recalling their joined hands as they were pronounced man and wife.

"I should like to see Miss Cordelia Haversham go into a cave like this." Isobel said, her eyes glittering with challenge. "I would wager she'd have none of it."

Beckett cocked an eyebrow. "May I remind you that you have yet to enter it yourself."

Isobel smiled back, calmly. "Quite right. I'll remember those words when I'm forced to drag you out bodily, sir, when you yourself are undoubtedly overcome with an attack of nerves."

He grinned.

Slowly, they entered. Beckett's torch cast shadows everywhere, but provided enough light to show the cave's incredible interior.

Beckett had never seen anything like it. The whole of the cavern ceiling was comprised of what looked like huge, dripping icicles, which seemed to glitter and glow with unusual, otherworldly colors.

"What on earth are those?" Isobel asked softly.

"Stalagmites and stalactites, if I remember my lessons correctly." Beckett whispered to her. "Look, over there."

He pointed toward an underground waterfall nearby, the torchlight illuminating more of it as they approached. Water flowed and bubbled over the odd-looking rocks, down to more of the formations which seemed to grow out of the cave's floor like strange mushrooms.

160

"My heavens, I've never seen anything like it."
Isobel's eyes traveled over the torchlit cave.

"Believe it or not, I've heard there are caves like
these all over Barbados. Or should I say under?"
Beckett peered into the darkness. "Who knows
how deep this one goes?"

"Shall we keep going?"

"We may explore a bit farther, but not too
much. As I said, caverns can be very unstable. At
least the ones in England are."

"I have been in a cave before, Beckett."

"Just trying to watch out for you, my dear—"

His words were cut off as a huge stalagmite
ripped away from the ceiling high above them
with a resounding crack. Beckett's head jerked up
to see it falling right toward them.

He seized Isobel in his arms and rolled them
both out of the way. He grunted as his back took
the brunt of the hard, rocky terrain.

The stalagmite smashed into the floor, its sharp
point piercing the muddy ground a few feet away
from their faces. It stood straight up, its tip
buried deep into the damp floor.

An eerie, high pitched squeaking flooded the
air and came closer, from somewhere deep in
the cave.

"I don't like the sound of that, Beckett! What in
God's name is it?"

"Bats!" Beckett yelled, and quickly shielded her
body with his own. The deafening sound of flapping wings surrounded them.

The air compressed and a huge gust of wind
blew overhead. A thundering clamor filled the air
as thousands of bats swept through the cave. Isobel buried her face in Beckett's chest and clung
tightly to his body. He pressed her into the
ground and covered her head with his arms.

Then, like a summer storm, the squeaking and flapping ceased as quickly as it had come. Slowly Beckett raised his head and looked around. Their torch lay flickering a few feet away.

He looked down at Isobel lying beneath him. They were molded together. "Are you alright?"

"Fine—I think."

"You're not hurt?" Beckett rolled off her and pulled her up beside him.

"No, just a little shaken. Was that your attempt at making me swoon?" Isobel brushed the dirt off her dress.

"Yes, but as you can see, I failed. You have not swooned, and I shall lose my chance to carry you out of this dangerous cave and look the hero."

She slapped at him playfully. "But you protected me from the bats—and the falling rock. That was very gallant." Isobel paused and studied him with cocoa-brown eyes. "Have I thanked you, Beckett?"

"For throwing you to the ground just now? I do not think many ladies would."

"No. For all that you've done for me. Not just today. For everything."

"A gentleman does not expect to be thanked, nor does he need to be." He felt suddenly uncomfortable—as if he'd just realized he was swimming in deep water.

"But perhaps one should be." Isobel touched her lips to his, then, lips as soft as a rose-petal, and kissed him with maddening delicacy. Beckett felt himself melting and hardening at the same time. Devil take him, how he wanted her!

She broke the kiss and touched his face, her eyes glowing up at him in the flickering torchlight.

"Are you trying to give me that attack of nerves, wife?" he said softly.

"I don't know." She stroked his cheek.

"Well, you are doing a damned fine job of it. But two can play at this game."

Beckett's mouth descended to claim hers and he deftly parted her lips with his tongue. He heard her quick intake of breath as he pressed her body tight against his and skillfully explored the secrets of her mouth.

Isobel trembled in his arms. He felt a surge of male vanity and kissed her more ardently. It felt as if she'd been made for his hands and mouth alone.

"Don't swoon, now," he said, "or I'll have to carry you out after all. Like this." He lifted her up and she squealed adorably.

Isobel struggled briefly in his arms as he carried her toward the mouth of the cave. "Put me down! I will not have you say that I have swooned when I have not."

"No, but you soon would have, trembling and sighing as you were in my arms."

"I did no such things!"

Beckett set Isobel down at the entrance to the cave. "Would you like me to demonstrate again, my dear?"

Isobel glanced quickly at him. "That might be most unwise, I should think."

Beckett felt a pang of disappointment. He offered his hand to help her down the rocky slope and found himself agreeing with her. "Most unwise, with dinner but an hour away. I'm sure a demonstration like that would cause us to be late. Shall we go back to the house then?"

Isobel nodded.

They made their way to the horses, who were still nuzzling each other amorously. Beckett helped Isobel up onto her saddle before mounting, himself.

As they trotted down the road, Beckett fumed.

Despite the stern talking-to he'd given himself, his resolve was weakening. Each day it became more and more difficult to resist his wife's charms.

His *wife's* charms, he repeated to himself. She was his wife after all, wasn't she? Where was the harm in consummating their marriage? He wanted it. It didn't mean he was in love with her.

Yet, he had sworn to himself not to take Isobel to his bed until he was certain she was innocent of the accusations against her. And that was hardly the case.

But what if that day never came?

What if his body gave in to its desires before he finished protecting his heart?

# Chapter Fifteen

Isobel lay in her bed gazing idly up at the ceiling. It was quite late in the morning, she knew. But she had been having such delicious dreams. Why couldn't she stay in bed and think about them for awhile?

She hadn't known what had come over her when she'd kissed Beckett so brazenly in the cave. But she didn't regret it. She'd wanted to thank him, and it seemed a perfectly natural thing for a wife to do to her husband. Besides—being in his arms was the most exciting feeling she had ever known.

Still, Beckett had made it perfectly clear to her that he would never have feelings for her or any other woman. Falling in love with him would be like stepping off a cliff to see if she could fly. While providing a unique experience, both would lead to her destruction.

And what of Sir Harry? If Alfred couldn't find evidence against him, the despicable man would be free to torment her for the rest of her life. It didn't bear thinking about.

Her cat meowed his morning greeting and came to sit near her head. Isobel was glad for the distraction. When she made no motion to get out of bed, the beast reached over with his paw and softly batted her cheek.

"Oh! You've got quite the nerve, Captain Black, even if you are a heathen pirate!" Isobel shoved the feline playfully, and he meowed in protest, jumping back and then trying to pounce on her hand. She hid her hands under the bedclothes and moved them as if there were a mouse scuttling beneath. The cat leapt about, his tail swishing back and forth as he stalked the mysterious lump beneath the covers.

Isobel laughed merrily, then even louder as she covered Captain Black with the sheets. The cat bounced about inside the bedding like a frog, then looked surprised when Isobel threw the sheets back and set him free.

Seemingly tired of Isobel's game, the haughty feline leaped off the bed and headed for the door, trotting quickly away.

"Oh, don't leave in a huff." Isobel stared after him, but he didn't respond with so much as a meow.

"Men!" Isobel scoffed, finally getting out of her comfortable bed and going to look out the French windows. She opened them and sighed with pleasure as she breathed in the unique scent that could only be called Barbados.

Throwing on her dressing gown, she went out onto the verandah and took a seat in one of the house's white wicker chairs. She let her eyes travel over the grounds, seeing the sugar fields rolling far off into the distance, speckled with men working under the bright morning sun.

She looked over the gardens, and wondered what her next drawing should be. She had done so many of the island's different flowers and plants. Perhaps she should try some human subjects.

Perhaps Beckett. . . .

No, she told herself. You will not find an excuse to stare at his wickedly handsome face any more than you have to!

It was as if he had cast a spell on her. Beckett plagued her when she was awake as well as asleep. And she highly doubted that he had spent any time dreaming about her.

Then, as if called up by her very thoughts, her husband appeared around the corner of the verandah and approached.

Isobel sat up straight in the chair, realizing too late how little clothing she had on. She had only meant to stay outside for a few minutes. Now she was trapped. Perhaps he would go quickly when he saw the state of her dress. Knowing her spouse, he would enjoy making her squirm, for a little while at least.

He strode leisurely across the verandah until he came near enough to notice her attire. Isobel saw his eyes travel over her body slowly, then rest on her face, an appreciative grin curving his lips.

"Good morning, Isobel. I see you couldn't wait to greet the day. It is a lovely one." To her, his voice was like a physical caress.

Isobel met his eyes. She would not let him torment her. At least, she would try not to let him torment her. "Yes, I'm sure it is going to be a beautiful day."

"Did you sleep well?" His eyes flashed.

"Yes. And you?"

"I was restless. I had the most bothersome dreams . . . they kept me awake half the night."

Beckett's gaze traveled over her body. Isobel felt her nipples harden beneath the thin fabric of her nightdress and wrap as if he had touched them. Knowing just how naked she was underneath these flimsy clothes made her heart beat like a hummingbird's wings.

"I should be going in, now." Isobel looked toward the open door.

"Unfortunately, that is true." Beckett gave her his usual infuriating smile and waited for her to move.

He was going to enjoy every minute of watching her. Well, if he was going to enjoy it, so was she. Isobel met his teasing eyes, then turned. She walked slowly back to the open door, letting the gauzy fabric of her dressing gown show what it would.

Reaching the doorway, she turned around. Beckett's eyes met hers, and in them she saw both amusement and respect. He paused, then turned away with a chuckle and disappeared from sight.

Isobel closed the doors and searched her wardrobe for something prim and proper to wear. Determined to keep her thoughts respectable, she donned a suitably somber dark blue day dress and headed downstairs for breakfast.

Isobel walked to the kitchen to inform Josephine that she would take her breakfast in the dining room, but was nearly bowled over by the woman as she stormed into the hallway. Josephine held Captain Black aloft as if he were a creature from hell itself.

"M'lady, you must keep dis cat away from my kitchen, now! He's eaten two of my frogs. We need dose frogs in de house to keep away de insects. And de lizards! I found him hanging off de cabinet trying to get one on de ceiling."

Josephine deposited the animal in Isobel's arms and dusted off her hands. "And if I catch 'im at it again, I be making soup out of his sorry skin!"

Astonished, Isobel watched Josephine hurry away. The woman had been so irate she hadn't even asked Isobel about breakfast.

Holding Captain Black up so she faced him directly, Isobel scolded the cat. "I am afraid it's the barn for you, my dear man. You shall have to do your hunting elsewhere from now on. I'm sure Josephine has every intention of making a nice soup out of you."

The cat meowed and squirmed in her arms. She let him down unceremoniously and gave his rump a tap with her toe. "Off with you, then!"

Hurrying downstairs, she finally convinced Josephine to feed her, and afterwards Isobel hung about the kitchen, which was buzzing with activity.

"Whatever is going on, Josephine?" Isobel plopped a cube of pineapple into her mouth. "It looks as if the house is being laid out for a feast."

"It's Cropover, m'lady." Josephine smiled at her, the episode with the cat seemingly all but forgotten. "We gonna harvest de sugar soon, and we be needin' all dis food for de celebration."

"Oh, *do* tell me about that, Josephine. It sounds wonderful!"

"Well, dere's dancin' and singin', and a whole lot of eatin'! We be startin' dis evenin'."

"Really? I'm sure I've never done anything so thrilling before. Will you tell me what to do?"

Josephine smiled at her and reached for another passionfruit. "You'll know what to do, m'lady."

\* \* \*

Later that night, the feast began. Torches burned in the gardens, and huge tables were laid out with a delicious array of roasted pig, beef, chicken, baked fish, rice, spiced vegetables, fruits, cheeses, puddings, sausages and a variety of hearty breads. To drink, there was a selection of ciders, ales, juices, port wines, and sherries.

Traditionally, Josephine said, all the workers were invited, along with their families. Isobel watched them talking and laughing with each other, their lilting voices floating on the air like music. They were dressed in colorful native clothing with wild designs. Many wore beads in their hair and around their necks.

It was all so strange and exotic, like something out of a novel. Isobel loved every moment of it.

She bit into a slice of mango and smiled at the strange, sweet taste. As Isobel wiped a bit of juice from her mouth, she looked up and saw Beckett walking across the grass. He wore his usual white shirt and tan buckskins, but had added a multi-colored sash around his waist that made him look rather piratical. Isobel didn't even attempt to keep her gaze off him. He looked like Adonis himself.

The tawny waves of Beckett's hair shone in the torchlight, as if daring Isobel's fingers to touch it. As he made his way around the garden, Beckett laughed and talked with the workers, who greeted him with genuine smiles. Every now and then, he caught Isobel looking at him. Somehow his smile always seemed to fade, then. He seemed to regard her with unnerving seriousness.

Isobel had dressed in a decidedly native style as well, in a turquoise blue frock that shimmered like the sea. Her hair was wound into an exotic style and adorned with a string of tiny seashells. Josephine had arranged it for her beautifully.

Suddenly, floating out of the hot Bajan night, the drums pounded their wild rhythm. It was time for the dancing to begin. Isobel stood back and watched, captivated, as the torchlit garden pulsed with writhing bodies.

The Bajans danced feverishly to a chorus of drums that was unlike anything Isobel had ever heard. The men and women swayed to the music, and through some sixth sense seemed to move perfectly in time with each other. Truly, it was like watching music in a physical form.

How she envied them.

Her body longed to be as free, as vibrantly alive.

Isobel saw Beckett being pulled into the crowd, led by a beautiful young Bajan woman with masses of curly black hair and a fetching smile.

Isobel's heart gave a surprising lurch. She could see primal sparks traveling between her husband's eyes and his partner's as they began to dance. Though she tried to fight it, she felt a stab of ugly jealousy.

Isobel watched their bodies pulse and sway and felt an unbidden desire to dance like that with Beckett. She wanted to see his eyes glowing blue fire at *her* as he held her close and moved to the drums' driving rhythm. She wanted to feel the heat of the music moving in *her* veins. To close her eyes and throw *her* head back, and let the drums take her like a lover.

Suddenly Josephine grabbed Isobel's arm and pulled her into the middle of the pulsing throng. Isobel tried to protest, but her voice couldn't be heard over the drums and the screeching of the crowd. So she kept moving along, feeling out of place and vulnerable.

Comfort came slowly, bewitchingly, but Isobel began to sway. Her mind seemed to be in another place as her body had its own exquisite way, moving to the beat of the drums as easily as the people around her.

Then, she saw Beckett.

He still danced with the other young woman, but now his eyes were locked on Isobel—with a heavy gaze that seemed to pull her toward him.

Isobel feared she might really swoon. If she were back in England it would have been a certainty, but she refused to do so here. She was going to let her pulse race, let her breathing become heavy, feel the muscles in her legs and arms, and let the drumbeat sing in her veins.

She was going to experience her body in a way a proper Englishwoman would never dream.

Beckett moved toward her through the crowd. Isobel stood transfixed. She was in his spell as surely as if he'd used obeah.

He danced around her slowly, holding her gaze with his. She let him move around her, realizing for the first time the power she also held. It was new. It was reckless. And it was thrilling beyond words.

Beckett danced in front of her, his body surprisingly fluid, his strong arms reaching out to touch her. But Isobel side-stepped him and twirled around, just out of his reach. His eyes burned brighter as he watched her, and a dangerous smile played upon his lips.

Again he tried to touch her. Again she moved out of range. Isobel relished the power that flowed through her. She twirled around again, then abruptly found herself pressed up against his hard body like a wet sheet.

It took her breath completely away.

He gripped her arms and held her to him, his eyes travelling over her body. His hips pressed against hers and for an awful moment she worried about such a sensual exchange in public. But when she glanced about them, no one had taken any notice. They were all too involved with their own dancing.

Beckett extended one arm and cradled the back of her neck in his hand, while the other held her hips glued to his. All the while his eyes bored into hers. She looked back at her husband, too spellbound to do anything else.

The drums grew wilder, more insistent, and their movements followed the frantic beat. Beckett pressed her forcefully against his thigh, and pushed his leg between hers as they danced.

She couldn't stop herself from grinding against him. Her eyes were closed. Beckett pressed harder against her, and she felt her skirts being raised, his hands on the bare skin of her thighs, running up towards—

Her eyes flew open, and she saw Beckett's face inches away from hers. Desire glowed hot in his eyes.

"Shall I make you burn for me, Isobel?" he asked, his voice dangerously quiet. "Shall I worship you with my body, the way I vowed to do at our wedding?" He pulled her closer. "Shall I finally make you my wife?"

Isobel stared at him, speechless, held prisoner by Beckett's body, his words, his gaze.

Her husband seized her hand, pulling her back toward the house. She could barely recall how they arrived in her chamber. Through the gauze draperies, the torches lit the room from outside with a warm glow. The sound of the drums continued their relentless rhythm.

Isobel heard the door latch click into place. The finality of the sound made her pulse race faster. Beckett turned around and gazed at her as he began to unbutton his shirt, and the sight sent a thrill up her spine. He reached for her hand and brought it slowly to his bared chest, placing her delicate palm on his warm, masculine skin.

In one quick motion, Beckett slammed her body against his, his mouth possessing hers feverishly, his hands roaming over her with intensity. He pressed his thumb against the hard tip of her breast.

Isobel tried to catch her breath. His dizzying touch intoxicated her; his hands were everywhere, circling her waist, in her hair, pulling her dress up to touch the bare skin of her thighs.

Beckett's hands moved upward and he pulled her dress down over her shoulders, uncovering her breasts. Isobel shuddered as he lowered his head, kissing her neck lightly, teasingly. She could hear herself breathing as if she'd just run a great distance. *Good Lord, what was he doing to her?*

His lips closed around a hard nipple, then he flicked his tongue mercilessly back and forth across it, and her knees went weak at the exquisite agony.

As she clutched at him, he lifted his head. "You like that, don't you, my sweet?"

Isobel whimpered as an almost painful desire teased the tips of her breasts and snaked down to curl between her legs.

"Should I continue?" He kissed her mouth hard, then turned his attention to her neck.

"Yes," she gasped, breathless and weak, though she would surely die if this torment did not soon stop! But did she want it to stop? Curiously, the more unbearable the sensations were, the more of them she wanted. And she didn't even know what it was that she so desperately needed.

Suddenly, she was as wild and feverish as he was, her hands running over his bare back, down over his hips and over the buckskins that covered the round muscles of his buttocks.

Beckett groaned at her challenging touch, and responded in kind, gripping her bottom and pulling her to him. She felt his hard arousal through his buckskins.

Her arms tightened around his back as his hands went up and under her dress. Isobel's eyes flew open as his fingers stroked her in a place for which she didn't even have a name.

Her heart beat so fast she thought it would burst. All her muddled brain could think of was how terribly good it all felt, and how much she wanted to continue this mad, incredible game.

"I think it's time I took you to bed, wife."

Beckett swung her up into his arms and carried her to the bed. She wanted him to hurry, though she feared what that would mean. Had this island's powerful spell turned her into a wanton? However it had come to be, when Beckett put her down on the bed, she pulled him on top of her, wanting, *needing* to feel the weight of him.

"Soon, sweet," he whispered, and she heard a hint of laughter in his voice.

Oh, how could he be laughing at a time like this—when she was dying!

"Let us dispense with this bothersome garment," Beckett said, quickly undoing her laces and sliding the dress over her head. "Ah . . . and this one, too."

She twined her fingers in his hair as he peeled away her underthings, her body wriggling shamelessly beneath him. His own clothes joined hers on the floor. Isobel felt the length and hardness of him, and her hands slid down to explore this body that was so different from her own.

Beckett hissed a breath inward, and she felt him shudder as she stroked the softest skin she had ever felt. She marvelled at how something could be so very hard, and yet silky-soft.

Beckett moaned and pulled her hands away, holding them above her head as he whispered, "Eager little vixen, aren't you? But I'm not done with you, yet."

Now it was Isobel's turn to moan, and she struggled to touch him again but he held her hands fast. She opened her eyes, imploring him.

Beckett took one hand away, but kept both of her wrists imprisoned in the other. With his free hand he teased her sensitive nipples and she arched her back. She heard her own short, desperate panting. Dear God, she was losing her mind!

He ran his hand down her hip and along the inside of her thigh, and then stopped just before . . . before. . . .

Her eyes flew open and she tried to kiss him. He moved his head back just out of reach . . . and then he smiled at her.

"What do you want, Isobel?"

She whispered feverishly, "Don't you know?"

"No, I don't know. You'll have to tell me."

Oh, she would throttle him for this! But as she stared up into his heated blue eyes, she knew he was the master of this game. For now, anyway.

"Tell, me," he insisted.

She bit her lip. "I—I want this aching to stop."

"Aching. And where are you aching, my beauty?"

"Inside. . . ."

"Oh, *inside*. I can make that sweet ache go away, Isobel. I can make you feel better. If I do this." His fingers delved between her legs.

She gasped and closed her eyes as he stroked her.

"And this." He rolled on top of her and spread her legs with his knees. He released her hands and positioned himself above her, piercing her with the intensity of his gaze.

"And this."

Isobel whimpered as the hard silk of him slid inside her. She closed her eyes in disbelief but gave herself over to the invasion of her body. Because she wanted it. More than anything else in the world, she wanted *him*.

Her back arched against the pain and she gasped and clutched at him, but as soon as it had come, it was gone. The only thing left was his delicious thickness inside her and the pulsing rhythm of the drums driving them on.

Her hands roamed over the straining muscles of his back and buttocks, his skin slick with sweat. She pulled him hard against her, trying to take in more of him. His tongue penetrated her mouth, mimicking his sex, and she thrilled at how completely he possessed her.

The burning that had tormented her for so long became hotter, but it also held a sweetness, like warm honey. The sensation traveled through her veins and warmed her whole body, all the while getting hotter and sharper at its core.

The violence of his thrusting shocked her, but it seemed even more unbelievable that she was a partner in this raw exchange.

Then a thundering pleasure so elemental, so complete, burst outwards from her very soul and left her trembling in its wake.

Beckett groaned as he gave a final thrust. He buried his face in her neck, and his body relaxed on top of hers. He stayed there for a moment, panting.

With a soft kiss he rolled off her, pulling her close in front of him. And though it had been the last thing she'd meant to do, Isobel fell asleep exhausted in her husband's arms.

* * *

Beckett lifted one of Isobel's golden curls in his fingers and watched the light from the window play upon it. It shone as bright as a moonbeam. Pale moonbeams . . . that was the color of her hair.

It must be the middle of the night, he thought. They had both fallen asleep after—

He felt a smile come to his lips.

Her response to his lovemaking had been hotter and wilder than any husband had a right to dream. His little wife had been as uninhibited as one of the undulating Bajan dancers last night at Cropover. And her passion had excited him unbearably.

Now, she slept in his arms, her warm, naked body curved into his, her round little buttocks deliciously pressed against his hips. He felt himself getting hard just thinking about her, about what they'd done together in this bed.

Perhaps he would wake her.

No. A good husband would let her sleep.

As he played with her hair, he doubted he was anything resembling a good husband—though perhaps he was making too much of this. It would have only been a matter of time until he had given in to his desire for her. What difference did it make if it was sooner rather than later? He had warned her not to expect more from him.

Suddenly, his thoughts skipped to Cordelia.

During their engagement they had never made love, though it hadn't been for his lack of trying. But she had always turned prudish in his arms, and he'd thought her to be just playing coy, protesting her virginity for form's sake. Now, he had the feeling that Cordelia would never have warmed to him as Isobel had done. It simply wasn't in her nature.

*Oh, but these were preposterous thoughts.*

He did not want to let any lustful feelings for Isobel trick him into thinking he was the slightest bit in love with her. Nothing would make the *ton* wag their tongues faster, than if he came back besotted with his new bride.

Though Isobel had proven a superb bedmate, it didn't mean she was any different from Cordelia, deep down. Certainly, Isobel was beautiful, but Cordelia also had been beautiful. He had fancied himself in love with Cordelia. Hell, he *had* been in love with her, with a woman who had never truly loved him. And he had been pitifully blind to the truth. He would not let that happen again.

Cordelia had lied to him, and so had Isobel. He mustn't let himself forget that. Naturally, they would have to be bedmates. They would have to produce an heir. They might even become friends. But he would never let himself love her.

In her sleep, Isobel squirmed her bottom against his hips, fully hardening his arousal. *Oh, damn.* How would he be able to get back to sleep now?

She did it again, and he decided to take it as an invitation. Perhaps she was dreaming about their lovemaking, and wanted nothing more than what he was about to do.

Beckett slid his hand down and tenderly touched her nipple.

She moaned.

Gently, he pressed his hardened sex against the softness of her buttocks.

She sighed.

Then he reached down and softly stroked the velvet flower between her legs.

She whimpered adorably.

He flicked his tongue out to tease the edge of her ear, and heard her intake of breath as she awoke.

"Hmmm . . . Beckett?"

He chuckled lightly. "Were you expecting someone else?"

She looked back at him, and he smiled at her sleepy face in the moonlight. "What are you doing?" she mumbled.

He resumed his caresses and she closed her eyes.

"*That* is what I am doing. But only if you want me to, sweet. I'm afraid you've been wiggling your bottom against me in your sleep, and damned if it didn't harden me up like stone." He kissed the back of her neck. "Are you ready for more of your husband's loving?"

"I think so." She started to turn to face him.

"No, you can stay like this." He pressed his chest against her back. "I've had dreams about loving you this way, and I would dearly like to see them become reality. If you agree."

He gently pinched her nipple between his thumb and forefinger and heard her gasp.

"You see, I can pay your lovely breasts all the attention they deserve this way, and I know how greedy those beautiful little darlings can be."

He snaked his other hand down to keep stroking between her legs, and she reached back and grabbed his hip, pulling him against her.

Beckett nuzzled the softness of her hair, caressing her neck with his cheek. She moaned as his fingers slipped into her. Damn if the feel of her so hot and wet didn't threaten to make him spill right now.

"I can't wait any longer, sweet. I've got to be inside you. I've got to—" He groaned as he slid from behind into the slick heat of her.

Then, thrusting with long hard strokes, he drew out his pleasure until it was an unbearable madness.

*Oh God, she felt good.*

He was near release, now, and he wanted her

with him, wanted her breaking as he was going to, and he stroked her little pearl of pleasure until she cried out.

He groaned, then, pushing himself deep into her. As the wave of his own pleasure approached, he thrust wildly, until finally he gave in to surrender. He let out a shuddering breath and pulled her close, squeezing tightly and kissing her shoulder, whispering, "Oh, my beauty. You make a man lose his senses."

Sated, he settled against Isobel. As he drifted off to sleep, he thought it was a good thing he'd promised himself that he wouldn't fall in love with Isobel. A very good thing indeed.

# Chapter Sixteen

Isobel curled up on her side, watching the sunlight stream through the ivory curtain and onto the floor of her room. She sighed, feeling as warm and weightless as the light itself.

Was this the way every woman felt after the first time?

Just saying his name in her head made Isobel thrill uncontrollably. Beckett. Her husband. Last night he had made love to her, had taken her body with his own, had truly made her his wife. And she had enjoyed every moment of it.

Her only regret was that she had awoken in this bed alone. How she had wanted his arms about her this morning, hugging her tightly. How she had wanted to feel his lips waking her with a kiss.

Well, it would not be the least good manners to be greedy, she admonished herself. Beckett did not have all day to lay in bed with her. Doubtless, he had to see to the business of the plantation.

There would be plenty of time later for these wicked games. Plenty of time, indeed.

Thoughts of Beckett danced in her head. The texture and warmth of his skin, the strength and thickness of his hands, the muscles in his forearms, the way his eyes held the light of the torches as he'd watched her dance—these were the things that made him so beautiful, so powerfully masculine.

Isobel sighed as she remembered his hard hands on her body, pressing her hips against his as they danced, and later as he had loved her here in this bed. Beckett had awakened something in her—something she had never known existed. It was mysterious and powerful and made her quite giddy.

Not like the distasteful business with Sir Harry at all. The vile touch of Sir Harry had made her want to be sick. She shuddered involuntarily.

Isobel rolled onto her side, clutching at the bed linen and pushing the memory away. She was safe from that blackguard, now. Safe with her husband, thousands of miles away. She would never be Sir Harry's wife, and he would never be able to do *that* to her. No matter what he had threatened.

With Beckett it had been like a dream. She had not been afraid. She had welcomed her husband's instruction in the art of physical love. And she had received him with an open heart.

Isobel wanted to shake herself. These thoughts would not help matters and she should not pursue them.

They had *made* love, not fallen in love.

*They* had not. But had *she*?

Isobel recoiled from the answer to that question. Beckett had warned her that love was not part of the bargain. For him it would undoubtedly be true. But for her?

The thought sobered Isobel quicker than a dousing of cold water.

Her heart pounded in her breast. *Oh, this was a mistake!* To fall in love with Beckett would be a *terrible* mistake. She had agreed to the terms of the marriage. They were to lead separate lives—he in London and she at Hampton Park. After this was done, she would spend the rest of her years alone on her estate, pining for a husband who had sworn never to love her.

And yet, it was too late. Last night had simply revealed the awful truth to her, removing the last barricade from her defences. . . .

It was true.

She *was* in love with him.

The warm wind lightly caressed Isobel's skin as she rode with Beckett down a quiet road that led to the beach. The smell of the sea floated on the breeze, and the sound of the gulls beckoned.

They ascended a rise and Isobel smiled as she beheld the breathtaking ocean beyond. The brilliant turquoise of the water held a vibrancy she had never before seen. The swirling colors reminded her of Beckett's eyes—their beauty could bewitch and their depths could swallow one whole.

Beckett stopped his horse near some swaying palm trees and dismounted, reaching up to help Isobel off her mount. His hands on her waist felt firm and strong and made her stomach thrill.

"This seems a good spot." Beckett guided her toward a grove of trees.

"The view is magnificent," Isobel agreed, gazing at the white, sandy beach and at the water that stretched as far as she could see. This was a paradise.

Beckett took the horses to a nearby patch of

grass and picketed them. With an unhurried air, he strolled back to the palm trees, spread out a blanket and plunked himself down.

Isobel joined him as he opened the basket that Josephine had prepared for them. A wonderful aroma drifted up from the delicious lunch of cheeses, roasted chicken and hearty brown bread. Beckett took a bite of cheddar and offered her some.

"No, thank you, I had a late breakfast," she said.

Beckett grinned. "A late breakfast, eh? Why were you so late to rise this morning? Now, tell me."

Feeling herself blush, Isobel looked away.

"Was that husband of yours keeping you up 'til all hours?"

Isobel met his eyes and saw the playful light dancing in them. Her stomach did flip-flops. "Yes, my lord, he did. He even woke me in the middle of the night to—"

"To. . . ." Beckett moved closer to her.

"To continue with his—"

"His. . . ."

"His husbandly rights."

A subtle change flowed through Beckett's eyes, a dimming. "*Husbandly rights*? Is that what you call what I did to you last night? I'd thought I was making mad, passionate love to you, Isobel. And that does not even consider what you were doing to me."

"Me?" she said, taken off guard. "I did nothing to you."

"I beg to differ, my dear, you did quite a lot. Such wiggling and squirming. What is a poor husband to do when his wife insists on being serviced at all hours? Ignore her demands upon his person? I ask you."

"Oh!" Isobel felt her cheeks burning.

"Not very kind of me to tease you so, is it?" He

leaned back and lifted a morsel of bread to his lips. "Is there much pain today?"

She paused, but answered him truthfully. "A little."

He nodded. "I've heard it's often so for a woman's first time. I'm sorry to say, nature is often cruel to the fairer sex. For isn't it the woman who must carry and bear the child that the coupling of the two sexes might create? You could be carrying my child right now, as we speak. Have you thought of that?"

Isobel's heart skipped a beat. Last night had happened so fast, had been so intoxicating, she truly hadn't considered it. She'd thought only of the pleasure, of the way he'd made her whole body hum with passion.

And now, she felt a primal rush of pride at the possibility of carrying her husband's child. Beckett's child.

"I see the idea sits well with you, and that pleases me," he said. "Because as the earl and countess of Ravenwood, we have a duty to perform, Isobel. You must conceive my child and heir. And that could take months. You know, my friends Lord and Lady Secord had to engage in this type of behavior every day for almost a year until Letty conceived. And the whole time, both she and George wore the silliest smiles about town. Come to think of it, they're still wearing them. Well, that stands to reason, as they've had a child each year since their marriage four years ago. Would you object to doing our duty as devotedly?"

"I would not, my lord."

Beckett lifted her hand to his lips and kissed it softly, gazing into her eyes. "Nor would I, my dear. Nor would I. But I shall be a good husband to you tonight, and let you recover from your first

186

taste of the marriage bed. It would be rather
boorish of me to force my attentions on you,
wouldn't it? And you still tender from last night's
loving."

*No, it wouldn't!* she wanted to reply. All this talk
was making her skin positively tingle. Oh, why
was he teasing her so?

Beckett turned his attention back to the picnic
lunch beside him and picked up a leg of chicken.
"Now that we've got that settled, I think I shall eat
my lunch. I'm famished. Are you sure you don't
want to join me?"

*She wanted very much to join with him. Right
here on the beach, if that's what he wanted.*

"No, I'm fine," she replied. "I'll sit here and
draw."

Isobel arranged her pencils and paper in a bid
to avoid watching Beckett lick the crumbs from
his fingers. Oh, why hadn't she brought her fan?
It was decidedly hotter than before.

Isobel concentrated on the white sheet of paper
before her. She did not want to be seen staring at
her husband like a love-sick cow. He must not see
the raw desire in her eyes. Nor how easily he
could arouse her passions.

She picked up her pencil and began to draw
the face of this man who drove her to distraction. She glanced up at him occasionally, his features quickly appearing on the paper in front of
her. There was the arch of the eyebrow that
sometimes taunted her, the regal nose, the sen-
suous mouth in that sly half-grin. Eyes that
seemed far too intense to accurately transfer to
paper.

Isobel completed the portrait, regarding the
finished result with a mixture of satisfaction and
embarrassment. The drawing of Beckett showed
a man brimming with raw sexuality. A man who

could fulfill any woman's desires. It looked indecent. She certainly didn't want to show it to him.

But her reservations came too late. He was already reaching for it.

Beckett turned the portrait so that he could see it.

"Well, what do you think?" Isobel brushed a flyaway hair from her face.

"Is this how you see me, Isobel?"

She swallowed. "I suppose it is."

"I look like a male courtesan. We should send it back to London and have it published in the Times. Imagine my reputation after the *ton* sees this. And my wife who drew it!"

Isobel snatched it back. "You will do no such thing!"

"Quite right. A full nude would be a far greater scandal."

"What? I most certainly will not draw you nude."

Beckett laughed, and it was a moment or two before Isobel realized he'd been teasing her once again.

"Shall we go down to the water?" he asked. "I'll bet it's warmer than the English Channel."

Isobel paused, then nodded in agreement as Beckett began removing his boots and stockings. She slipped off her shoes and silk stockings, picked up her skirts and trotted down to the beach, with Beckett following behind. It would be good to get her mind off her husband's teasing.

They splashed into the warm, foamy water, and Isobel gloried in the refreshing feeling. The tropical breeze sighed against her bare legs as Isobel lifted her skirts to keep them out of the water. She turned to see Beckett staring at her.

"You're making it damned difficult for me to keep my word about leaving you alone tonight."

"Perhaps I don't wish you to keep your word." She trotted off ahead of him, splashing through the water and back onto the sand.

Walking quickly down the beach ahead of Beckett, feeling deliciously light-hearted, Isobel drank in the blue sky overhead with its white, puffy clouds. The heady scent of the island's exotic flowers floated on the breeze.

Though she knew most ladies of the *ton* would rather give up their opera boxes than come to such a wild place, Isobel was enchanted by this island. It was stunning, serene and haunting all at once. It was so unlike London with its measured rows of townhouses, soaring cathedral spires and noisy cobblestone streets.

Isobel's thoughts turned back to that day she'd fled to London. She had been so frightened then, of Sir Harry, of the dangers that surrounded her in the city streets. And then Beckett had found her, and saved her.

Rounding a curve in the shoreline, Beckett stopped and looked down at the sand, kicking it with his toes.

"Now, what have we here? Footprints? Must have been four or five men at least, and they lead down to the water, there. Perhaps Mr. Cobb's talk of pirates wasn't just flummery after all. There, you can see where their boat was dragged up onto the sand."

"Might it not be local fishermen?" Isobel asked, seeing the marks in the sand. An unsettling shiver ran up her back.

"Mr. Cobb said the fishing is done farther down the coast, where the waters are calmer. Of course, I'm most likely assuming the worst. It might not be pirates at all. But you must promise me not to come down here alone." He looked down at her with serious eyes.

189

Isobel nodded. "I promise."

It was not a difficult promise to make.

They turned back toward the grove of trees, and as they neared the horses, Isobel tried to silence her fears. Surely, it wasn't possible. It couldn't be Sir Harry. *Could it?*

She pushed the thought from her mind.

They packed up the picnic basket and her drawings, and mounted the waiting horses.

As they neared the plantation, Isobel noticed an oppressive smell in the air. Beckett seemed to notice it too and they stopped the horses. They heard shouts of alarm floating on the breeze.

Beckett's eyes suddenly turned deadly serious. He kicked his stallion into a gallop, and Isobel followed as closely as she could.

As they approached the plantation, they saw the pandemonium.

"The fields are on fire!"

# *Chapter Seventeen*

Beckett jumped off his horse and ran toward the burning sugar cane fields. Isobel struggled to keep up. Around them, but not yet burning, were the dried cane stalks left from Cropover. She and Beckett stopped short when they saw Mr. Cobb running toward them.

"What's happened, Cobb?" Her husband shouted. "You said the fields weren't supposed to be burned until next week!"

"Not sure, m'lord!" Cobb yelled, his face and clothes blackened by soot. "Started 'bout an hour ago down in the south field. No one supposed to be down that way. Don't know what coulda happened. I've got all the men out there, and some o' the women, too. We've got to put it out, or the house'll be next, sir."

Beckett ripped off his jacket and rolled up his sleeves. "Tell me what to do, Cobb. I'm not going to lose Ravenwood Hall!"

"We're diggin' ditches 'round the fields so the fire won't spread. Got some o' the women to wet down the sides and roof of the house and barn. Don't want flying sparks to ignite the buildings."

"I'll help Josephine and the others up here." Isobel squinted her eyes against the heat from the fire.

Beckett nodded and touched her arm. "Whatever you do, don't get too close to the flames."

"But you're going down there!"

"I have no choice, Isobel. But neither do you! Mark me." Beckett turned and followed Cobb toward the heart of the fire.

Isobel coughed from the smoke in the air and sought Josephine, who would be in charge of the women.

She found her quickly; the woman was already busy issuing orders. "You girls go and get all de buckets you can find. *Big* ones!" Josephine shouted. When she saw Isobel, she said, "M'lady, come wit me."

She led Isobel over to the well as the other women ran back with the buckets.

"Make a line to de barn," she told the staff, coolly directing the panicking servants like an army colonel. "M'lady and I will pull de water up from de well."

Isobel and Josephine worked together to crank the water up, handing bucket after bucket to the first woman in line, while the ladies at the other end doused the barn.

They worked as fast as they could to wet down the structure and get to the house before floating sparks landed on the roof. Making a line toward the manor, bucket after bucket passed down the line until the house was dampened, too.

Isobel had no idea how much time had passed since they began their back-breaking work, but she could see the fire still burning down in the fields. She turned to Josephine, panting and wiping the sweat from her brow.

"We must go down and help the men dig." *And see whether Beckett is safe.*

"Dat would be a good idea, m'lady," Josephine agreed.

After assembling the other women and taking what shovels remained, Isobel led the women down to help out.

The men had split up into small groups, each group concentrating on one side of the field. But the flames were getting closer, and there weren't enough men to control the fire's progress.

Beckett looked up as Isobel and the rest of the women approached. He wiped his forehead, hands and face blackened by ash.

"Isobel, take the women away—I told you it was too dangerous down here!" Beckett yelled over the crackling of the flames.

"You need our help!" Isobel insisted.

"Don't you be arguin' wit m'lady, now!" Josephine shouted in agreement. Her dark eyes flashed a warning.

Beckett paused and leaned on the handle of his shovel. "Alright then, split your women up into four groups and go join the men."

Isobel and Josephine quickly divided the women up, and Josephine took the others to where they were needed. Isobel's group began to dig near Beckett's.

As she worked, Isobel was surprised to feel herself getting stronger again after a period of near exhaustion. At the start, she'd felt clumsy with the shovel. But after a short time she found her rhythm, enjoying a new awareness of her body. She discovered muscles in her arms, back and legs of which she had been previously quite ignorant; she enjoyed the sensation of really using them.

Isobel had never had to apply herself in such a physical way before. Except for dancing with Beckett at the Cropover feast. Back in England, it was considered most unladylike to engage in any activity more strenuous than waving a fan. But this sort of physical exertion made her feel more alive, more capable than ever.

Isobel glanced at Beckett, who had taken off his shirt. Although covered in ash and dirt, with his chest streaked in sweat, her husband had never looked more capable or strong. How could he have hidden such a form beneath tailored jackets and silk neck cloths? Did all the gentlemen of London look thus without their fancy clothes?

Helpless to look away, she watched his body as it worked. The muscles in his arms and shoulders flexed as he dug into the brown earth. His hard thighs and buttocks strained against his buckskins and made her catch her breath.

She kept digging, though her initial stamina was fading. It was fruitless to be vain at a time like this, but she wondered what she must look like as she wiped the perspiration from her brow, undoubtedly smearing dirt and ash all over her face.

Finally their efforts were rewarded when the fire, contained by the network of ditches and almost out of fuel, began to recede.

"Good work, everyone," Beckett called out, resting his elbow on the handle of his shovel. "Split yourselves up, now, and let's finish this up." As they walked past, he patted several workers on the back.

Beckett threw his shovel on the ground and walked over to Isobel. He looked down at her, brushing the hair away from her face. "What would the *ton* say if they could see us now?"

"I'm sure I don't care a whit." She liked the way he was looking at her. His eyes shone in his grimy face, and she barely noticed the soot anymore.

Beckett nodded toward the smoldering field. "We still have work to do. Come help me start cleaning up."

Isobel obeyed and took up a position near her husband. She wanted to laugh as she tried to picture any other countesses digging ditches alongside their husbands. Lady Whitcomb, the hostess of the party they'd attended for instance. Perhaps it was the absurdity of that notion, her exhaustion and her relief now that the danger seemed past, that made her think of such things.

As she scooped up a shovelful of earth and heaved it, she saw some of the dirt land on Beckett's boot. She nearly burst into giggles, glancing at his face to see if he had noticed. Thankfully, it seemed he hadn't.

She continued her work, but was startled when a flying clump of earth caught the edge of her skirt. Isobel slowly looked over to see Beckett continue to dig.

Casually, she lifted her shovel, filled it with dirt, and sent the whole thing sailing over to strike Beckett's chest.

Her husband stopped for a moment, looking down at himself. Dirt was stuck to every inch of him.

Isobel was suddenly afraid she had taken it too far. Beckett would be furious with her. Unsure of what to do, she bent to continue her digging.

A huge load of dirt hit the back of her head with so much force that it nearly knocked her off her feet. Isobel spun about to find Beckett smiling at her, proud as a peacock.

Bellowing in a terribly unladylike manner, Isobel threw down her shovel and charged. Her husband instantly dropped his shovel and ran, laughing. He easily evaded her pursuit by changing directions and dashing around the edge of the ditch.

He stopped long enough, however, to pick up a handful of dirt and throw it at her. It covered the front of her dress so that her state of cleanliness now resembled his own.

Isobel quickly grabbed some dirt herself, and lobbed a handful at Beckett's head. She just missed. His return volley landed in her hair and she shrieked unhappily.

Beckett laughed and pointed, but was duly silenced when a soggy clump of earth pelted his face. Now Beckett charged at Isobel, who knew it was impossible to out-run him.

The dirt kept flying in both directions, until they were out of breath from running, and merely stood hurling handfuls at each other.

Finally, Isobel stopped and pointed at Beckett, laughing uncontrollably. "You look as if you've been rolling in a pig sty!"

Beckett laughed too, pointing back at her hair. "Well, I'm afraid your hair is now as dark as horse dung, my dear. You know, I believe I'll have to start calling you the countess of Ravendirt."

Isobel attempted to catch her breath and glanced around to see Mr. Cobb, Josephine, and about twenty men and women staring at them completely dumbfounded.

"I daresay that's enough mudslinging for today." Beckett dusted off his hands. "Besides, we are attracting quite an audience."

Isobel made a feeble attempt to straighten her filthy dress. Thankfully, no one could see her blushing beneath all the dirt on her face.

Beckett took her hand and placed it in the crook of his arm, as if they were about to leave a dinner party. He cleared his throat and paused, glancing down at Isobel. Then, he opened his mouth to speak but said nothing.

Josephine's face broke into a smile that rivaled the sun's gleam on the ocean. Her booming laughter rang out over the field. The others joined in as well. Soon Beckett, Isobel, Mr. Cobb, and all the other workers were laughing and pointing at each other's dirty clothes, faces and hair.

Josephine held her stomach and doubled over in laughter. "I be surprised if 'dere be any dirt left in the field, now! Ha, ha! Oh, my . . ."

"Indeed, Josephine," Beckett chuckled.

"By the way, m'lord," Mr. Cobb said, grinning. "The fire's put out."

At this the crowd erupted in hoots of wild laughter. Beckett and Isobel couldn't help but join in.

"You both be wantin' a nice bath, now," Josephine said, wagging her finger. "I'll run up to de house and get de water boilin'."

"That won't be necessary, Josephine." Beckett pulled Isobel close.

Josephine looked unconvinced. "It will be if you want to get dat dirt off yourself."

"Oh, we shall get ourselves clean, but with a little help from Mother Nature instead. I couldn't bear to have any of this tracked indoors. Have some soap, towels, and clean clothes brought down from the house. I think it's time Lady 'Ravendirt' became acquainted with our natural spring."

Isobel felt butterflies flit through her stomach. Was he suggesting what she thought? She looked up at him, and the twinkle in his eyes confirmed it. Good Heavens, they were going to bathe together.

In a few moments, a girl from the house appeared with towels and clothes in her arms and a yellow cake of soap in her hand.

The servants and workers looked at each other sheepishly before being dismissed by Josephine: "What you all lookin' at, now? You go and clean yourselves up and let de lord and lady do what dey please."

Isobel watched their knowing smiles as they turned away, and wondered why she wasn't mortified. Strangely, there seemed no need for such worries here.

Josephine's eyes twinkled at Beckett and Isobel as they turned to go. "I be servin' dinner soon. Dat is, if you still be *hungry* after your *bath* . . . Ha-ha!"

Beckett led Isobel across the lawn to the path, with the servant girl following behind at a respectful distance. Isobel's heart skipped with excitement and she clutched his hand. Beckett glanced back at her and smiled, then led her deeper and deeper into the dense greenery.

Soon, the spring appeared, encircled by a lush array of colorful flowers and shiny green leaves. A wall of rock rose up on one side and over, and a glistening waterfall spilled down it into the pool.

As Beckett waved a hand in dismissal, the servant set down their clothes, made a curtsy and left.

"My, my, but you're filthy." Her husband chuckled, looking Isobel up and down.

"The countess of Ravendirt must dress appropriately."

"Take off your clothes, then." He bent down to remove his boots.

Isobel felt gooseflesh cover her skin at Beckett's words, but found herself obeying as if she had no will of her own. Soon she was down to her lawn undergarments.

"Everything, Isobel." He gazed at her with intense eyes while he unfastened the buttons of his buckskins.

She swallowed. She had never stood naked in front of anyone before—at least not without any sort of covering. And certainly not in broad daylight. When she and Beckett had made love, it had been blissfully dark. But now?

As Beckett peeled off his buckskins and drawers, he looked up at her. She watched the last stitch of clothing fall away, and her uncertainty faded . . . replaced by desire.

He stood proudly nude, watching her. His arms and chest and face were covered with dirt, and the rest of him . . . oh, the rest of him!

Isobel let her eyes feast on the wonderfully masculine body before her. She had never seen anything so *impressive* before. Had God made man for the sole purpose of tempting woman?

Isobel's eyes traveled unashamedly over the body she'd explored with hungry hands the night before. Her gaze lingered over his thighs, and up, and she saw that he was powerfully, beautifully aroused.

"Come on. It's your turn," he growled.

As if under a spell, Isobel slowly removed the rest of her undergarments, and felt the warm air touch every part of her body.

Beckett smiled and held his hand out to her. Silently, they entered the water and walked in until they were waist deep.

Beckett turned her to stand in front of him and dipped the soap in the water. He brought it up again and lathered it between his hands. "Close your eyes, tight."

Isobel did as he asked and felt his hands gently rubbing her face. The sensation was wonderfully soothing. She felt herself smile through the suds and Beckett laughed, presumably at her.

**199**

"Dunk your head, now, like a good little girl."

Isobel giggled and sank down into the water. When she came up again, she wiped the water away from her eyes and saw Beckett regarding her. His expression was more serious than she was accustomed.

"Now, your hair."

Beckett moved to stand behind her, and she closed her eyes again as he ran soapy fingers through her slick wet hair. He scrubbed her head gently, and it was so relaxing Isobel thought for a moment she might fall asleep.

As she rinsed her hair, Beckett still stood behind her. She felt his strong hands on her back, sliding through the suds and massaging her tired muscles. A sigh escaped her and she heard Beckett chuckle.

"Enjoying this, my sweet?"

"Oh, yes," she whispered.

"I'm sure there aren't many husbands who engage in personally bathing their wives as I do. They should know what they're missing."

Beckett turned her to face him. If it was possible, his eyes blazed even more intensely than before. He looked like a lion about to pounce upon his prey. Taking her hands in his, he placed the slippery round soap in her palm.

Isobel lathered the soap between her hands and felt a thrill as Beckett closed his eyes. Reaching up, Isobel smoothed suds over his chest, reveling in the feeling of his wet skin, his hard muscles, and their latent power.

She washed his face and his hair, as tenderly as he had done hers. She felt possessive of him, of this body that he seemed to offer like a gift. Did he feel the same way when he looked at her?

Isobel waited as Beckett dipped beneath the water to rinse the suds away. When he stood again, water running down the firm lines of his body, she found herself looking into eyes as dark as the sky before a storm.

"You know, Cobb said the fire looked suspicious." Beckett ran his fingers through his wet hair, brushing it back. "It may have been purposely set."

He held out his hand to Isobel and headed out of the water. On the grassy bank they dried themselves off and donned their dry clothes.

Even though the sun warmed them, Isobel felt a chill move through her. "Those footprints we saw in the sand. Could Sir Harry have found us?"

"You think he could have found you? I suppose it is possible. . . . You must not venture about alone, not even the grounds. Is that understood?"

Isobel nodded, unwilling to believe the serpent had found its way into their Eden. "If it *is* Sir Harry—"

"We don't know that yet."

"But if it is . . . what will we do, Beckett?"

"We'll do what we have to. *I'll* do what I have to in order to keep you safe, Isobel. I promise."

As they headed up the grassy path back to Ravenwood Hall, Isobel tried to quell the uneasiness in her heart.

Was Sir Harry here in Barbados?

Beckett seemed unconvinced, but of course, he was not as well-acquainted with Sir Harry Lennox as she was. The villain reminded her of a mastiff that used to live on a property near Hampton Park. Once the dog caught the scent of his prey, he would not give up until the creature he hunted lay limp and lifeless between his jaws.

Though she tried to convince herself otherwise, Isobel couldn't dismiss the feeling that Sir Harry had found her after all.

The footprints on the beach, so close to their

estate . . . the suspicious fire shortly thereafter . . . were these just subtle calling cards her enemy was using to announce his presence?

And if so, when and how would he pay her and Beckett a formal visit?

# *Chapter Eighteen*

Beckett leaned against a palm tree and stared out at the windswept ocean. The turquoise water crested into white foam and spread toward him on the sand, only to roll back and disappear from whence it came.

Looking at a sight of such awe-inspiring beauty, he knew his heart and mind should have been at peace.

But they were not.

He was about as far from peaceful as he was from England.

He had been happy these past weeks with Isobel. Far too happy for his own liking. And it unsettled him.

They had fallen into an easy friendship. Each morning, he and Isobel awoke in each other's arms after a night of passionate lovemaking. They flirted and teased. They made each other laugh.

For all intents and purposes, one might think they were in love.

Except for the fact that Beckett knew it to be impossible.

Love was an illusion. He'd vowed never again to let Cupid's arrow play havoc with his good sense. He had done it once. And he'd learned from his foolish mistake of loving Cordelia.

At least he'd thought he had.

But didn't his actions speak louder than words? And if he continued acting as if he were in love with Isobel, he just might wake up one day to find that it was true.

When they returned to England, he would be sending her off to Hampton Park with a settlement and an heir to raise just as they'd agreed. Only now, to his surprise, that plan lacked its former lustre. And when he asked himself why, he refused to hear the knowledge that emanated from the depths of his heart.

It simply would not do.

Especially now, with the possibility of Isobel's nemesis having followed her here. But surely there was only a slim chance of that. Lennox couldn't have found out where they had gone. Could he?

The thought of Lennox only served to remind Beckett of the danger Isobel might be in—both here in Barbados, and back in London. There was still that murder charge to be taken care of. And if Alfred was unable to find proof of Lennox's guilt in the matter, there was a possibility that Isobel could be arrested upon their return.

It was his duty as a husband, however business-like their arrangement, to protect her from Lennox. And the best way to do that was to distance himself from the dangerous feelings that were growing in his heart, which, like a poison flower, made him weaker with every new bloom.

For if Lennox ever put his filthy hands on Isobel, Beckett would never forgive himself. Just the thought of that blackguard touching her made his stomach harden into a tight knot.

Beckett turned and saw Isobel coming up over the rise, her golden hair blowing in the wind. She wore a gown of palest pink. Even from here, he could see that she radiated beauty as effortlessly as the sun itself.

*Damnation!* Why did his heart feel so damn heavy? As she came closer, his mind bucked from the answer.

Isobel smiled brightly when she reached him, and pushed her windswept curls back from her face. "I've been looking for you everywhere."

"Have you?"

"I missed you at breakfast, and now it is past luncheon. Shall we go back? Josephine has made a lovely cucumber soup."

He stepped away from the tree and offered his arm to her.

Isobel curled her arm through his. They strolled down the wind-swept beach in silence. From the corner of his eye, he noticed her looking up at him questioningly.

"You seem rather preoccupied," she said.

He kept staring at the sea, as if in its depths he would somehow find his answers. "You are most observant, my dear. Being an artist, that is quite natural for you, I'm sure. I am indeed, preoccupied."

"What is it, Beckett?" He heard the concern in her voice. She touched his arm tenderly, just like a loving wife would.

"I expected to hear from Alfred by now. And I must confess, I am concerned for his safety, especially since we are not ruling out the possibility that Lennox could have learned our location."

He felt Isobel stiffen.

"And . . . there is something else that I must speak to you about." He stopped, turning her to face him. He looked down into her warm brown eyes, and suddenly wished he hadn't. It would be more difficult now, having let himself glimpse the beauty there. "This has gone too far, Isobel. And we must put a stop to it."

"What has gone too far? I don't understand."

"*This*. This sham of a marriage that we are starting to pretend is real. And we must stop it, now. Before one of us gets hurt."

She held him with a steady gaze. "One of us? Oh. *Me*, you mean."

He swallowed. *She was not going to make this easy, was she?*

"Yes. I suppose I do."

"Because you feel nothing. That is why you make love to me every night with such passion it threatens to turn us both to cinders? Because you feel nothing?"

"I didn't say that I felt nothing. Only that we have been playing at a dangerous game. And we would be deluding ourselves if we continue." He looked out over the water in a bid to escape Isobel's accusing expression.

"I've been looking ahead to our eventual return to England," he continued. "We shall have to discuss your settlement, et cetera. And depending on the situation at home—whether or not you'll be required for appearances at court or that sort of thing—you may accompany me or go to Hampton Park directly, as you like."

"Is that what you want?"

Beckett fought the tightness in his chest. "Of course it's what I want. It is what we agreed upon. And though we have proven to be suitable bedmates and do not lack for conversation, we must

206

remember the terms of our arrangement. This is a marriage of convenience. It is *not*, and never shall be, a love-match. And that suits me splendidly."

Her eyes flashed, dark and dangerous. "Now I know why you never sought a career on the stage, my lord. You are a very poor actor." Isobel turned on her heel, but Beckett seized her arm and spun her back to face him.

"What is that supposed to mean, madam?"

"I mean to say that you are liar, my lord. Yes, you heard me. A liar. This marriage doesn't suit you at all. That is why you are trying to deny the truth of it."

"I am doing nothing of the sort. I am merely trying to remind you of the arrangement we made—"

"What are you afraid of?"

He tried to mask his shock. "*Afraid?* I am not afraid."

"Oh, yes you are. It's a strange thing, Beckett, but in my experience, a man doesn't run away from something unless it's got him scared witless."

His stomach clenched like a fist. Good God, but the little chit could irk him! Didn't she know that he was doing this for her own good? It seemed he would have to make it very clear to her.

"What do you want from me, Isobel? You want me to profess my love to you?" He gripped her shoulders and pulled her closer, as if that would make her understand. "I gave you fair warning when we struck this bargain. Love would have no place in our marriage. I have held true to that. I have kept my promise. And I can't help it if you haven't."

"I know what you're trying to do, Beckett." Her voice sounded strained. "You're trying to push me away—to make it easier on yourself somehow. So you won't have to risk anything!"

"Why would I do that when there is nothing to risk?"

He saw the shock in her eyes—the hurt. But she did not look away. She took a deep breath, and went on.

"Of course, you are right. There is nothing to risk for you. But for me . . . I know that I am not supposed to love you. It is regrettable—*but I do*. And though you have said you don't want my love, I cannot simply end such feelings."

Beckett cleared his throat, as it had somehow become thick.

So, he had her love, did he? The one thing that he could never trust in, never accept, never believe in. He had believed in love once, and found it to be a trickster, a sprite—playing on the weakness of the human heart. He would not be fooled by it again.

"I am sorry to hear it. And I am sorry if I gave you false hope that I might one day return the sentiment. Even if I could love a woman again— it could never be you, Isobel. How could I love a woman I can never fully trust?"

Isobel closed her eyes and stepped back as if he had struck her. She took a moment, then opened her eyes to look at him again.

"You have a right to say that. It's true, I did lie to you before. And perhaps that will always stand between us. But there is something I want you to know. I want you to understand that even now, hearing these hurtful words coming from your lips—lips which have kissed and loved me in the night—even now my feeling for you is still as strong. It is still there."

Her eyes burned brightly with emotion as she spoke. "You are in my heart. You are there *every moment*. I cannot get you out. Do you not think I have tried? But there is no cure. You *are* my heart."

Beckett fought the urge to take her into his arms and crush her to him. "A pity."

He thought she might slap him, then. In fact, he wished that she would. But she just looked up at him with her sable eyes. The hurt and anger he saw swirling there was more painful than any blow she could have given him.

Isobel turned and stalked away. In her haste to leave, she stumbled over a rock and almost lost her balance.

Beckett stepped quickly to help her, but she shook him off.

"Leave me alone!"

"Isobel—"

"Don't touch me." Her voice held an edge of warning.

"Let me help you, please."

"No. You've helped me quite enough, I think." She headed up the little hill, Beckett following behind.

Oh, why did his heart pound painfully in his chest—as if it were actually punching him from the inside out?

She stopped short, turning around to face him. "If you want to push me away, that is your choice. But make no mistake, Beckett. It is *I* who pity *you*."

He stopped and let her walk on alone, shocked that he was the one trying to recover from their interview, instead of the other way around.

Isobel's indomitable spirit astounded him. So, she would not be frightened off by his attempts to hurt her. If only she could understand that he was pushing her away for her own sake! Surely, she would come to see that.

He looked up ahead. Where was she? He couldn't see her anymore. Trying to catch up, he broke into a run and dashed down the path to the road. He came around the trees, and his heart froze at the sight before him.

There, in the middle of the road, Isobel stood surrounded by pirates.

# Chapter Nineteen

Isobel ran down the path, eyeing rocks upon it with the thought of stopping to hurl a few at Beckett. But that would only prove to him that he'd hurt her. And she would rather eat broken glass than embarrass herself further.

He'd had every right to say what he did. Love hadn't been part of their arrangement. But she had fallen in love with him, anyway. Though she'd known it was foolish, she'd nurtured the fragile seed of her love, hoping that one day Beckett would feel the same. But all hope was lost now.

He would never, ever love her.

She burned with hurt and anger. She wanted to kick herself! How could she have let herself fall for a man who was nothing more than a good-looking block of ice?

She heard Beckett calling from somewhere

behind on the path. Isobel picked up her pace. She didn't want him to catch up with her now, because if he put his arms around her and tried to comfort her she would let him.

Isobel turned onto the road and ran headfirst into someone rather tall. She looked up and saw a huge man with shaggy red hair and a beard that had been twisted into braids. He looked down at her and smiled. He was missing several teeth.

A thread of fear shot through her and she turned back toward the path, but it was blocked by three other men who looked just as scraggly and menacing as the one in the road.

Isobel's heart raced as the realization hit her. *Pirates!*

"Hello, my dear." A silky voice floated from behind her. She knew that voice. But it couldn't be!

Isobel turned and her stomach lurched.

Sir Harry Lennox walked toward her, looking for all the world like a gentleman just stepping out of a London club. His eyes were dark and glittery, and a smile snaked across his thin lips. "Happy to see me?"

"Can't you tell?" She made her voice sound hard and fearless.

"No? And after all the trouble I went to in order to find you." Sir Harry eyed her reproachfully. He grabbed her arm and jerked her towards him. "You've led me a merry chase, my dear, and I intend to make you pay for such foolishness. In very interesting ways."

"You're a murdering swine. Let go of me!"

Annoyance flashed in Sir Harry's eyes. "I advise you to behave, my dear. We are, after all, in public."

"Isobel!" Beckett shouted. Isobel turned to see her husband at the end of the road being overpowered by Sir Harry's men.

"Ah, the dutiful husband has made an appearance, I see." Sir Harry smirked. "How considerate of him."

Isobel screamed.

One of the pirates punched Beckett in the face and Isobel saw his head snap back. He staggered, but stayed on his feet, even broke free to land a punch of his own in the man's face. But then the others had him and the bellowing pirate struck Beckett over and over in the stomach.

"Please, don't hurt him anymore." Isobel cried, but Sir Harry just laughed.

"Don't hurt him? But my dear, I intend to kill him."

Isobel felt the color drain from her face and forced down the nausea in her stomach. She looked at Sir Harry, beseeching him with her eyes. All this time, she'd thought she had the courage to face this man when the time came. But seeing Beckett being beaten made her courage drain away like blood from a wound. "Please . . . I'll do whatever you say."

"You'll do whatever I say anyway." Sir Harry looked quite unconcerned. "And when I do kill him, you will watch every moment of it. Bring him here, Fergus!"

Isobel stared helplessly as the men dragged Beckett toward them. Her husband was hunched over, obviously in pain from the blows to his stomach, and Isobel had to struggle to remain in control as they approached. One of the other cutthroats held Isobel while Sir Harry stepped away from her.

Fergus, the pirate whose nose had been bloodied by Beckett's punch, grabbed her husband's hair and wrenched his head back. Isobel's hand flew to her mouth to stifle a cry. Beckett's eye was already swelling, and blood dripped from his mouth.

He glared at Sir Harry and his voice rasped with pain. "If you touch her, I'll—"

Sir Harry smashed his fist into Beckett's face. Isobel screamed again as her beloved finally crumpled to the ground. Sir Harry bent down toward Beckett and put his hand to his ear.

"Sorry—you'll what, old chap? I didn't quite catch that." Sir Harry lifted Beckett's head, and seeing no response, let it drop. "The man's at a loss for words, it seems. Oh, and just so you know. I *do* plan on touching her."

"I'll kill you first!" Isobel cried, struggling hopelessly against the pirate who held her. She stared down at Beckett's lifeless form and felt her heart break.

Sir Harry reached out and touched her face.

"Still my little spitfire, I see. Just as I liked you."

Isobel lunged at him with an unknown strength, breaking free of her captor's grasp. She dug her fingernails into Sir Harry's face as they both toppled to the ground. Isobel screamed in rage, thrashing and clawing at him like a wildcat. Sir Harry let out a yell as Isobel drew blood.

Her foe struggled for breath as the men pried Isobel off him. Slowly he stood up, looking quite unsteady on his feet. He tried to straighten his dishevelled clothing. Reaching up to touch his face, he stared with disbelief at the blood that stained his fingers.

"I hope I've left you a nice scar, you loathsome blackguard!" Isobel spat.

"You will pay for that, as well. Very dearly indeed."

"As you will pay for your crimes."

He cocked one eyebrow. "We'll see."

Motioning to the men, Sir Harry led them down the road and onto another path. Soon they reached a secluded cove that Isobel didn't recognize. A large rowboat waited for them in the clear water, its front pulled up onto the pink sand like the nose of a sleeping dog.

The pirates dumped Beckett into the end of the boat as if he were no more than a sack of potatoes. Two of them lifted Isobel in and she decided not to struggle. There was no question now of attempting to escape. Beckett was unconscious and she had to stay with him. Sir Harry climbed in and the last pirate pushed them off and took his place at one of the oars.

Isobel twisted around to watch Beckett, who lay crumpled on the bottom of the boat. The sight made her heart tighten with wretched pain.

Isobel stared out at the turquoise sea and watched the shoreline recede. Suddenly, she thought she was going to be sick.

This couldn't be happening! Now, Beckett's life was in danger because of her. Perhaps there was a way to change Sir Harry's mind. Perhaps she could convince him that Beckett should live. She knew that she'd do anything—submit to any vulgarity that Sir Harry wished to inflict upon her—if it would save her husband's life.

They neared the pirate ship, and Isobel felt the hopelessness of their fate like a great stone in her gut. She closed her eyes and prayed.

The rowboat came alongside the ship and a rope ladder dropped down next to them. The pirates clambered up the ladder, as agile and quick as monkeys. One of them, the big red-haired man, hoisted Beckett over his shoulder and climbed up easily despite the extra weight.

Then it was Isobel's turn. She stood, and when Sir Harry tried to play the gallant gentleman and assist her, she shook him off, wishing her eyes were daggers. Apparently it had some effect, because Sir Harry allowed her to climb up by herself.

When Isobel reached the top of the rope ladder, the red-haired pirate pulled her aboard the ship with strong arms and set her down on the deck.

Her eyes searched for Beckett and she caught sight of him being dragged down below. She whirled around to face Sir Harry. "Where are they taking him?"

Sir Harry smirked. "To the brig, my dear. Don't worry, no harm will come to your husband until I am good and ready to inflict it."

"Please, leave him out of this," she begged. "It is *me* you want, and now you have me. You don't need Beckett. Let him go."

"Ah, but I don't have you, yet, precious one. I cannot make you my wife while your husband still lives. So I intend to see that you are widowed before this voyage is over. Then we shall retire to Hampton Park, and live out our lives in perfect happiness."

"That is what you think these twisted plans will bring you? Happiness?" Isobel asked, incredulous. "How can a man without a heart ever be happy?"

"Make no mistake. I have one, and it beats only for you. You shall understand that one day."

As she stared at Sir Harry in disgust, another man approached them—a man who from his bearing was undoubtedly the captain of the ship. He had a fierceness that made Isobel tremble. Though he only looked to be in his forties, his hair was white as snow. He wore it tied back in a bloodred ribbon.

He held a cat curled in one arm and Isobel recognized the animal at once—Captain Black!

But how had the cat come to be here?

"You must be Lady Ravenwood," the ship's captain said.

"I am the countess of Ravenwood."

"I am Captain Worthington, and this is my ship, the *Revenge*."

"I've heard of you. Forgive me if I am less than delighted about our meeting under such circumstances, Captain. And would you please explain how you have come to be in possession of my cat, sir?"

"Of course." Worthington nodded and smiled smoothly. "Firstly, Madam, he is *my* cat, as I'm sure you know. Be assured, I am most grateful to you for taking care of him. When I paid a visit to Ravenwood Hall earlier today, I found him living like a king."

Isobel's stomach knotted in fear as she thought of Josephine and the others at Ravenwood Hall. "Was anyone hurt while you were absconding with Captain Black?"

"No, no." The pirate shook his head as if the idea were ludicrous. "They did not even know that I was there."

He seemed to notice Sir Harry then and regarded his scratched face with raised eyebrows. "Had a little trouble did you?" He turned back to Isobel. "I applaud your efforts, madam."

Sir Harry stood taller, eyes narrowing. "A man must not be afraid to shed a little blood in order to get what he wants, Captain."

"Hmm. Especially if what he wants is what shed the blood in the first place, eh?"

Sir Harry grabbed Isobel's arm and pulled her next to him. "It does seem that my little kitten has claws. But they shall soon be trimmed. It is nothing I cannot handle."

"Undoubtedly." Worthington gave a humorless smile. "We have calm seas, Sir Harry. I'm sure you'll find the seasickness that plagued you on the journey over will be less of a nuisance—for the time being."

Sir Harry snarled. "I told you, Captain, it was the *food*."

"Ah, yes. So you did."

Isobel felt somehow reassured by this exchange. It seemed that Captain Worthington had no love for Sir Harry, either.

"I would like to go below now, Captain," Sir Harry said, petulantly. "As you can see, I'm in need of a change of clothes. I shall leave Isobel to your care for a few moments, if you think you can manage her?"

Sir Harry pulled Isobel close and whispered in her ear. "Behave now, my darling. I'm sure Captain Worthington will not be so indulgent of your antics as I."

Isobel stared straight ahead until he released her arm, then watched with relief as Sir Harry went below.

Worthington turned to Isobel, his fierce gray eyes holding her prisoner.

"Lady Ravenwood, you strike me as an intelligent young woman, so let us come to an understanding. I am a businessman. I work for profit. If, let's say, a sack of coffee beans fell overboard, no one on this ship would bother to fish it out. And since you are a piece of cargo that I am being paid to transport, I'm afraid my crew and I have as much interest in you as we would in a sack of coffee beans."

Isobel felt her heart sinking even deeper, but tried not to let it show.

He adjusted the cat in his arms and continued. "So if at any time, you are considering trying your luck with the sharks, be warned, no one from my ship will come to your rescue. Of course, if Sir Harry wants to play the hero, he is welcome to it."

"It would almost be worth it to have Sir Harry gobbled by sharks, too." Isobel laughed bitterly. "Oh, what does it matter? The truth is, I would welcome such a fate, compared to the one that awaits me."

"With Lennox?"

"He will murder my husband, sir, and force me to be his bride. I have already seen him commit murder. He is a madman."

"I am sorry for you."

"Are you? And you would allow him to do this? Have you no conscience?"

He smiled in a cold, businesslike manner. "You ask a pirate if he has a conscience, madam? Then I truly *am* sorry for you. Sir Harry has promised me a substantial sum for your passage back to England. It is none of my business what he does with his goods."

"I'll wager this isn't the first time you've transported human cargo, is it, Captain?" she challenged.

"No, it isn't. And it won't be the last."

"I'm sure. You likely did so under Captain Black." She stepped closer to the white-haired pirate and reached out to stroke the cat in his arms. "Captain Mayfield told me much about you and your former captain—wild stories of obeah, and strange ceremonies of transfiguration. You know, Josephine, our housekeeper at Ravenwood Hall also told me many stories of her own. Of course, they must be whimsy. For we all know that such transformations are not possible. But if they were . . . Ah, well, I'm sure Josephine was just spinning stories. Don't you think?"

She saw something flicker in the man's grey eyes, then quickly cloak itself. Worthington held the cat closer and regarded Isobel with a thoughtful expression. "I would like to hear these stories, Lady Ravenwood. Captain Black seems to be quite legendary in these islands. And he is just a silly cat, after all."

Captain Black meowed sharply and looked up at Worthington, batting a paw at the man's chin.

"Silly, indeed," Isobel muttered, trying to hide her smile.

Worthington looked unamused, and transfixed her with his stare. "We shall continue the conversation over dinner, then. And you must tell me more of these 'folk-tales' regarding Captain Black."

*Could those stories really be true?*

"Ah, Sir Harry has returned." Worthington made a bow. "I shall leave you under his 'care.' But I shall see you both tonight at my table for dinner. Until then, Lady Ravenwood." He strode across the deck with Captain Black peeking at her over his shoulder.

Isobel felt her heart sink as she watched the pirate exchange a few words with Sir Harry. They both glanced at her for a moment, and she looked away, staring out at the azure water as they headed out to sea.

Surely, having Captain Black here was a good omen. She'd seen the look in Worthington's eyes. Had it been one of fear? Of course, the man was a pirate and the captain of this ship. He was obviously adept at cloaking his reactions and maintaining a cool veneer at all times.

But he'd given her a weapon, however small. And hadn't David slain Goliath with a rock the size of an egg?

It was obvious that Worthington thought she knew something rather important. She would find a way to use the stories about Captain Black to her advantage.

And she would find a way to see Beckett. To *save* Beckett.

Or she would die trying.

# Chapter Twenty

Beckett moaned.

Ugh. Why was the room rocking so? What was that smell? And why did his entire body hurt?

He opened his eyes.

*Dear Lord, I've gone blind. . . .*

He opened and closed them a few times, his eyes adjusting to the dark. And then he remembered.

*Isobel.* He sat up and tried to get to his feet, but fell back down. He knew what the pain in his side meant. Broken ribs. Oh, bugger.

Beckett lay on his good side and clenched his teeth in frustration. He ignored the pain and struggled at the bonds that held his hands behind his back. It was fruitless. He was trussed up like a Christmas turkey. Beckett felt a knot of fear and anger harden in his gut.

Where was Isobel? If Sir Harry had hurt her,

had even touched a hair on her head . . . just the thought of the bastard's hands on her made Beckett growl in fury.

He had to do something or he would go mad.

Beckett heard scuttling across the floor, and knew it was a rat. Well, who had he expected to meet in the hold of a pirate ship? *Prinny?* He felt like laughing. This would be the first time he'd gladly trade present company for that of the prince regent.

Trying to ignore the pain in his side, Beckett thought back to the Battle of Salamanca during the war. He and his men had been cut off from the main force by a legion of French dragoons. His colonel had panicked and led half the battalion to their deaths.

Beckett had taken command then, and though the situation had seemed utterly hopeless, he'd led the remaining men to safety by keeping a cool head and not letting his fear get the best of him.

He would do the same now.

The first thing to do was escape from this cell.

The second was to find a way for himself and Isobel to escape.

And the third was to kill Sir Harry Lennox. Of course, the second and third items might change order, depending on circumstances.

This obviously proved the validity of his wife's previous claims.

Beckett stared at the dingy floor in the murky darkness. He decided not to contemplate the origins of the sticky substance that covered it and smelled like the back end of an ox. This would be his home for a little while. Still, he'd lived through worse things in the war.

He heard the scurrying again. It seemed the rat had brought its friends to meet their new cellmate. Well, it wasn't polite to complain about one's neighbors.

The sound of keys rattled outside the door, and Beckett sat up, wincing from the pain in his side. Warm yellow light streamed into the cell and momentarily blinded him. He squinted, trying to focus on the looming shadow in the doorway.

"Lord Ravenwood," said Sir Harry Lennox, stepping into the cell. "So glad you're awake."

Sir Harry stepped into the brig, followed by a large red-haired pirate who stood and blocked the entire door with his towering form.

"Your accommodations are comfortable, Ravenwood?" Sir Harry asked, looking about the cell.

"Quite." Beckett fought the urge to attack the weasel-gutted peacock strutting before him. It would be no use while he was injured and with "Redbeard" standing just feet away. He'd learned during the war to pick his battles; this wasn't one of them.

It was apparent Sir Harry had something in mind. And it was not killing him—not just yet. Lennox would have simply thrown him over the side by now if he wasn't saving Beckett for something else.

"Your wife's accommodations are very different, you'll be pleased to know. Not like this dung-hole. But what else could I provide for a thief like yourself?"

"Thief?" Beckett spat. "I suppose I'm somehow responsible for stealing my wife and myself, then?"

"I have only recovered what is mine, Ravenwood. You'd do well to remember that."

"Isobel is not yours. She never was yours. She will never *be* yours."

"Oh?" Sir Harry smiled easily. "How do you know that I haven't made her mine already?"

Beckett refused to take the bait. "Because there

are not enough marks on your face, and you can still walk. If you had tried to possess my wife, I daresay you'd be much the worse for wear. Though I applaud her for the gash she gave your cheek back on the island."

Sir Harry self-consciously raised his hand to the fresh wound on his face and stared down at Beckett darkly. "Don't worry, Ravenwood. I do plan to tame the little cat, and take much enjoyment from it."

"Do you? It's obvious that you do not know my wife, sir. She is tenacious as a terrier. I don't doubt she will have you for luncheon." Beckett laughed even though it hurt his ribs to do so.

"Brave words from a man who is destined to spend his last days in a dung-hole. We'll see how brave you are on the day of your execution, Lord Ravenwood."

"Oh, have you a date in mind, then? Do be good enough to let me know so I can have my clothes in order. I wouldn't want to swing in anything other than the latest fashion. Perhaps you might lend me something of yours, Sir Harry, as we look to be the same size?"

The man looked smug. "Who says I'm going to hang you?"

"Well, a hanging may be unimaginative, yet it does hold a certain amount of drama, as well as being easy. I thought it would suit a coward like you perfectly. Just think of it. The yard-arm extended over the water, my hair blowing in the wind, all your pirate cronies assembled on deck waiting to watch me gasp my last. You know, it sounds just like Mr. Norton's new play I saw at Drury Lane but a month ago. I must say, it *was* a boring affair."

"I can assure you, Ravenwood, your execution will be anything but."

"You have your work cut out for you, then. I'm afraid fighting in the war against Napoleon has made me ever so hard to impress."

"Then I shall do my best to entertain you, my lord. And Isobel, of course, as she will be present to watch your long, painful death. You may spend the rest of the voyage in this miserable cell, with nothing else but that prospect to occupy your thoughts. Oh." Sir Harry stopped as he turned to go. "That, and wondering which part of Isobel's body I have my hands on at any given moment. Good day, Ravenwood."

Beckett clenched his teeth and fought against leaping to his feet and hurling himself at Sir Harry. But with his hands tied behind his back, the gesture would be useless. Instead, he watched the slimy coward take his leave, followed by Redbeard. The cell was again plunged into darkness and Beckett heard the key in the lock.

He sat back and leaned his head against the wall, fighting the awful knot of dread that had balled itself in his stomach.

*Isobel.*

The sight of her face as they'd stood on the beach swirled in his mind. His heart tightened painfully at the memory, and of the things he'd said to her.

What a wretched excuse for a husband he was. He had sworn to protect her, had given her his word. And he had been unable to keep it. Now she was in danger and he was in the brig, wounded and unable to help her. And God only knew what Sir Harry planned.

Beckett had only been fishing when he'd said the lack of marks on Sir Harry's face proved the man hadn't forced himself on Isobel. *Yet.* Oh, God, the very thought of it made Beckett want to rip the heavy oak door from its hinges.

He'd kept his head, but at what cost? Should he have tried to escape just now, and thrown caution to the wind? Maybe he could have succeeded.

But they were on a pirate ship. Even if Beckett had somehow succeeded in killing Sir Harry and Redbeard, if he himself were killed, what would happen to Isobel? He doubted that the pirate captain, whoever he was, would return Isobel to England unharmed.

No, he had to stay alive until his ribs were a little better and he was able to fight. Then he would get both himself and Isobel to safety. Or at the very least, Isobel.

His eyes were adjusting to the little bit of light that crept in under the door from the companionway, but he closed his eyes. All of a sudden there was a lump in his throat. He breathed deeply to try to get rid of it, but it didn't work.

His mind filled itself with images of her, laughing merrily at a shared joke. Covered in dirt, but radiant and indomitable as they'd fought the fire together. Panting and helpless in his arms as he'd made love to her for the first time.

Like a slap in the face, the realization of such feelings stung him. And how ironic that he'd denied having any feelings for her at all, only hours before on the beach.

Was all this to be torn away from him?

Could he allow his bride, his *friend* to be taken from him forever because of the wickedness of a madman?

He would rather cut off his own arm.

# *Chapter Twenty-one*

In the week that passed—at times unbearably slowly, and at others so fast it made her head spin—Isobel had not been able to see Beckett even once.

She had tried twice. Once, she'd feigned sickness and headed back to her cabin alone, but the man with the red beard had found her. He hadn't said anything; he'd merely taken her arm, gently but firmly, and returned her to the deck. And the other time, she had attempted to convince a burly pirate that he would guarantee himself a place in heaven if he assisted the cause of true love. That hadn't worked either.

She was allowed a semblance of freedom, however, after proving on the first day she wasn't going to throw herself overboard. And since a sudden seasickness kept Sir Harry cabin-bound, she'd been put in Captain Worthington's charge, and he usually was too busy with the running of the ship to notice her.

At least she had a companion in Captain Black. Though he spent a fair amount of time sitting on Worthington's shoulder, her old feline friend would seek her out as well, always appearing when her heart was darkest with worry.

He would purr and nuzzle his face against her neck, and gaze at her with knowing green eyes. Once, when a teardrop escaped and trickled down her cheek, the cat had reached up and touched it gently with his paw.

*A cat who could wipe away your tears*, she'd thought.

Perhaps the stress of her bleak situation was fooling with her senses.

To keep her mind occupied and her sanity intact, Isobel had taken to sitting up on deck, drawing. But today she was finding it especially hard to concentrate.

As Captain Black lounged beside her, Isobel looked out at the empty sea that surrounded the ship and tried to summon her eyes back to the sketching paper that Captain Worthington had provided her. But she felt lifeless as a rag doll.

She forced her hand to the paper. She would sketch and try not to think about Beckett, or if she would ever see him alive again. She would stay calm, and not think about what might be happening to him in the hold of the ship.

Perhaps nothing was happening to him. Perhaps he was already dead.

As for Sir Harry, from Captain Worthington's account the man was green to the gills—just as he'd been on the trip across.

*Good*. She hoped it was fatal.

Surprisingly, she hadn't encountered much

trouble from the pirate crew. Though she had noticed some leering glances and muttered comments, Isobel always noticed that a glance from the captain or first mate stopped the ragged sailors cold. The sailors were too busy working most of the time to take much notice of her, anyway, and she thanked God for it.

Isobel began sketching without really knowing what she was doing, but soon a face emerged before her. It was no surprise to see Beckett staring back out at her. Something shone from the eyes on the page. Hope? Love? Was it hers or his?

Her hand faltered and she inadvertently slashed a mark across the beautiful face she had just sketched. Immediately, her heart throbbed with pain as she regarded the ruined picture in her lap.

A terrible fear struck her. Would she ever touch Beckett's face again? Would she ever feel the heat of his blue eyes as they looked at her as only he could? Would she ever feel his mouth on hers or his strong hands caressing her body?

She shut her eyes tight, valiantly trying to stifle the growing panic that rose in her chest like the waves of the sea that surrounded her.

Her thoughts went back to the loss she'd felt when her parents had died. She'd loved them so much. If she hadn't loved them, the pain would have been negligible.

It seemed the world was built on opposites—land and sea, sun and moon, man and woman, pleasure and pain. Each was a part of the other, and to accept one was to accept its opposite as well. One could not enjoy the sun all day and tell the moon to stay away at night. That thought comforted her.

Isobel looked out at the sea and remembered the hot intensity of Beckett's eyes. She had drowned in their depths long ago, and would not be sorry now. If the price of loving Beckett included a life of misery, she would pay it. And if being Sir Harry's whore would save Beckett's life, she would do it gladly.

There must be a way to convince Sir Harry to spare her husband's life. She would sign over the deed to Hampton Park. She would tell Sir Harry there was more money hidden away somewhere, anything to buy Beckett some time.

But perhaps he would try to play the hero and refuse to leave without her, even if she won him the chance. Yes, she could see that happening. Beckett might not love her, but he would never leave her to a fate with Sir Harry in order to save himself.

She stared at the skyline and shook her head. None of this would be happening if she hadn't run away that night. Beckett would never have found her, or taken her in, or made her his wife. Now, she was back where she'd started—doomed to a life as Sir Harry's plaything. But the man she loved would be killed because of her.

Isobel turned her head toward approaching voices from the lower deck. It seemed to be a good time to return to her cabin. She picked up her pencils and started to leave, but stopped as she heard whispering.

"I tell ye, we must move tonight, McGregor!" the whispered voice said forcefully.

Something told her to hide then, and she crouched down by the crate on which she'd been sitting. The only place remotely plausible was behind a huge coil of hemp near the railing.

Isobel scooted behind it just in time and crouched as low as she could. As if sensing the tension in the air, Captain Black made himself scarce. Holding her breath, she listened to the pirates' hushed conversation.

"I 'aven't got enough men yet," a gruff voice replied. "I needs a few more days, still."

"In a few more days it'll be past the turn. I told Brinkman we'd be in Jamaica to pick up the cargo next week, see? If we don't move now we'll not make it in time!"

"Styles, 'ave ye gone daft in the knob? If we move without enough men, neither of us will make it to Jamaica!" McGregor hissed. "Now, d'ye want the ship, or don't ye?"

"Of course I do, ye dung-head!"

"Then ye'll have to trust me, old nodder! In a few more days, I tell ye. We'll 'ave most o' the men on our side then, and it'll be much easier to slit the cap'n's throat if 'is lackeys are with us."

"Alright, then," Styles said. "But don't disappoint me. I want Worthington's 'ead on a platter. And that little miss 'e's been protectin' will fetch a nice price in Kingston market . . . after we've all had a few turns between 'er legs, o' course."

Isobel's blood turned icy cold, and she stared helplessly at the rough, damp rope in front of her. *Was there no end to her woes?*

"I'll do what I can tonight," McGregor said. "Meet me in the galley after grub n'grog. I'll know more then."

"The sooner, the better. Shite, someone's comin'!"

Isobel heard their footsteps scramble away, but could only sit numbly behind the coil of rope as she contemplated her bleak future. The situation was going from bad to worse, rather quickly.

There was only one thing to do.

She *had* to reach Beckett. *He* might know how to turn this situation to their advantage. And if he didn't, it might be the last time she would ever see his face.

Isobel peeked over the crate and, seeing that it

was safe to move, quickly grabbed her pencils and stood. Purposefully, she walked across the deck toward the doorway that led down to the sleeping quarters.

"I'll be going to my cabin, now," she said to no one in particular. The pirates there ignored her as she walked past.

She searched the deck for sight of Captain Worthington, but didn't see him. The red-bearded first mate seemed to be in command at the moment. That meant Worthington was in his quarters, working on charts, or counting gold coins . . . or doing whatever pirate captains did.

"Yes, I *am* tired," Isobel continued saying to the air. "I think I shall have a long nap."

She reached the doorway and yawned loudly before she went through. As she'd become used to the steep stairway, she descended it as quickly as a monkey. There was no one about in the companionway.

She went to her cabin and left her papers and pencils on the small table, then peeked out the door. It was still clear.

Quickly and silently, Isobel scuttled down the companionway. She went in the opposite direction she'd tried before, hoping that this was the way to the brig. Her heart thumped hard in her breast as she went deeper and deeper into the bowels of the ship.

As she came around one corner she saw a big, burly man fiddling with some keys near a door. Ducking back, she waited and listened.

"Damn. I needs me pipe," the pirate said to himself. "Been too long without a smoke. Oh, bugger."

Isobel heard him shifting around on his feet, snorting and clearing his throat.

*Go. Go and have your pipe.*

"Devil take it," he said, as if to her, "I needs me pipe! Now, ye be a good chap and behave yerself while ol' Williams is gone. A man has to have his pipe now and again, or like as go mad, eh?"

*Chap? Could he see her?*

"So right, Mr. Williams. Be a good fellow and fetch me back a cigar, won't you?"

*It sounded like Beckett's voice!*

Williams laughed. "Yer a right funny one, ye is, m'lord. Tell ye what. I'll have an extra smoke in yer honor. 'Ow's that, eh?"

"Take your time, my good man. Take your time."

The man chuckled. "I shall, sir. And not a word o' this to the cap'n, now. Wouldn't look good if he thought we was becomin' friends, eh? Might toss me overboard, he might. An' I needs this job."

"Don't worry, Mr. Williams. If the captain comes by, I shall do my best to quake in fear if your name is mentioned."

"Right good of ye, sir. I'll be off then." Williams turned with a snort, and headed towards where Isobel stood at the end of the passage.

She looked behind her frantically for a place to hide, but there was none. She backed up all the way into a set of stairs. There was no place to go!

She looked again. There was a small crevice next to the stairs she thought she could squeeze through. It was a risk, though. If she got stuck, Mr. Williams would find her, and what explanation would she have for being wedged between the stairs and the bulkhead?

She heard the man's heavy footsteps approaching, and knew it was now or never. She squeezed herself sideways against the narrow opening and wiggled an arm through. It was going to be tight.

234

He was getting closer. She could hear him coughing only feet away around the corner. She closed her eyes—though what good that would do she didn't know—sucked her stomach in, and shoved.

Like a pearl through a button-hole, she popped through the opening. Isobel crouched down in the shadows just as Williams's foot touched the first step. He clomped up the stairs with heavy feet, and soon disappeared out of sight.

Isobel breathed a sigh of relief and quickly went about squeezing back out of the opening. There was no time to lose.

She peeked around the corner again and breathed a sigh of relief when she saw the passageway was still empty. Beckett was here, just a few feet away. Isobel crept closer as silently as a cat. She reached the sturdy oak door and saw a small square opening near the top. It was blocked with sturdy iron bars.

"Beckett!" she whispered. "Beckett, it's me . . . Isobel."

His head popped up in the opening like a Jack-in-the-box, and Isobel felt tears come to her eyes.

"Isobel?" She saw the disbelief in his eyes as he looked down at her.

Her hands flew up to the bars and Beckett's fingers threaded through to twine with hers. The touch of his skin sent a jolt through her body. She was laughing and crying all at once.

"I didn't know if you were still alive. Oh, Beckett!"

"Are you alright, Isobel? Lennox, has he—"

"Sir Harry has a terrible case of seasickness. He's been in his cabin for most of the time, and other than that, he hasn't had the strength to do much more than scowl. I'm quite well."

Beckett closed his eyes in relief, then looked back at her with that fiery gaze that made her heart skip. "I've been going mad with worry."

"As I have." She squeezed his hand through the bars. "Are you alright?"

"I had some broken ribs, but they're on the mend. It's too bad Williams didn't leave his key. Don't suppose you feel like breaking down the door, do you my dear?" He chuckled.

"Don't try anything foolish, Beckett. You must promise me."

"I will try anything if it will get us out of here."

"Well, that is the least of our problems now, it seems."

"What do you mean?"

Isobel took a deep breath. "I overheard two men talking just now about a mutiny that is going to take place very soon. They plan to kill Captain Worthington, and I can only imagine what they mean to do to us."

"Damn!" Beckett cursed. "Where is the captain?"

"I haven't seen him about. I assume he's in his quarters."

"You must go and warn him. It's too risky to hope we could escape in the midst of a mutiny. Though I'd most likely be safe in here, you would be in great danger. No, you must warn the captain. I'll give odds that he won't believe you at first. He'll think you're trying to help me or yourself escape. But you must find some way to convince him. Do you think you can do that, Isobel?"

"I can if it means our lives. *Your* life. Oh, Beckett, I am so sorry you've been mixed up in this. If only you hadn't taken me home that night. If only—"

"If only you'd stop saying 'if only.' I wouldn't change it for the world. All of London will be terribly jealous when they find out we have sailed on a real pirate ship, and survived. I imagine Prinny will have us to dinner just to hear the tale."

Isobel laughed, though tears dampened her eyes again.

Beckett squeezed her fingers, his eyes glowing with their intensity. "It will be alright, Isobel. I promise. Now find Worthington."

He pulled her fingers to his lips and kissed them tenderly through the bars, his gaze burning with emotion.

Isobel reluctantly pulled away, unwilling to give up even one moment of feeling his touch. She finally turned to go down the companionway, but stopped. This could be the last moment they ever saw each other alive. . . .

She turned back and pressed herself against the heavy door, wishing it was Beckett's body she clung to instead of the barrier that separated them. "I have to tell you. I can't leave you here, not knowing if I'll ever have the chance again. And I know you don't want to hear it, but I must."

Beckett's fingers came through the bars and reached for her. She stretched up on tiptoe as high as she could, and she felt him stroke her hair. The look in his eyes threatened to melt her where she stood.

"No, Isobel." He kissed her through the bars, so tenderly it almost broke her heart. "This won't be the last time we have together. I promise. You must believe me."

"I'm afraid of losing you!" She kissed him back fervently. She felt as if she were drowning, and Beckett was the very air that her body—her entire being—thirsted for.

"You won't lose me, Isobel. And I won't lose you—not to Sir Harry Lennox. As long as there is breath in my body, I won't."

Beckett's words sent a chill through Isobel's heart. *As long as there is breath in my body. . . .*

"Beckett, I love you." Her voice was no more than a whisper. "Even though you don't want it to be true. Even though *I* don't want it to be true. And I don't care if you don't want to hear it. I love you more than life itself. So you better take care, do you hear? Don't take any foolish chances with my husband's life. I want him in one piece when this is over."

His expression was strained—his blue eyes dark as a dusky sky. He kissed her fingers, then abruptly released her hand. "You must go now, Isobel. We're running out of time."

She nodded. A numbing coldness washed through her heart.

Isobel stepped back. She didn't know what else to say. And she couldn't will herself to smile as she looked upon her husband's face for what could be the last time.

Finally, Isobel turned away, and slipped around the corner. She paused for a moment and stood with her back against the bulkhead before she continued. Hidden from Beckett's sight, she felt her heart aching, as if the love and pain inside would overflow and burst it open like the banks of a swollen river.

*He still didn't love her.*

Even now, when their lives were in such danger, when they might never see each other again, he'd said nothing.

It shouldn't matter. Not now. But it did.

She swallowed and steeled herself against the tears that threatened to fall. She had no time for them now. She had a mutiny to stop.

# Chapter Twenty-two

Isobel walked purposefully down the companionway, taking deep breaths and trying to calm herself. But she didn't know if it was from the danger she was facing or from the scene with Beckett.

How she had wanted to believe that he loved her! And she had foolishly thought he would answer her declaration of love with one of his own.

She had to clear her head of such notions. Now was not the time to lament her unrequited passion. Beckett had made his feelings plain on the beach. And if they did get out of this together, she could not expect anything more from him.

She came around the corner and saw the dark, sturdy door to the captain's quarters and stopped. As usual, there was a fearsome looking brute standing guard outside. Apparently, Worthington's trust went only so far—and rightly so.

"I need to see the captain, if you please," Isobel said firmly.

The big man looked at her, unimpressed. " 'E's not to be disturbed."

"It is of the utmost importance," she insisted.

The man moved his face close to hers, and the strong smell of his unwashed body penetrated her nostrils. The stubble on his face almost scraped her cheek as he spoke again, slowly and quietly. "I said, 'e's not to be disturbed . . . didn't I?"

Isobel tried not to look at the rotten, jagged teeth that sparsely filled his mouth. "Good sir, I *must* see the captain. If you will not knock on the door, then I shall."

The big man blocked Isobel's approach and grabbed her outstretched arm, pulling a wicked-looking dagger up just inches in front of her eyes.

"Ye see this, Miss?"

Isobel nodded mutely.

"Well, the cap'n, see, 'e tol' me to put it through the heart of anyone who come near that door, there. An' I would hate to dirty yer lovely dress." He pushed her away but held the dagger up threateningly. "Now, ye be a good lass, and shag off, before me and me dagger poke holes in ye."

Oh, bother! This was not going at all well.

"I shall return, then." Isobel's eyes flashed with as much haughtiness as she could muster. "And if the captain emerges, please tell him that I must speak to him right away."

The man grinned at her as if she had just asked him to perform *Hamlet* in its entirety.

" 'Course, Miss. I'll do that."

Frowning at her failure to talk her way past the guard, Isobel turned on her heel and made her way down the narrow passageway. Not knowing what else to do, she headed back to her quarters.

She would wait for a little while before insisting on seeing the captain once more. And if the man wouldn't let her past, which he probably would not, what would she do then?

Fighting the urge to return to Beckett's cell, Isobel forced herself back to her room. She would wait a quarter of an hour or so, then try again. Feeling terribly powerless, she sat on a chair and looked around the room, as if the answer to her troubles might be lurking somewhere.

Her eyes came to rest on the tray that held her luncheon dishes. Usually, it was removed right away, but someone had neglected his duties and hadn't picked it up.

Isobel looked at the plate. It was made of cracked porcelain, and looked quite old and dingy. But perhaps it could be more than that. She wanted to laugh at herself for not thinking of it before.

She picked it up and hit it against the side of the table. The plate broke into a few pieces that fell to the floor, and consequently broke into more. Reaching down, Isobel picked up one that was long and sharp, like an oddly shaped knife. She ripped some of her underskirt and wrapped it around the end, making a handle to grip. At any rate, the cloth would protect her hand from the jagged edge.

Lifting her skirt, she tucked the makeshift weapon into the laces that wrapped around the top of her boot. She arranged it as best she could, and hoped she wouldn't inadvertently stab herself in the foot.

She picked up the rest of the broken plate and hid the pieces under the lumpy straw mattress of her bunk. As the services she received consisted only of having food brought twice a day, she didn't think the pirates would be changing her bedding anytime soon. Hopefully, her crime would be well-hidden there.

241

She waited for more time to elapse, and when she was wringing her hands in frustration, decided she could wait no longer. Armed as well as she could be, Isobel set out on her mission once again.

Walking down the passageway, Isobel tried to look as carefree as possible. She didn't want to raise any suspicions. The knife she carried made her feel self-conscious, as if it were visible to all, though hidden beneath her skirts.

As she neared the captain's quarters, she noticed that the man who had previously stood guard outside was nowhere to be seen. Instead of reassuring her about any chance of seeing Captain Worthington, instinct told her this would be worse.

Isobel slowed her pace, listening for any sound beyond the door, when a big dirty hand clamped over her mouth and yanked her around the corner.

"And where d'ye think yer goin', Missy?" a voice rasped in her ear. Isobel grimaced at the stench of the man's breath. Strong, beefy arms held her easily and pressed her back against a solid chest. The man's forearm mashed her breast, and from the way he rubbed his arm against her there, Isobel guessed that the pirate was enjoying it.

Infuriated, Isobel kicked and thrashed about in the man's iron-hard arms. The pirate only laughed and squeezed her tighter.

This couldn't be happening. Not now—when Beckett's life depended on her reaching Captain Worthington!

Using all the willpower she could muster, Isobel sank her teeth into the meaty hand that covered her mouth and bit as hard as she could.

The pirate bellowed and tried to pry her mouth open with his other hand, but Isobel's jaws held tight. She tasted blood in her mouth, but refused to let the revolting hand go.

The pirate's hand curled around her neck, and she felt his fingers dig into her flesh.

"Let go, ye bloody bitch!" the man hissed.

"Leave off, Murray!" another voice said. "No marks on 'er skin, remember? Styles will have yer tongue cut out if ye bruise 'er."

"To 'ell with Styles! Help me get 'er off," Murray groaned.

The two men struggled to pry Isobel's jaws apart. When they finally succeeded, both regarded her with shock. Isobel could feel the warm wet blood running down her chin, and knew she must look quite a sight indeed.

"Me 'and—look what she done to it, Dobbin!" Murray held his wounded hand as gore dripped from it onto the floor.

"You should have the surgeon look at it." Isobel spit out some of the blood in her mouth. "While I was on Barbados I contracted a rare disease—*Caribbean parrot fever!*"

It was a bold-faced lie. There was no such disease as far as she knew. Nonetheless, it had the desired effect.

Murray's face turned white and he looked at Dobbin accusingly. "Why didn't *you* grab 'er? Now I've got 'Caribbean parrot fever'!"

In truth, Isobel thought she probably had more chance of having contracted a disease from Murray.

"Gag 'er, and put 'er in the galley," Dobbin ordered. "That should keep the baggage out o' trouble for a time."

"*You* gag 'er, Dobbin! I've had me fill o' bein' her dinner, thank you very much. The little bitch can take a bite out o' you."

243

"Hold 'er hands then, and I'll gag 'er."

The men roughly turned Isobel around, and Murray pulled her arms back painfully as Dobbin approached.

Isobel glared at the man. "Fever symptoms can be hideous. It won't be long now."

She saw a flicker of fear in the pirate's eyes and felt a small thrill of victory.

Dobbin bent down and ripped off a piece of her skirt, then stood, twisting it into a coil. Slowly, he brought the gag to her face.

Isobel shook her head like a terrier, but he managed to get it between her teeth and tied it tightly around her head in a secure knot.

She heard another tear of her skirt and soon her hands were bound behind her back, as well. At least Dobbin hadn't seen the porcelain knife in her boot when he'd ripped her dress. Thank goodness for underskirts!

Roughly, the men dragged Isobel down the narrow passageway and into what was obviously the galley. She had never seen it before and was surprised at how small and cluttered it was. Everywhere, pots and pans hung from the low ceiling, along with various ladles and other cooking utensils, which all clanged together as the ship rocked.

A galley with no cook? So, the mutiny had begun.

The pirates dragged her over to the table, pushed her down into a sitting position on the floor, then bound her hands to the table leg. Isobel kept her boot hidden under her skirt, but wondered if her makeshift knife would do her any good. With her hands tied behind her, she couldn't reach it.

Isobel glared up at the pirates, truly wishing that looks could kill. Strangely, the overwhelming emotion she felt was anger, not fear. But that would most likely change when the reality and hopelessness of the situation set in. When she heard the mutiny going on around her, *then* she would feel fear.

*What would happen to her—to Beckett?* She hoped that Sir Harry Lennox would be consigned to eternal torment for this!

"She should stay out of harm's way in 'ere," Dobbin pronounced. "If a pot doesn't fall on 'er head!"

"Per'aps we should take a pot to 'er noggin and knock 'er out now." Murray nursed his wounded hand. "I don't trust 'er."

Isobel tried to calm her fears as she pictured Murray taking a skillet to her head.

"Don't think so—might make her go daft, see? T'would lower 'er price in Kingston."

"Oh, and she's not daft already?" Murray asked looking unconvinced. "Said she 'ad parrot fever after all. Her an' me both, now."

"Ah, quit yer cryin', Murray. I say our job's done 'ere. McGregor will be wantin' us, now. Come on." Dobbin motioned toward the door.

The two men took a last look at Isobel and closed the door behind them.

Isobel struggled against her bonds but it was of no use. She tried lifting her boot up to her mouth to retrieve her knife, but could not stretch that far. Even if she could get the little weapon, she realized she would not be able to use it with her hands tied so. Frustration made her want to scream. But the sound she made came out like a muffled mewling and that made her fume in aggravation even more.

Hearing an odd squeaking noise, she twisted her head but could not see anything.

Then she saw it.

A little gray mouse scuttled straight toward her across the rough plank floor.

After fighting bloodthirsty pirates, Isobel wouldn't have thought she could still be frightened by a mouse. Not so. And now she would spend her last moments being terrorized by one. How fitting.

She squealed a little as the tiny rodent scurried in front of her. It began to sniff around the edge of her skirt, which had been soiled with spilled food and drink from the floor of the galley.

Then, with an other-worldly growl, a cat sprang from the shadows.

*Captain Black!* He truly was her knight in furry armour.

The mouse squeaked and scuttled across the floor in a blur of grey fur. Captain Black darted after the poor creature, and though it had surely been about to nibble her to death, Isobel feared for the rodent's life.

Just as Captain Black was about to pounce, the mouse disappeared through an opening in the planked flooring. The cat meowed and batted at the mouse-hole with his paws, unwilling to give up the chase.

Though gagged, Isobel attempted to get the cat's attention by making sounds that came out as a series of unladylike grunts.

Reluctantly, it seemed, Captain Black abandoned his hunt and returned to her side. *Oh, I wish you could help me . . . I wish you could set me free,* she thought, looking at the cat in desperation.

Since she knew no other way to convey her message to the feline, she kept grunting and wriggling, hoping that would do the trick.

Captain Black regarded her with his jewel-green eyes, meowed a few times, then moved behind her.

Holding her breath, Isobel waited. And hoped.

She felt his whiskers brush against her hand. Then she felt a tug on the fabric that tied her wrists. Her heart leapt with hope—Captain Black was chewing on the bonds!

*Could the cat really set her free?*

Captain Black continued with his task and Isobel felt the bonds begin to give way. She pulled gently. Using a bit more force, she felt the cloth rip and in a moment was free. She reached back to untie her gag, and turned to thank her valiant friend.

Pulling the cat into her arms, she placed a kiss right on his nose. He purred loudly and nuzzled her chin.

"Thank you, Captain Black. I shall have to give you a very large fish for this."

Standing, Isobel smiled at her four-footed friend. "Captain Mayfield was right. You *are* watching out for me, aren't you?"

The cat meowed, and she shook her head, chuckling.

Grabbing a skillet as she scrambled to the door, Isobel wondered what she could possibly have to smile about.

# Chapter Twenty-three

The ship held an eerie silence as Isobel walked quietly towards the captain's quarters. Captain Black bolted down the companionway and disappeared from sight. Isobel had no idea where Sir Harry would be in all this, but with any luck he would be mortally wounded during the melee. She only hoped Beckett would be safe in his cell.

As Isobel approached the door to Captain Worthington's cabin, she heard snarling voices from within. Taking a deep breath for courage, she crouched down in front of the door and peeped through the keyhole.

What she saw made her gasp.

Captain Worthington sat tied to a chair. The pirate she knew as Styles held the tip of his saber dangerously close to Worthington's throat.

*Oh, he couldn't be killed now.* Worthington's death would mean much worse for herself and

Beckett. She had to do something . . . anything! It was their only hope.

Isobel knocked on the door, then wondered what exactly she was going to do when it opened.

She heard footsteps approaching and stood back.

"Who is it?" a raspy voice asked.

Isobel used the gruffest voice that she could muster. "Message for Styles," she croaked.

She heard a grunt from behind the door. Resheathing her knife, she crouched a little and held her skillet ready.

The door opened and a large, ugly head popped out.

With all her strength, Isobel swung the skillet, smashing it into the pirate's face.

Perhaps she should have used the knife, but the truth of the matter was that she hadn't felt quite up to stabbing someone. The skillet produced the desired effect, however, as the large pirate crumpled in a limp heap across the door's threshold.

Isobel peeked around the door and saw Styles pause for a split-second.

It gave Worthington a chance. His boot flew up and connected with Styles's crotch. The man let out a bellow and dropped his saber, his hands covering his injured privates. Worthington kicked the saber into a corner as Isobel dashed in. There was no one else in the room.

"Hurry up!" Worthington commanded.

Isobel dropped the skillet and ran over to cut the captain's bonds with her little knife.

Styles was recovering. Like a bull, the pain seemed to have fueled his anger.

Isobel cut as fast as she could, but the ropes were thick and her silly piece of porcelain was not very sharp.

Styles approached slowly, his eyes blazing like a madman's as he pulled out a long thin dagger from his boot. He fingered it idly.

"Per'aps I *won't* sell ye, little whore! I shall carve ye up and feed ye to the sharks . . . after I've done with *him*."

Isobel worked frantically on the last rope, and as Styles neared, she finally cut through it.

Worthington sprang up like a panther. He easily dodged Styles's lunge and landed a few well-placed punches in his opponent's ribs.

Then the captain's leg shot up and he kicked the dagger out of Styles's hand. Worthington swung his boot around to land in the mutineer's stomach. But Styles was far from beaten, and in their hand-to-hand combat, he did some damage to Worthington, as well. Both men panted as they stared at each other, waiting for their opponent's next move.

Isobel glanced down and saw Styles's dagger by the wall. She scurried to retrieve it. As the men locked in a deadly embrace, Isobel jumped out of the way and dashed behind an armoire. The men crashed backwards onto a table, sending books and papers flying in all directions. The two rolled over it and onto the floor.

There was a shattering of glass and Isobel peeked around the armoire. Worthington lay pinned to the floor, and Styles hovered over him with a broken bottle, poised above the captain's face.

Isobel sent the dagger sliding towards the captain, and prayed that Worthington would be able to reach it in time. It bounced off the captain's thigh and he struggled mightily to make a grab for it, but with Styles above him it was impossible.

Isobel looked around quickly and spied a heavy barometer rolling around on the floor. She picked it up, took aim, and launched it at the back of Styles's head.

It was just the advantage Worthington needed. In an instant, Styles was not only stunned by the hastily thrown projectile, he was on his back with Worthington hovering over him, his own dagger now pressed against his throat.

"Mutiny can be very bad for your health, Styles. As you'll soon see." Worthington growled.

Isobel shuddered as the captain drew the blade across his opponent's throat.

She turned around, shutting her eyes and covering her ears. Death was not something she wanted to witness again, even that of an enemy. She heard muffled groans and gurgles, and in a moment Worthington was grabbing Isobel's arm and lifting her to her feet. He wiped the blade against his pant leg and regarded Isobel with eyes like ice.

"My, my. You are truly full of surprises, Lady Ravenwood." He cocked an eyebrow. "And how did you know to come here, may I ask?"

Isobel gulped, feeling a new uneasiness spreading through her gut. *Would Worthington think she'd a hand in this?*

"I heard some men plotting against you, and when I tried to warn you, they tied me up and left me in the galley. I escaped and came here . . . just in time, it seems."

"It was fortunate for me that you came to my rescue. Very brave of you to attempt such a thing."

"Bravery had nothing to do with it, sir. I heard them saying they were going to sell me in the Kingston market—after getting to know my acquaintance better, of course. If you were killed, Captain, I would most probably face a fate worse than death."

Worthington folded his arms across his chest. "Quite so. What else did you hear? Did Styles have any accomplices you could name?"

"Yes—a man named McGregor was recruiting the men against you. He wanted to wait. He said he needed time to get more men on their side, but Styles insisted they move now. And the men who tied me up in the galley were named Dobbin and Murray. That's all I know for certain."

Worthington nodded. "McGregor . . . I should have known that malingering skulker would be involved." He looked at her with newfound interest. "Is that blood on your chin, my lady?"

"I bit Mr. Murray."

He laughed. "Good. Though I'm sure he tasted terrible."

Isobel smiled in spite of herself.

"Now, we must leave. I must gather my men and stop this mutiny before it starts."

Taking Isobel's hand, Worthington led her to the door. Stepping over the other unconscious pirate, only pausing briefly to bind him, they quickly made their way into the narrow passage.

They stopped in front of Isobel's cabin, and Worthington opened the door.

"You must stay here while my men and I sort out this business, my lady. I will lock you in so no harm will come to you."

"But—my husband . . . will he be safe in the brig?"

"He will be, for the time being." He opened the door and pushed Isobel in. "Until we meet again, madam."

"Wait—" Isobel protested, but the door slammed in her face. She heard the key turn in the lock and she slapped at the door with her hand. "Oh!"

Fear and frustration boiled inside her.

She sat on her bunk and in a futile gesture, covered her heart with her hands, trying to keep it from bursting with pain. *Oh, Beckett . . . Beckett!*

Isobel felt him inside her heart. Saw his face floating before her eyes. Why was the cost of loving someone so terribly high? She wanted so much to feel his arms around her, and his mouth kissing hers at least one last time. If they were to die in this mutiny, she hoped Beckett would know how much she had wanted to be a true wife to him.

She heard shouts and bodies crashing on deck above her head. Isobel ducked instinctively, as if they might fall through on top of her. The clanging steel of their sabers rang through the ceiling planks, along with the sounds of death.

Fear clutched at her heart with its cold, icy fingers. She curled her knees up to her chest and prayed.

Beckett paced around in his cell. He was finding it more and more difficult to keep his mind occupied. And more and more difficult to keep his hopes up.

His heart ached painfully in his chest.

Isobel.

He had failed her. His stomach contracted in wretched frustration and fear—at being unable to rescue Isobel, not knowing what was happening to her even at this moment, and wondering if he'd ever get them off this damned ship alive.

His ribs had healed sufficiently to attempt an escape, but so far he'd been unable to swipe the key from his guard's belt. And there had been more than one guard, lately. That meant trying to overtake one or both of them would be virtually impossible. He wanted to avoid physical combat—not only would his chances of victory be slim without a weapon, the noise of a fight would undoubtedly bring reinforcements.

He'd felt it important to wait for the right time to strike, as he had learned to do in the war. But each day that passed meant one more that Isobel might be suffering at the hands of Sir Harry Lennox.

Still, bad odds usually guaranteed failure. If he made a premature attempt and got himself killed before he could rescue Isobel. . . .

Beckett closed his eyes in despair, wondering why he'd even bothered to open them in this awful cell. His heart felt just as dark and hopeless as this mean little room, and he hated it. He tried to think of other things, to take his mind away from the problem at hand.

He saw her face then, floating in front of his eyes, her golden curls lifted on the wind. He remembered the softness of her skin underneath him as he covered her body with his own and loved her. He heard her cries of pleasure as she shuddered in his arms.

Oh, why was he torturing himself like this? When one or both of them might be killed? The thought made his heart twist like a wet cloth being wrung out.

He missed her. He missed Isobel's friendship, their talks, the way she laughed when he teased her. He missed her hand crooked in his arm when they walked . . . the smell of her skin . . . even the way she chewed her toast at breakfast. And he missed her passion, her innocence, her warm little body curled up beside him after a night of loving.

It was almost too much for him to bear, to think that he might never be able to know Isobel like that again.

He wanted to spend his life loving her.

Beckett's eyes opened slowly again. Though it

was still dark as always, it seemed that in his heart the light of a thousand candles burned brightly and illuminated the room.

He said it again in his head: *I want to spend my life loving her.*

It was so simple. And so true.

Beckett felt the enormous weight he'd been carrying deep inside his heart push itself through, and out, and lift—flying away into nothingness.

It had been like a physical thing weighing him down—making him immobile, unable to go forward. It had been a part of him, like a useless, mangled limb. And now, it was gone.

Gone.

*"Oh . . . oh."* He groaned and felt his head droop as tears dampened his face in the dark.

He'd fought against it for so long. It had been as fruitless as trying to fight against the tide, and just as exhausting.

But now, he had given up the fight. And he felt relief, and a joy so pure, so indescribable, that soon he found he was laughing even though tears still flowed from his eyes.

He *loved* her. He loved Isobel, his wife.

"I love her . . . ," he said, sounding somewhat stunned, even to his own ears. Then, he laughed, and bellowed, "I *love* her . . . do you hear? I love Isobel!"

He smiled as he stood there in the dark cell, thinking if anyone could see him, they'd be convinced he was a raving lunatic. It made him laugh anew. He *had* been a raving lunatic—*now* he was completely sane.

Earlier, when Isobel had come to his cell, he'd been so close to saying it then, but he hadn't. He hadn't known.

Those three little words had held him prisoner far better than this cell ever would. And he had

Michelle McMaster

escaped them. He was no longer in their power.
Now, they were in *his* power. The most important
words in the English language were no longer a
thing of fear, but of beauty and freedom.

And now, looking back, he wondered what he
had been so afraid of. Losing himself? Believing
in something that could not possibly be true? But
the alternative had been closing his heart to the
most powerful gift of all.

He thought of Cordelia then. Of how he'd
thought himself in love with her. But that hadn't
been love. It had been a feeling that masqueraded
as love, and had been quite convincing . . . like
drinking cheap wine and being told it was cham-
pagne. You could only know the difference when
you'd tasted the real thing.

And Beckett *had* tasted the real thing. Now that
he knew the difference, he'd never go back to
shoddy imitations. Like cheap wine, imitation
love left one feeling quite sick and empty inside.

His thoughts went to Isobel, of their confrontation on the beach just before Sir Harry had
snatched them. The things she'd said about her
heart being full of him, about not being able to
remove him from there . . . he understood, now.

Now that he'd opened his heart to her, fully,
completely, he knew that it would be impossible
to remove her. But that was fine. It felt good to
have her in there.

He wanted to see Isobel, to tell her. He grabbed
the bars in the little window and though he knew
it was no use, tried to shake them, as if that
would have any effect. He peered out and tried to
see down the passageway. His guard was absent,
and there was no one else about.

He frowned. The ship seemed quiet. He hoped
that meant the mutiny hadn't yet started. He

256

stretched up again and tried to see if his guard was asleep on the floor, but no one was there.

Then Beckett heard the familiar sound of Williams's heavy footsteps coming down the passageway. He heard the man whistling a jaunty tune as he approached, and unfortunately also smelled the pirate well before he came around the corner.

Williams's large round face appeared in the window.

"Brought ye some dinner, m'lord."

Beckett heard the sound of the key in the lock and was about to thank the man, when Williams made a strange gasp. A look of surprise came over his face and he fell forward against the door, looking at Beckett in confusion, then sliding down out of sight.

"There, take that, Williams, ye old bugger!" a voice hissed.

Another voice said, "Ye sure we was s'posed to kill him?"

"O' course I'm sure, ye cork-brained git!" the first man said. "Come on, now, there's more killin' to be done."

Beckett flattened himself against the wall beside the door, waiting for it to open.

It didn't.

He heard quick footsteps echo down the passageway until they were gone. Then, there came the sounds of scuffling on the deck above . . . the sounds of close combat, of men screaming and yelling, of metal blades clashing.

Gads, the mutiny had begun. A chill of fear ran up his spine as he thought of Isobel. Had she been able to warn Worthington? Where was she in all of this?

In anger and frustration, he grabbed the bars of

the little window as he had before and pushed and pulled against them. Surprisingly, the door opened.

He jumped back, waiting to see who had opened it. But no one appeared. The door just creaked open slowly, gently inviting him into the passageway . . . and freedom.

Beckett peeked around the door and saw the key sticking out of the lock. There was no one else about, and he hopped over Williams who lay crumpled on the floor. Beckett crouched down and turned the pirate over. He was dead.

"My condolences, Mr. Williams." Beckett removed a long dagger from the man's boot. "I don't think you'll be needing this anymore. But I most certainly will."

With that, Beckett turned and trotted down the hall to where he thought Isobel's quarters were. There seemed to be no one at all below-deck—at least on this end of the ship. But he would be ready if he encountered any resistance.

He turned another corner, hoping to find Isobel's quarters, and instead looked straight into the black eyes of Sir Harry Lennox.

# Chapter Twenty-four

"Ravenwood," Sir Harry hissed, stepping back and bringing his own dagger up to flash in front of his face. "I must say, I'm surprised to find you here. I was just coming to see you. To see you *die*, that is. Thank you for saving me the walk."

Sir Harry slashed out with his dagger as Beckett quickly side-stepped.

"You bastard!" Beckett growled, feeling his anger blaze. This was the blackguard who meant to take away his beloved. He hated this man with absolute clarity.

His enemy snarled and slashed at his stomach, but Beckett nicked him on the wrist with a return cut. Good. He wanted Lennox to bleed a bit before he died.

Beckett had fought men like this before. Men without much training, but who were mad enough to be as dangerous as a loose cannon. Such men could be goaded into making a mistake.

Sir Harry smiled as he prepared to strike again. "When Isobel is my wife, Ravenwood, I'm going to make her pay for every drop of blood you make me spill today."

"Isobel will never be your wife, Lennox. *Never*."

Sir Harry's expression darkened like a forboding sky as he lashed out again with his dagger. He nicked Beckett's elbow. Beckett ignored the minimal pain, though Lennox seemed overly pleased by the blow. Beckett would let the man tire himself out a bit before he attacked in earnest.

Sir Harry's eyes glittered unnaturally. "You stole my bride, Ravenwood! I swore I'd make you pay for touching what was mine, for defiling her. And I shall."

"Oh, I beg to differ with you there, on both counts." Beckett slashed and caught his opponent's thigh, who gave a groan. "Isobel was never yours, Lennox. But she *is* mine. We love each other, you see. That's something you'll never understand."

Beckett heard a muffled voice shouting from down the passageway. And pounding on a door. He thought he heard his name.

"Isobel?" he shouted, deflecting Sir Harry's thrust once more.

"Beckett!" Isobel's voice sounded far away.

"Yes, it's your beloved husband, Isobel," Sir Harry shouted over his shoulder. "Say your good-byes, my dear. And listen to him die!"

"No!" Her muffled shout echoed through the ship.

Sir Harry attacked like a mad bull. Beckett moved quickly, landing a hard kick in his opponent's groin. This was a dagger fight, and he doubted Lennox would hold to any gentlemanly rules of conduct. Better the first surprise should be his.

Sir Harry was doubled over in pain, still keeping his weapon out in front of him. Beckett kicked again, and knocked the dagger from his enemy's grip. In a moment, he was on him, pulling Lennox up by the scruff of his neck and placing the tip of his own knife to the base of the man's throat.

"I can't say that I'm sorry to do this." Beckett prepared to deliver the killing stroke.

"But I can," a voice said from behind him.

Beckett heard the sound of a pistol being cocked near his head. He felt the cold tip of the barrel against his skull, and knew victory was being snatched from him like a toy from a child's hand.

"Worthington! It's about time," Lennox croaked.

"My apologies, Sir Harry." The captain stepped around Beckett and took the dagger from his hand. "Had a bit of a mutiny to take care of, which Lady Ravenwood was good enough to warn me about. It is because of her that I didn't shoot you dead just now, Ravenwood."

"Let me see her. Please," Beckett asked, looking down the barrel of Worthington's pistol. The man was flanked by other pirates.

"I'm afraid that would be unwise. Your wife is safe in her quarters, and that is where she will stay," Worthington answered.

"Not for long," Sir Harry said, smiling.

Beckett made a lunge for him but was stopped by Worthington's men. "If you touch even a hair on her head, Lennox, I'll hunt you down like the dog you are!"

"Too late." Sir Harry gave a sickening grin.

Beckett struggled anew, but Worthington stepped

between them, resheathing his pistol in his belt. "Be assured, Ravenwood, your wife will remain unharmed while she is on my ship. I owe her that, at least." He nodded to his henchmen. "Take Lord Ravenwood back to his cell."

One of the pirates put a pistol to Beckett's head, and then yanked him back down the passageway. Out of frustration, he struggled against them as they headed back to his cell, but he knew it was useless. He would not be able to escape now, that was certain. At least Worthington had promised that Isobel would be safe for the duration of the voyage. That would give him more time.

Soon, they were at the door to his cell, and the pirates pushed him in. The door creaked loudly behind him and he was back in the familiar darkness. How long had he been out of this mean little room ... fifteen, twenty minutes? Surely, that had been the world's shortest escape.

Beckett heard the key turn in the lock and the muffled sound of men dragging Williams's body down the passageway. He turned around and slammed his fists against the wall. It hurt, but the pain felt good, so he did it again. And again. And again.

"Isobel!" he yelled into the darkness, and unable to do anything more, hung his head in despair.

The wind whipped Isobel's hair mercilessly around her face. She pushed it behind her ears for the hundredth time, and wondered why she attempted to put it up each day.

She pulled her shawl close around her. The wind had gotten colder the closer they got to England. And now they were almost there. Isobel looked out across the horizon, seeing land loom in the distance. She tried desperately to fight the despair that had been growing in her heart steadily since yesterday. Their voyage was almost over. And Sir Harry had promised to make her a widow before they reached shore. A widow!

She had been unable to see Beckett after the attempted mutiny. Worthington had come to her quarters with Sir Harry in tow, to thank her for warning him.

She had begged to be able to see her husband, then, but the pirate captain had refused. All he would say was that Beckett was in good health. Her only consolation was that he'd assured her of her safety while she was on board his ship, and by his purposeful glance at Sir Harry, she knew that meant safety from him.

Since then, she had been able to move about only with a guard, and not anywhere below-decks except her quarters. So she had gone up on deck to try to clear her thoughts. It wasn't working.

Isobel turned, and when she saw Sir Harry approaching, turned back again toward the water. There was no use in trying to get away from him. He would merely follow her. At least up here, she would be under the protection of Captain Worthington.

"You should not spend so much time in the sun, my dear," Sir Harry drawled. "It will darken your freckles."

Isobel refused to look at him. "Then I shall stay out in it all day, if only to displease you."

He chuckled, but there was no warmth in it. "Still bent on defying me at every turn, I see. That's alright. You'll learn soon enough. And I shall relish teaching you."

Sir Harry lifted his hand to her face and tried to stroke her cheek. Isobel jerked her head away as if his hand were a burning iron. She glared at him, wishing the power of her hatred could kill.

"Oh, the fire in your eyes excites me, Isobel." His own glittered dangerously. "I shall *so* enjoy putting it out."

Isobel turned and faced him squarely. "You shall not extinguish the fire in me, Sir Harry. If you try, you'll be *burned*."

Sir Harry's eyes darkened and he came closer to her, bending his face down near hers. "You are so like your mother, Isobel . . . in countenance, as well as in spirit." He reached into his jacket pocket and pulled out something small. Smiling tenderly, Sir Harry held it up in front of Isobel's face.

She looked at it cautiously. Her stomach twisted into a hideous knot when she saw that it was a miniature portrait of her mother. "What are you doing with that?" Fear whispered up Isobel's spine.

"Your mother never told you about us, did she?" Sir Harry's voice purred as soft as a cat's, and he tilted his head slightly as he looked down at her.

Isobel remained silent, not wanting to give Sir Harry the satisfaction of a reply. But her heart grew icy with fear as he continued.

"No, I suppose she wouldn't have wanted you to know that your father was not her first love. It was *I*, Isobel. Oh, yes. At one time, your mother and I were engaged to be married."

Isobel felt nausea swirling in her stomach, and she clutched the railing for support. She did not want to hear this.

"Then I lost my fortune in bad investments, and I admit, a bit of gambling as well. But I ask you, what young buck doesn't like to gamble, eh? Suddenly, your grandfather decided *I* was a bad investment. The old fop made her break the engagement. Then your father, *my friend,* came along to save the day. He had fortune and position. Your grandfather approved of the match, so they were married." Sir Harry's lip curled in a hideous sneer.

"Of course, I told them they had my blessing. But that very day in the church, before God, I swore that they would both pay for betraying me. My plan was simple. And it would have worked if not for your mother's foolishness . . . a trait which you have obviously inherited."

Isobel shook her head, trying to make sense of Sir Harry's story. Could her mother really have been drawn in by this monster? And was he responsible for much more than her guardian's death?

Sir Harry grabbed Isobel's wrist, and she struggled against him, but he held her fast.

Her foe smiled his reptilian smile and continued. "You remember the highwaymen who attacked your parents' carriage that night?"

His voice was heavy and cold, like a dull blade cutting open Isobel's heart with excruciating slowness. She shook her head. No, this couldn't be true!

Sir Harry held her chin and turned her face so that her eyes met his. "I sent them," he said simply.

Isobel shut her eyes and bit her lip as tears flowed silently down her face. This could not be. She would not hear it.

"Shall I tell you more?" Sir Harry asked, his voice mocking. "The highwaymen were to stop the carriage, rob it, and in the process shoot that inconvenient husband of hers—your father. Which they did. But your mother attacked one of them. And during the struggle, the pistol went off. Everything would have gone according to plan if it hadn't been for your mother's stupid actions! If she hadn't gotten herself killed that night, we all would have lived happily ever after. But now, all I have left of her is *you*."

"You *monster!*" Isobel cried. She clawed at his face, but she was no match for the man's strength. He easily grabbed her wrists and crushed them together with one hand.

"Unlike your mother, you are not going to escape me. And how fitting that the daughter will pay for the mother's crimes. Though you have quite enough of your own to answer for."

"I hate you!" Isobel bucked against him. "You have taken everything that I have ever loved away from me! My parents, my guardian. And now my husband—a man that I love more than life itself."

Isobel raised her chin, staring defiantly into his coal-black eyes, and saw the displeasure there.

"But there is one thing you can *never* take away from me, Sir Harry. And that is love. The love that my parents gave me and I gave them. The love I feel for Beckett, and the love we've shared as man and wife. Those are moments you will never know. And they are mine . . . *forever*."

Sir Harry took a step back, released her wrists and sneered, "Cherish them, Isobel. Cherish your precious moments of love. They are yours, forever . . . just as you are *mine*."

He turned to go, but Isobel took a step toward him and grabbed at his sleeve. "Please . . . let Beckett go. If it's me that you want, then no one else need suffer. I will go with you willingly, but please, *please* set my husband free. I beg you to do him no harm. He is innocent in all of this!"

"Innocent. *Innocent*, you say?" Sir Harry spat. "He has defiled you, Isobel. Defiled my bride. And he will pay very dearly. You shall see. I have decided to hang him." He pointed up at the masts. "Tomorrow, he shall swing from the yardarm."

"No! No, *please!*" Isobel cried, shaking her head.

"Oh yes, and you shall watch it! Tomorrow at dawn, Isobel, your dear husband will be executed."

# Chapter Twenty-five

Beckett squinted at the bright light that came into the brig from the doorway. He shielded his eyes and made out a tall figure standing in the doorway. It was Redbeard.

"Up an' at 'em, m'lord. Cap'n wants to see ye on deck, now."

"What's the occasion?" Beckett asked groggily.

"Oh, there's to be a hangin'." Redbeard smiled. "Some say it's to be yours."

Beckett rose to his feet. "Mine, eh? Too bad. I always found a hanging to be a damned inconvenient way to start the day."

Redbeard laughed. "To be sure, m'lord, to be sure. Now, don't you be givin' me no trouble, an' I'll make sure yer face stays pretty 'til ye put it through the noose, alright?"

"Very kind of you . . . ah, what is your name, if I may ask?"

"Josiah Cox, sir. First mate."

"Well, Mister Cox, it has been nice knowing you."

"Been lovely knowin' ye, too, sir," Cox said, chuckling. "Now, if ye don't mind, they're waitin' for ye."

Beckett stepped through the door and tried not to squint at the bright light. As he walked down the passageway, his mind raced, and his heart—damn the bloody thing—pounded in his throat. This was undoubtedly his last chance to save Isobel and himself. He would have to keep his head, find an opportunity, and grab it. It would be bloody difficult surrounded by armed pirates, but there was no choice. He had to succeed.

So many memories of Isobel whirled before him. Some he could see, and some he could only feel. They all seemed to flow together and blend into one, like the everchanging colors of a sunset. The silkiness of her hair, her warm cocoa-brown eyes, the timbre of her voice . . . bathing each other in the spring, exploring the cave, kissing her neck that night in the Whitcomb garden, the sound of her gasping beneath him, dancing with her to the drums at Cropover. The images all swirled together in his head, in his veins, his limbs, his heart.

Would she be up on deck to watch him hang? If Sir Harry had his way, Isobel would most certainly be there. Beckett put his foot on the first step and looked up the stairs. He would find out soon enough.

"Ah, I see the guest of honor has arrived." Sir Harry smirked at Isobel. "Though I must say, he looks like he hasn't dressed up."

"Beckett!" Isobel cried. Instinctively she tried to move toward him, but Sir Harry's strong hand clamped down on her shoulder and held her firm.

"Now, now, my dear. You must stand back in order to appreciate the view."

Isobel stared helplessly at Beckett, feeling her heart burn in her chest as though consumed by flames. He met her gaze with his own, and though his face was pale, unshaven and thin, his eyes still held a depth and intensity that touched her soul.

*Dear God, help us!*

Isobel turned toward Worthington, who stood nearby, and wrenched herself free from Sir Harry's grip. She ran to the captain's side, and sinking down onto her knees, grabbed his hand and pressed her lips to it. Tears dampened her face as she looked up into the wolf-gray eyes of the pirate lord.

"Please, *please* . . . don't let him do this! Don't let him kill my husband. I would do anything to save his life. *You* can stop this. I beg you to stop this, Captain, please!" She kissed his hand again and tried to choke back sobs of despair, but they jumped out of her throat and echoed forsakenly across the deck.

Worthington looked down at her and pulled her to her feet. For a moment, she thought she'd seen something flicker in his eyes—compassion, or sympathy perhaps. But it had only lasted a moment. It was gone.

"I am sorry, Madam. I can do nothing to help you."

Isobel cried out and tried to strike his face, but Worthington easily grabbed her wrist and held it immobile.

"You mean you *won't* do anything! You are a coward, sir—of the first order. I'm sure you are the only pirate in the world who is afraid to stand up to the likes of Sir Harry Lennox."

"I am not afraid of anything, madam." Worthington raised an eyebrow in warning. "Except of course, ruining my reputation—which I have no intention of doing by interfering with a paying customer. Not for you, not for your husband."

Isobel spat, "Then I will pray for your soul, Captain, for it is surely destined for hell."

Worthington's eyes narrowed. "You do that." His gaze flicked over to the men holding Beckett. "String him up."

Isobel looked about in desperation. Could no one help her?

Captain Black crouched on the nearby railing. His green eyes watched her, stoic.

"Wait."

Isobel turned to see Sir Harry approaching with his reptilian smile. And as he walked toward her, Isobel thought that he moved like a snake . . . so smooth, so dark and menacing. The only things missing were scales.

"Perhaps my future bride has a point. I am, after all, not without some feeling. I see no reason why you shouldn't be allowed to say goodbye to your first husband, Isobel. Would you like that? I know *I* would enjoy seeing it. The tears, the final kiss . . . oh, I *do* love romance."

Isobel stared at him, horrified, but unable to resist the promise of touching, kissing Beckett for one last time. She nodded mutely.

"Shall we, then?" Sir Harry grabbed her arm and yanked her toward her husband, who struggled anew against the pirates who held him.

Sir Harry pulled her up in front of Beckett, so she stood just out of reach. Her eyes devoured the sight of him, trying to memorize every line, every curve of Beckett's face, the exact color of his eyes, the shade of his lips. She tried to get closer to him, but Sir Harry jerked her back.

"But you said we could have one last kiss," Isobel pleaded.

"I lied."

"Get your hands off her, you bastard," Beckett growled.

"Oh. You mean *these* hands, Ravenwood?" Sir Harry slid his palms over Isobel's shoulders and pulled her against him. "You mean, the ones that are going to be undressing your little wife on our wedding night, while you rot in hell?"

Beckett thrashed against the pirates who held him.

"I won't let him hurt you, Isobel—I promise you that! Whatever happens, I'll come for you. Do you believe me?"

Isobel nodded. "I love you, Beckett."

"And I—"

"*Now* you can string him up," Sir Harry ordered, dragging Isobel away while her husband struggled against his guards.

"Beckett!" Isobel cried out over her shoulder, trying to see him.

"Isobel," his muffled voice answered, drowned out by the scuffle.

"Get him up there, now!" Sir Harry shrieked.

Isobel watched in horror as the pirates dragged Beckett toward the side of the boat, where the noose hung off the yard-arm and swung mockingly in the breeze.

"*No!* Oh, please, no." Isobel stood transfixed, not wanting to watch, but helpless not to.

"For goodness' sake, he could at least have the decency to put his head in the noose like a gentleman," Sir Harry complained.

Catching the man off guard, Isobel shoved him as hard as she could, and spun around to do more damage. But the escalating noise behind her made her turn around, and her heart leapt at what she saw.

Beckett seemed to be breaking free of his captors!

272

Two of Worthington's men had been trying to force his head through the noose, and Beckett had taken one of their daggers. It now flashed before him and glinted in the early morning light as he fought against the remaining guard.

But the tide was turning yet again.

Soon five, then six armed pirates swarmed around Beckett, and Isobel screamed.

He would be sliced to ribbons by their swords!

Beckett climbed up the rigging like a monkey, his dagger swishing through the air behind him as the cutthroats clambered after him in pursuit. The clanging of blade on blade rang out from above and made an eerie music for this strange dance.

"Damnation!" Sir Harry growled from beside Isobel, his injury now forgotten as he watched the action high above, along with the rest of those on deck.

Isobel ignored him. Her heart, her entire being was too fixed on the deadly ballet going on above to pay Sir Harry any attention now.

Beckett had stopped climbing, desperately fighting off the closest of the pirates. He kicked out and the man went flying off the rigging and fell to the deck below. The pirate landed with a great thud, then lay inert. She looked back up and saw another pirate closing in on her husband and their blades clashed anew.

Then, Beckett threw his head back to avoid a blow and lost his hold, falling through the air. Isobel screamed. It seemed so unbearably slow, but she heard him yelling, and herself screaming, and then, a great splash as he hit the water.

Isobel ran to the side, joined by the entire crew. Frantically, she scanned the water for his head, but saw nothing.

"Beckett! *Beckett!*" she cried.

Someone's hand grabbed her arm and tried to pull her away, but she fought hard.

"Where is he? I can't see him! *Beckett!*"

Worthington's voice spoke from behind her, and she realized it was his hand that gripped her arm. He peered over the side down into the water that offered no answers.

"He's gone, my lady."

"No!" Isabel shook her head, willing herself not to believe.

"A fall from that height . . . he went straight down. Or broke his neck when he hit the water. Your husband is dead."

"No. I don't believe it. I *won't* believe it!"

Worthington shook his head. "He is dead, madam."

"Well, I certainly hope so," Sir Harry spoke up, adjusting his cuffs. "Though I must say, I am not pleased with the way it went. I would have liked it drawn out a bit more, at least. But, as you say, Worthington, dead is dead. Now, we can be married, my dear." A smile snaked across his lips. "As soon as we reach Hampton Park, which, if we continue to make good time, may be tonight. Can you imagine? Widowed and married in the same day. How very *macabre*."

Isobel, unable to speak, turned and looked out at the calm water that surrounded the boat.

The idea that Beckett was gone—it was too painful to even think about. Instead, she would stare out at the water, looking for a glimpse of him. She would not think about Sir Harry or his plans.

The truth was, she didn't care anymore. If Beckett was dead, then so was her heart. Sir Harry could do whatever he wanted to her, and none of it would matter.

But she wouldn't think about that now. She couldn't.

She wiped away the tears that stained her face. Her heart ached so painfully. Now she understood what it meant to feel your heart bleed, for surely that's what hers was doing.

The thought of losing Beckett forever chilled her so completely, she began to shake, her teeth chattering noisily. She had lost so much already . . . how could she bear to have lost the only man she would ever love, as well?

Not knowing what else to do, Isobel stared down into the cold blue water and prayed.

Worthington motioned to one of his sailors. The man quickly came to the captain's side.

"Launch the rowboat, Mr. Ross. Wait for me on shore—near the caves as usual. And Mr. Ross—"

"Yes, Cap'n?" The burly pirate stepped closer.

"If you should find anything *interesting* floating in the water, fish it out and hold it at the caves until I get there. Understood?"

"Yes, sir, Cap'n." The man nodded and made to go about his orders.

Worthington reached out his hand, stopping him. "Be sure and have a good look out there, will you? There is a rather large 'fish' in these waters that I should very much like to catch."

# Chapter Twenty-six

*Soon.*

They would be there soon. And then she would be lost forever.

Isobel stood on the deck, watching the pirates preparing to drop anchor. The gulls overhead seemed to be speaking for her as they cried out in haunting lament to the skies above. It was fitting music for this day.

The *Revenge* bustled with activity as it prepared to unload both its passengers and its smuggled cargo. It had hidden itself in a secluded cove that would have been dangerous for any other ship to enter. But it was obviously a spot well-known to the *Revenge* crew.

Feeling a presence behind her, Isobel turned to see the cool stare of Captain Worthington. He held Captain Black in one arm and extended the hand of the other. She made no move to take it.

He smiled, acknowledging the snub. "I wish

you well, Lady Ravenwood. You would have made a splendid pirate, I think. If you are ever in need of employment, perhaps I could find a place for you on my ship."

"Is that intended as a compliment?"

"It was, indeed."

"If you truly want me as a crew member, throw Sir Harry overboard. Then I'll be happy to join you."

Worthington chuckled. "A noble attempt, my lady, but I wouldn't want it to get 'round that I double-cross my paying customers. That would have a negative effect on my business."

"Ah, yes, your business." Isobel nodded and turned to look at the coastline. "Forgive me if I see my husband's life as rather more important than any financial transaction could ever be."

He cocked an eyebrow, stroking Captain Black's fur. "I am a pirate, after all. You underestimate yourself, Lady Ravenwood. I don't believe you need me at all. You have the survival instincts of a fox. You're clever, and you know when to stay hidden and when to run."

"Sometimes the fox gets caught."

"True. But whatever happens, the fox never gives up, does it? And that is how it escapes the hunters."

Isobel turned away, thinking of everything she'd left behind at Ravenwood Hall on Barbados. It all seemed like a twisted jest. Her life had been interrupted by a dream of love, safety and belonging. Now she seemed fated to be Sir Harry's plaything. It was as if her escape to London, her time with Beckett there and in Barbados, had never taken place.

She glanced at Worthington as he stood beside her, also gazing at the cold Atlantic. But as she gazed out over the forbidding sea, a faint hope still glowed in her heart. She would cling to that hope until her heart stopped beating.

Worthington turned to her. "There are stories of mermaids in these waters, did you know, Lady Ravenwood?"

"Mermaids? Indeed, Captain."

*What game was he playing at now?*

"Oh, yes," the pirate said, stroking Captain Black as the cat studied her with bright green eyes. "There are many stories of mermaids—and mer*men*, too. I thought I saw one myself, once. I should keep my eye open, if I were you, lady. One never knows what one might find in these waters."

Isobel looked at him quizzically.

*What was the man trying to say?* Was he trying to give her false hope? Or did he know something she didn't?

Just then, Sir Harry appeared on deck, fussing with his coat. He approached Isobel and Worthington. Isobel felt her stomach sink.

This was it, then.

"I say, Worthington—coaching my bride-to-be in the tricks of your pirate trade, are you?" Sir Harry's eyes darted from the captain to Isobel.

"Oh no, Lennox, she needs no coaching from me." Worthington's smile was mocking.

Sir Harry's eyes narrowed as he thrust his final payment towards the pirate captain. "You think to laugh at me, do you?" Sir Harry grabbed Isobel's arm and pulled her roughly beside him. "Believe me, Captain, *I* will have the last laugh . . . on *all* of you."

Captain Black hissed at Sir Harry, but Worthington held the animal fast. Sir Harry took a step back.

"Captain Black and I wish you luck in trying to tame her, Lennox." Worthington's voice was as cold as ice. "You'll need it." With that, the man turned away and walked to the open cargo hold to oversee the unloading of smuggled goods into their landing boats.

Sir Harry looked down at Isobel, his eyes dark and dangerous. His lips curled slowly, but it was more of a threat than a smile. "Just think, my dear—only a few more hours and we shall be at Hampton Park celebrating our wedding. And then our wedding *night*."

He pulled her close to him so that her breasts were pressed uncomfortably against his chest. Instinctively, she turned her head away from his leering face, but he grabbed her chin and forced her to meet his eyes.

"*I* shall be your husband now, as I was meant to be. And you will see that no man could ever love you as much as I can, Isobel. Soon . . . you will see exactly how much I love you."

He pulled her head towards his and she tried to squirm away, but he was too strong, and his vile lips covered hers and kissed her hard. Isobel felt bile rising in her throat and hoped it made its way up her throat and right into Sir Harry's mouth.

What would she do? What would she do tonight, if Beckett did not appear to stop this? He had said he'd come for her. He had *promised*. But for the first time since he'd disappeared into the dark blue waters, Isobel felt her fears grabbing hold of her faith and choking the life out of it.

Sir Harry released her and looked down into her eyes with a self-satisfied grin. "That was only a taste, my love. I shall show you much more tonight in our chamber. After you've been taught a lesson for cuckolding me, of course." He touched her cheek. "Until tonight, then."

Cold fear washed over her heart in icy waves as

Sir Harry led her toward the side of the ship and her new life.

*Oh, dear Lord . . . what if it's true? What if Beckett really is gone? Have I been deluding myself to hope that he might still be alive?*

Just then a gull swooped down from above, having apparently decided to use Sir Harry's head for target practice. The baronet stood stunned for a few moments, then scowling, he gingerly reached a hand up to investigate. His face seemed to curl inward as he grimaced in distaste.

"Oh! Bloody hell! Damned ignorant bastards, those *disgusting* birds." Sir Harry pulled out his handkerchief and ineffectively mopped his head.

Isobel couldn't help but laugh, and neither it seemed, could any of the pirates. Not only was it good to see Sir Harry in any kind of discomfiture, but surely the gull had been sent by the Lord Himself to give her a sign.

"Alright, the theatricals are over." Sir Harry growled at the crew. "Isobel, get down that ladder and into the boat. It's time to get off this bloody scow."

Isobel saw the captain look over at Sir Harry's choice of words. She and Worthington locked eyes for one last time before she descended the ladder. If she'd been hoping to see a change of heart, it was not to be found.

Stepping into the boat, Isobel sat silently while Sir Harry descended the rope ladder. The two pirates that he had hired sat in the middle, each one holding an oar. Soon, her abductor took his seat and the boat began to move quietly towards shore.

Isobel looked at the dark sapphire water around her. The oars dipped eerily into the water without making so much as a sound. For a moment, she had the urge to jump overboard and try to swim to shore herself. She knew it would be impossible—the men would be able to pick her up very quickly, if she didn't drown first.

No, she would not go willingly to her death. She must stay alive. Beckett might be coming for her. And there might be an opportunity for escape after they reached Hampton Park. She had grown up there, and knew all sorts of hidden passages that she doubted Sir Harry would. One way or another, she would escape this madman.

Until then, she would think of nothing but Beckett.

Hampton Park loomed dark and foreboding in the distance. The yellow moon hung low and eerily above the house as the carriage rattled over the bumpy road. This was certainly not the homecoming Isobel had hoped for.

She looked at Sir Harry across from her in the dark cab. He stared at her, and she saw his eyes flash in the dim light from the lanterns that bobbed outside the cab's windows. The man looked like the devil himself.

Chills went through her. Was this truly happening? Would this blackguard finally be victorious in his utter destruction of her and her family? Obviously, Sir Harry thought so. He'd sent word ahead to rouse the parson from his sleep to be ready to marry them when they arrived. Then they would finally enjoy their wedding night, he'd sneered.

Oh, just the thought of it made her sick with fear. How could she let Sir Harry touch her as Beckett had done? How would she survive something so horrible, with the memories of her husband's sweet touch swirling in her head and mocking her as this villain defiled her body?

Sir Harry leaned forward and took her face in his hands. Isobel stiffened, trying to keep calm, but the touch of his skin made her want to retch. He brought his face closer, trying to cover her mouth with his own. Isobel struggled against him, pounding his chest with her fists in a vain attempt at freedom.

"Stop it, Isobel! Stop this nonsense. You can't escape, do you not yet understand?" Sir Harry grabbed a handful of her hair in his fist and forced Isobel to look at him. Her blood ran cold. "You are mine! Ravenwood is dead, Isobel. Forget him."

"I can't forget him—I *won't*!"

"Yes you will, little wife. I will drive his memory from your head and your heart. I will drive him out of your body with my own. Beginning tonight."

Sir Harry pulled at his neck cloth and untied the elaborate bow. "It seems you need to be trussed up, my dear. I suppose it's just as well that you develop a liking for such things now."

Sir Harry yanked her arms in front of her, easily binding her wrists with the strong silk. Isobel struggled, but it was futile. He was much too strong for her. What would she do if she were too exhausted to fight him later?

Sir Harry pushed her back onto her seat and resumed his place opposite her.

"There." Sir Harry huffed. "Now, you shall stay put until we reach Hampton Park. And no more nonsense, Isobel." He took a deep breath, settling himself on the seat and wiping at his face with a handkerchief. "You *will* learn to obey me."

Isobel kept her face turned away from him and stared out the window. Her heart ached unbearably, her stomach seized in dread. Escape would be impossible, now. He would be watching her every move.

She heard a little thump on the roof of the carriage, and then a faint yowling sound. Were they to be attacked by creatures of the night as well? Nothing would surprise her on this terrible journey.

She looked across at Sir Harry and felt her heart turn to stone.

How could she face a life as Sir Harry's plaything? How could she bear the brutality that he would surely inflict on her for his own corrupt pleasure? If she knew Beckett were alive, she could endure any suffering, if there were any chance they would be reunited.

But without that hope, what was there to live for? No one had seen Beckett resurface after he'd fallen into the water. They all considered him dead. Had she, in her despair at the possibility of losing Beckett, simply refused to believe the truth?

She had been sure that Beckett was still alive. But now, everything was cloudy. She felt numb. Her life, or what was left of it, would be unbearable without him.

With her heart clenching in pain, Isobel forced herself to face the horrible truth.

Her husband was dead.

# Chapter Twenty-seven

Beckett sat on the damp ground, thankful that his trousers had already been ruined from his plunge into the ocean. It was one less thing he had to worry about.

After the pirates had fished him out of the water, they'd landed their rowboat on shore and held him prisoner. He'd been looking down the barrel of a pistol for at least a half-hour, since then. None of the pirates would tell him why they'd rescued him—only that he would be wise not to give them any trouble.

Since the odds were against him, he was obeying their orders—for the present. The fact remained that his wife was in the clutches of a despicable villain and that he was determined to rescue her.

And not even a band of pirates would keep him from doing that.

Another boat appeared out of the darkness. As it neared shore, the pirates leaped out and dragged the boat up onto the sand.

Beckett watched as the men approached. Instantly, he recognized the white-haired captain at the fore.

"Lord Ravenwood," Captain Worthington said, his teeth glinting in the golden moonlight, "may I be the first to congratulate you on cheating the Grim Reaper."

"Why, thank you, Captain." Beckett said. "I'm rather delighted by it, myself. I must thank your men here for fishing me out and keeping me company. And while I would love to stay and chat, I'm afraid I have rather important business to attend to."

"As do I, my lord. Some of it concerns you . . . and of course, your lovely wife."

"Save your breath, Worthington. If you plan to kill me now, I wish you luck. You may have me outnumbered, but I will most certainly be taking you with me."

Worthington smiled. "My dear Lord Ravenwood, you misunderstand. I came to offer my help. For a price of course." He motioned for the pirate guarding Beckett to lower his pistol.

Beckett stood slowly, considering the man's words. "Of course."

"For the right price, you could hire me and my crew to help rescue your lovely wife."

Beckett cocked his head. "Why the change of heart? You were willing enough to let me hang. Now you want to act the gallant hero?"

"You're right, of course. I would have let you hang. You see, I make it a point never to interfere with my paying customers. Lennox hired me to do a job. It was nothing personal, I assure you."

"And now that you have fulfilled your obligations to him?"

"I am free to offer my services to whomever can pay."

"What kind of price did you have in mind?"

"Oh, a thousand pounds or so."

Beckett paused. It would certainly be useful to have Worthington and his men along. The money was no object, at least now.

"You have a deal, Worthington—a thousand pounds to your bankers, post-haste. Shall we shake on it? I should like to go get my wife."

They stepped forward and sealed their agreement with a firm handshake.

"Pleasure doing business with you." Worthington nodded. "Shall we be off? I have a carriage waiting just up the road, there, and the horses are fresh. We'll be at Hampton Park before long, I'll wager."

Beckett followed Worthington toward the roadway, with the band of pirates close behind. "Lennox should be surprised to see you again. *And* me."

"So he should." Worthington chuckled. "He's an odious excuse for a man."

"Just stand there and perform the marriage, you idiot!" Sir Harry snapped at the parson, who was looking a trifle uneasy about the whole scene in the huge drawing room.

"Please!" Isobel implored. "You must help me. I am here against my will. I do not wish to marry this man!"

The little cleric eyed Isobel with uncertainty, then addressed her captor. "Forgive me, Sir Harry . . . but it would seem that the bride is voicing some objection."

"Don't listen to her, Parson." Her would-be-husband smiled, looking unconcerned. "She is nervous, that's all."

"I'm *not* nervous!" Isobel protested. "I'm mortally opposed to being in the same room with him, let alone becoming his wife. I'd rather be fed to an ill-tempered tiger."

The parson frowned.

Sir Harry merely shrugged. "A lover's quarrel."

"It is not a lover's quarrel, sir! Look! He has me here against my will." Isobel raised her wrists so the parson could see her bonds.

"Oh, my." He glanced at Sir Harry, alarmed. "It is *most* unusual for the bride to be bound in such a way, my good man. Most unusual, indeed."

Sir Harry looked at the parson with deadly eyes and spoke in a low voice. "My fiancée has just suffered a great loss. She has been beside herself with grief. The doctor has ordered her to be bound thus for her own protection."

"That is not true!" Isobel cried.

"You see?" Sir Harry nodded. "She is beside herself, as I warned you. Not that it is any of your concern. You know my standing in this community. Now, I wish to marry the girl . . . to bring some *joy* back into her life. Surely, you will allow me to do that by marrying us sometime between now and the next century!"

"Oh . . . oh, yes." The parson nodded, still seeming unsure. "Of course. The poor girl. Well, where was I, then?"

"You weren't anywhere! You haven't even started," Sir Harry spat.

"Oh . . . of course. Now, let's see," the parson said, slowly turning the pages.

Isobel looked away. It was no use. This country preacher would not help her. He would do as Sir Harry bade, no matter what she said.

"Oh, *give* me that, you buffoon!" Sir Harry

grabbed the book and flipped through the pages. "Here! Now, read it."

Isobel noticed the two pirates standing by the wall. They were here to act as witnesses, but they were chuckling. Stranger bridesmaids she had never seen.

Isobel waited for the parson to send her to her fate.

She absently looked around the drawing room. This place, where she had enjoyed so many quiet evenings with her parents, would now be the setting of a nightmare.

Suddenly, something in the corner caught her eye. It had looked like the shadows moving. Or something in them. *Was she imagining things?*

"*Ahem.*" The parson cleared his throat and looked at Sir Harry and then at Isobel. "Dearly beloved . . . we are gathered here, today. . . ."

Isobel watched the expression on the parson's face change slightly as he stared at something behind them. His expression changed quite quickly from confusion to fearful disbelief.

"Oh, what on earth is the matter, now?" Sir Harry huffed.

"How unkind of you," a familiar voice said from the doorway. "Not to invite a man to his wife's wedding."

Isobel turned.

*Beckett.*

Alive!

And standing in the doorway with Worthington and his pirates.

"You!" Sir Harry hissed, staring in shock.

"Yes, *me*, Lennox." Beckett stepped into the room, his powerful frame poised for action. "Very much alive, and very intent on reclaiming my wife, if you please. And even if you *don't* please."

Isobel felt life pouring back into her heart,

warm and light, coursing through her veins in a flood of joy. Her whole body sang with a love that was painful in its intensity.

Beckett was alive! And he had come for her as he'd promised.

She moved toward him, but Sir Harry grabbed her arm and whirled her in front of him. He whipped something off the table beside them. With one hand, he covered her mouth and with the other he held a letter-opener poised to stab her throat.

Beckett aimed a pistol at her tormentor, regarding him with ice-blue eyes.

"Let her go, Lennox."

The man backed toward the wall, taking Isobel with him. She knew where he was going and tried to tell Beckett, but Sir Harry's hand muffled her voice. So he did know about the secret—

"I said release her," her husband ordered, his voice commanding. "There's nowhere for you to go, Lennox. There is only one exit to this room and as you can see, it has been blocked. You're surrounded and outnumbered. You can't win."

Sir Harry's mouth curved into a belligerent frown. "I may be surrounded and outnumbered, Ravenwood, but I'm still going to win. If I can't have Isobel, no one will . . . including you!"

Sir Harry pushed back against the wall and the secret door opened. He pulled Isobel through and shut the portal behind them, bolting it quickly. They were plunged into pitch blackness.

Isobel heard pounding on the door and Beckett's muffled voice fading away as Sir Harry dragged her through the dark, narrow corridor. She struggled and kicked at him but he grabbed the silk bonds that tied her wrists and pulled her behind him. Isobel was forced to keep up or be dragged across the ground.

"I knew Beckett wasn't dead. He came for me, just as he promised." Isobel tried to catch her breath. "You've lost, Sir Harry. Do you hear? You've lost!"

He stopped short and Isobel slammed into him. In the pitch blackness, she heard his awful, menacing voice as his hand encircled her throat. He pushed her up against the wall.

"I have lost nothing! It is not yet over, I assure you. Just because your husband has risen from the grave doesn't mean he can't go back there just as quickly. The detestable man is like a cat with nine lives! But I assure you, my darling bride, his luck is about to run out."

Isobel gasped as she felt something furry move past her leg. A rat? Oh, what did it matter when she was in the hands of a madman?

Sir Harry released her and took hold of her bonds again.

But a strange, otherworldly cry echoed through the passageway, and Sir Harry was screaming in terror. Isobel shrank back against the wall, paralyzed with fear. *Something* was attacking Sir Harry. He cried out for help, and she heard his arms flapping uselessly as he tried to fight off his assailant.

Isobel could hear the mysterious presence hissing as it bounced off the walls near her. But it never touched her—it only seemed to want Sir Harry. He screamed pitifully for mercy. From the sound of it he was being ripped to shreds.

And it went on. Again and again, Sir Harry cried out, each sound more desperate than the last. Finally, she heard him sink to the ground, whimpering like a wounded animal, and the assault was over.

Would she be next?

Isobel stood against the wall, unable to move. Her shallow breathing made a light rhythm, and turned Sir Harry's eerie moaning into a melody that echoed down the dark corridor.

"Isobel?" she heard a muffled voice call from far away.

It was Beckett.

"Here! I'm here, Beckett!" she cried.

"I'm coming, Isobel." The sound of his voice grew closer.

She only hoped the ferocious creature wouldn't attack her before Beckett arrived. To be safe, she crept further away from where she knew Sir Harry lay.

Then, she saw light bouncing across the floor, and her eyes searched the shadows. And then—

*Beckett.*

His eyes—his face—all of him, his arms around her, his lips on hers, his hands in her hair, stroking her, soothing her, loving her.

She heard boots trample by and knew it was the pirates going to see to Sir Harry.

But she didn't care.

She didn't care about anything but this moment, and this man, and the love that threatened to burst her heart open with its beautiful power.

"I—I feared you were dead," she whispered, as tears filled her eyes.

Beckett held her in front of him, and she looked through the dimness into the brightest, bluest, most beautiful eyes she had ever seen. It set her to crying even more.

"I would have been, if I hadn't found you again, Isobel."

His mouth covered hers and he kissed her with such fierce passion, Isobel wondered fleetingly if they might shock the pirates. But she didn't care.

She was in the arms of the man she loved, and nothing else mattered.

Nothing else ever would.

"*Ahem,*" someone said.

Beckett broke the kiss and they both looked at Worthington, who stood with arms folded and an amused grin on his face. "My apologies for interrupting your reunion, Ravenwood. My lady. But there is something I think you should see." He motioned to where Sir Harry was lying.

They came closer, and Isobel couldn't stop a gasp from escaping her.

Sir Harry lay on his side, seemingly unconscious. His clothes were torn and bloodstains marred his shirt. His face and hands were covered in scratches and cuts, all of them bleeding. It looked as if someone had taken a knife to him.

Behind him, sitting just in the shadows, was a cat . . . calmly cleaning its paws.

"*Captain Black,*" Isobel exclaimed. "But how?"

Beckett shook his head, and grinned. "I'm certainly glad he turned up—though I have no idea how he did."

"He must have hitched a ride on Lennox's carriage," Worthington said. "After all, that cat does have a fondness for you, Lady Ravenwood."

At that, the cat looked up at his growing audience. His green eyes glowed, and as he walked toward Isobel, she could see bloodstains on some of the white patches of his fur. He stopped at her feet and meowed up at her. Isobel lifted him in her arms and snuggled him close.

"I guess Captain Mayfield was right—you *did* protect me." Isobel scratched his ears in gratitude. The cat purred and closed his eyes.

Beckett grinned. "Thanks for looking after her, old boy." He reached over and stroked the cat, too.

Isobel looked down at Sir Harry, then at Worthington. "Is he—?"

Worthington smiled. "Dead? No . . . the silly sap just fainted from the shock of it all. His wounds, while painful, are unfortunately not fatal. Still, he'll have some nice scars. Ought to fit right in with the lads at Newgate. I have 'connections' that will make sure Sir Harry is taken into custody." He sneered down at the unconscious heap at his feet. "I must admit, I never liked the man—"

Isobel took a step toward him. "But yet you did his bidding onboard ship. You kidnapped us because of him!"

"That I did, Lady Ravenwood, but as I explained to you, it was a business transaction. I had nothing personal against you or your husband. That is why I helped him to rescue you."

"Another business transaction?" Isobel asked, warily.

"Yes, Isobel," Beckett said.

"And what was the price?"

Beckett looked at her with a serious expression. "A thousand pounds. I thought it quite steep, myself—"

"What?" Isobel exclaimed.

Beckett smiled and pulled her close. "I'm teasing. I would have given up my entire fortune, my dear, if that was what Worthington had asked."

Now it was Worthington's turn to cry, "What? Damn me—if only I'd known!" He chuckled. "Ah, well, I still made a tidy profit. It should cover the ship's repairs. . . ."

He reached for Captain Black, and Isobel reluctantly handed him over.

"Now, you and your husband must be tired. You should get yourselves home. I and my men will take care of everything here."

"But this *is* Isobel's home." Beckett regarded her with concerned eyes. "Perhaps you want to stay here for the night?"

"No, Beckett, it is ours, now. But I don't want to stay here. Let us go to Covington Place."

Beckett kissed the top of her head. "I would like that very much indeed." Then he looked down at Sir Harry, who was still out cold, and addressed Worthington. "My wife and I are going home. Might I hire two of your men to drive us?"

Worthington held out his free hand and shook Beckett's. "Of course. Mr. Evandale and Mr. Martin will be happy to escort you. Best of luck to you, Ravenwood. My lady." He kissed Isobel's hand.

Isobel took one last look at Captain Black, and then she and Beckett headed out of the passageway. Soon they were rumbling down the road, away from Sir Harry and the nightmare that had almost come to pass.

But the nightmare wasn't over yet. There was still the false murder charge hanging over her head in London. Would Palmerston proceed with prosecuting her?

Oh, she couldn't think about that, now. She *wouldn't* think about it!

Beckett was alive. He was beside her, warm and strong and alive. She would let nothing else spoil this moment.

Beckett tipped her chin up towards him. His face looked unbearably handsome in the yellow moonlight.

"Tell me something, wife," he whispered.

"Yes?" She thrilled at the sound of his husky voice.

"Have you ever made love in a carriage?"

# Chapter Twenty-eight

Beckett knelt on the floor of the carriage before her, and in the dim light from the lanterns outside the windows, his eyes glowed like jewels. His hands reached up and slid her dress down over her shoulders.

Slowly, with exquisite control, he ran his hands over her breasts. Isobel heard her own intake of breath at the sensation of his skin on hers. Beckett closed his eyes as if she were hurting him, and he turned his head slightly as he caressed her with deft fingers.

His touch was maddeningly light as his fingertips drew circles around the sensitive pink tips. She held on to his arm for support as he took a breast in each strong hand and squeezed. With each thumb, he teased the hard peaks until Isobel heard herself gasping. And all the while, she stared at him, at this beautiful man's face with blue eyes that seared her like the heat of the sun.

Suddenly, his hands moved to the hem of her skirt. Beckett stopped for a moment, and the wicked promise in his eyes was almost too much for Isobel to bear. He smiled and pushed her skirt up over her knees. His hands explored her thighs, and Isobel arched her back and spread her legs, wanting so much for him to touch her. He pulled off her undergarments and threw them over his shoulder.

Beckett leaned forward and captured her mouth in a burning kiss while his hands stroked between her legs. Isobel felt herself becoming slick, and when his fingers went inside her she moaned and gripped his shoulder.

"I want to worship you," he whispered in her ear, and it sent shivers down her spine.

Beckett knelt back and dipped his head to kiss her inner thigh. He teased her with lips and tongue, bathing her like a cat. She jolted a little as his warm, wet tongue delved between her legs.

He raised his head and looked up at her. "It's alright, Isobel. Just lie back and let your husband love you."

His words sent a bittersweet pain through her heart.

It was dangerous to pretend that their love-making was anything more than a physical exchange. This dance of desire, this blinding pleasure was all that Beckett could give to her. She could not hope for more, no matter how he acted. He'd made that very clear long ago. If only she could keep her feelings at bay when he made love to her, and accept their coupling as pure physical sensation. But that was much more difficult than it seemed.

She closed her eyes as his mouth pleasured her. The sensation was so exquisite, so intense, she could never have imagined such beautiful wickedness. It was frighteningly intimate, almost too much to bear. But she would let him take her down this unknown road, for she was powerless to do anything else.

Beckett moved his mouth with a smooth rhythm, and Isobel heard her breathing quicken. The warmth spread through her body with maddening slowness, like cream travelling through coffee.

She spread her legs wider, her hands reaching down and holding his head as he worked her with his tongue. He lifted her legs over his shoulders. Isobel heard herself gasping. It sounded as if she were in terrible pain, so desperate was her response.

Two of his fingers slipped inside her and she thought she would lose her mind—the double pleasure was unbearable. She wanted to beg him to stop, but words were impossible.

Isobel moaned loudly and rocked her hips against his hand and mouth. Her head thrashed from side to side against the back of the seat. She bit her lip to keep from screaming.

Then, a mind-numbing pleasure seemed to rise and pass through her body from back to front. She felt it everywhere, in her legs, her arms, even her fingertips. It emptied her and yet filled her completely.

Beckett pulled his head away and she regarded him through half-lidded eyes. He unfastened his trousers and slid them down over his hips. Then he reached forward and lifted her towards him. He sat back on the opposite seat and lowered her down onto the hardness between his legs.

Instinctively, she wrapped her legs around his waist. His hands cupped her buttocks, his mouth joining with hers as their bodies moved together.

Isobel circled her arms around his neck as he

pumped into her. She closed her eyes and threw her head back as the pleasure of him filled her completely. Then she felt it coming again, that speeding, heady flood that would wash her away so completely, reducing her to skin and blood and sweat.

Beckett groaned and pounded into her with a blinding rhythm. His breathing was short. He moaned as he gripped her buttocks and thrust harder.

Isobel felt lightness overtake her—as though she were weightless and couldn't feel her body anymore. She cried out, bursting through glorious waves of pleasure.

Beckett groaned and crushed her to him, burying his face in her shoulder as he, too, found release.

They remained that way for awhile, unable to move. Then Beckett kissed her sweetly, tenderly, and looked into her eyes. He brushed the stray hair away from her eyes and stroked her face.

"You never answered my question, Isobel."

"What question?" she asked, dazedly.

"Have you ever made love in a carriage?"

She smiled. "Oh, yes."

"And how was it?"

"Very enjoyable."

"Hmm. Perhaps you'll want to go for more carriage rides, then. All about London. Perhaps we'll go through Hyde Park at five o'clock on a Saturday, and draw the curtains."

"We couldn't!"

"We couldn't draw the curtains? Wicked woman. Then everyone would see."

"No. We couldn't do *that* riding around Hyde Park . . . could we?"

Beckett pulled her to him and kissed her so

passionately, she thought he might make love to her again, right there.

"We shall see. Now, we should get ourselves dressed. I think we'll be entering the outskirts of London soon. And while I am entranced with your current state of *dishabille*, I'm afraid I'd rather not share the sight with Hartley when he opens my door."

Isobel laughed as he threw her undergarments at her head. Dutifully, she rearranged herself, all the while watching Beckett in the growing light as they neared the city.

When she was once again presentable, Isobel sat back on the seat and Beckett joined her. He encircled her with his arms and she leaned her head back against his chest. And though she hadn't meant to, relief and happiness overwhelmed her and she promptly dozed off.

Isobel rolled over and pulled the covers higher over her head, refusing to let the troubles of the world disturb her. She was certain that she could stay in this bed forever. It was so warm and soft. And yet, there was a niggling feeling in the back of her mind. *Where was she?*

Isobel sat upright in the bed and realized she was naked. Oh, yes. She was in Beckett's bed in the townhouse in Covington Place, *exactly* where this adventure had started.

But she didn't remember coming into the townhouse, let alone Beckett's bedroom. The last thing she remembered, she'd started to doze off in her husband's arms as they neared London. Could she have been asleep all this time?

Isobel looked up as a knock sounded at the door. It opened, and a pair of bright blue eyes peeked around it. They belonged to the most handsome man she had ever seen. Her heart did a flip-flop, and she smiled as her husband entered the room. Close on his heels was the most handsome dog she had ever seen.

"Monty!" She held her arms out to the dog as he bounded over to the bed, his great pink tongue lolling in his excited rush to see her. The shaggy brown dog skidded to a halt just before crashing into the bed, and plunked his rump down obediently, resting his chin on the coverlet.

"Good heavens, wife, I could have had Hartley with me instead of Monty." He pointed at her bare breasts and cringed in mock horror.

"But you didn't." Isobel scratched the dog's head and ears as the animal gazed at her with a look of unadulterated devotion. "Besides, I seem to have a strange habit of waking in your bed, wearing not even a stitch of clothing. Have I been asleep since the carriage?"

He sat next to her on the other side of the bed and leaned over to kiss her. She patted Monty's head and then turned her full attention to her husband. His hand absently fondled a breast. "Yes. I carried you in and put you to bed. Rather like the first night we met. Only last night I climbed in beside you in a most premeditated manner. Then I joined you in dreamland. It's no wonder we slept so soundly. We'd had a bit of an exhausting day, I think."

"Oh, Beckett . . . is it true? Is Sir Harry really out of our lives?" Isobel put her arms around his neck and he held her to him. It felt so good to be in his arms again that, for a moment, she thought she might still be dreaming.

"Yes, Isobel. I promise that no one will ever hurt you or take you away from me again."

"But what about Lord Palmerston?"

He put his hand to her lips. "We shall talk

about that later. Now you must get dressed. Alfred is due at any moment. Unless you prefer to entertain guests in all your natural glory."

Isobel gasped at the suggestion. "I shall reserve such wicked pleasures for my husband only."

"Wise woman. Perhaps I shall take you up on it tonight. I must confess, I have an urge to see you play the piano-forte thus."

Isobel laughed and pushed him away.

A knock sounded at the door, followed by Hartley's voice. "Lord Weston downstairs to see you, m'lord."

"Yes, Hartley, I'll be down directly," Beckett answered. With blue eyes sparkling at her, he kissed her hand softly. Then he rose from the bed and headed for the door, Monty obediently following. "Come down as soon as you're dressed. Oh, and there's something I've been meaning to tell you. Remind me, will you?"

Isobel nodded and watched them leave. She wondered at his words, trying to quell the uneasiness in her heart. Whatever he had to say to her, she would find out soon enough.

Isobel threw the covers back and walked to the washstand. Quickly she bathed and dressed. She chose a simple gown the same blue as Beckett's eyes. And as she headed downstairs, she thought to herself, there was one subject she would not bring up.

Since they'd been reunited, she'd been careful not to speak of love. Certainly, they had *made love* in the carriage, and they had made love before— but it was only the physical relations between husband and wife. She would not confuse it with real love.

It was enough, Isobel had decided, that she loved him. Though she would not speak of it, she would know that in her heart. And Beckett had an affection for her, even if he couldn't truly love her. He was her friend, and she was his.

She had so much to be thankful for. Beckett was alive, and Sir Harry was out of their lives. That alone was more than she could have hoped for, only a day ago.

Descending the staircase, she felt as she had on that first morning, hearing Beckett and Alfred talking and joking in the salon, and Caesar squawking noisily along with them. But, no—then she had been afraid. This time, she had nothing to fear. She was at peace with her marriage—a union that was and would always be an arrangement between friends.

Isobel entered the salon, and Alfred turned with an open smile on his face. He quickly crossed the room to greet her. Opening his arms, he embraced Isobel and kissed her cheek.

"Beckett has been telling me about your adventure. I must say, I can scarcely believe it."

"*Believe it! Believe it!*" Caesar shrieked from his cage.

"Oh, Caesar—*really*," Beckett admonished.

Monty barked his own disapproval at his feathered friend. Isobel laughed as the bird ignored both his master and the dog and kept squawking. "Nor can I, Alfred. Only yesterday, I was Sir Harry's prisoner and I feared that Beckett was dead. And now I am here at my husband's side where I belong."

"And what of Sir Harry?" Alfred asked. "As I was telling your husband, I acquired heaps of incriminating evidence against him while you were in Barbados. Blackmail, bribery, smuggling, swindling—I'm afraid the man is as dirty as a dung-heap. Where is he? Has he been taken off to the magistrate?"

"No." Beckett reached for a note on the table. He looked meaningfully at Isobel. "This came while you were sleeping, my dear. I thought you and Alfred would like to hear it."

Beckett opened it and began to read aloud as Isobel looked on.

Lord Ravenwood,

I write to you as the *Revenge* prepares to set sail for Jamaica. I hope you and your wife are well.

Sir Harry Lennox is dead. He was shot while trying to escape from Newgate. Fortunately, no one else was hurt in the escape attempt.

While he was in my custody, I was able to "persuade" Lennox to make a full confession regarding the murder of Edward Langley, the kidnapping of both you and your wife, and his manipulation of Lord Palmerston; a signed copy of which is attached. I will keep the other copy in a very safe place.

With Sir Harry's death, you and your wife are finally free of his threat.

Sincerely Yours,
Captain Richard Worthington
P.S. Captain Black sends his regards.

Isobel let out her breath, though she hadn't realized she'd been holding it in.

Beckett pulled her close and kissed the top of her head. "You're free, my dear. Lennox can never hurt you again."

Alfred reached for the letter. He looked over the confession and seemed satisfied. "Now that Lennox is dead, I should think the murder charge against Isobel will be dropped."

"Yes, I daresay it will. He was the one pulling Lord Palmerston's reins. I'm sure Palmerston wouldn't want it known that he'd accepted a bribe from Lennox in the matter."

Alfred turned to Isobel. "And what do you think, my dear lady? Do you think that justice has been served?"

She paused for a moment before answering. "Sir Harry was responsible for my parent's deaths, for the death of my guardian, and he almost took Beckett away from me. Sir Harry has earned his fate, and he has occupied more than enough time in my life. I have no more room for him. Only for happiness."

Beckett kissed her hand and he looked at her proudly.

"A remarkable woman you married, Beckett." Alfred smiled. "No doubt about it. Oh, and I have news about someone else who won't be bothering you anymore. Cordelia."

Beckett's eyebrows rose. "Oh?"

"She's gone and married Sir Montague Tate."

"*Tate*—why, he must be close to sixty!"

"He is. But Sir Montague must be in good health for he and Cordelia were—" he looked at Isobel "—forgive me, my dear, but they were caught in a disastrously close embrace at Lady Ashbrook's ball not two weeks past. I must take some responsibility, as I was the one who misinformed her about Tate's fortune. You see, Cordelia had set her cap for the Marquess of Rutledge, who, as you know, is enormously rich, and also a very good friend of mine. What could I do? I simply *had* to intervene.

"Word was that Cordelia was beside herself after the fiasco with Tate. But what could be done? Her father wisely forced the match. They were married in a little church in Huxley Lane, and removed to Sir Montague's modest—meaning *terribly small*— estate in Shropshire. Can you imagine Cordelia in Shropshire with all those sheep?"

Beckett shook his head, but smiled. "No, but I wish Cordelia and Sir Montague well in their marriage. As Isobel said, we must let go of the past. Let only happiness into our hearts."

Isobel looked at her husband. His beautiful face, his sea-blue eyes that bewitched and calmed her, and let her glimpse the beauty of his soul. He made her heart sing with joy.

Yes, she could let go of the past. She could let go of the need to be loved by Beckett. She would let only the happiness of loving him every day into her heart, and that would be enough.

It would have to be.

# Chapter Twenty-nine

Isobel stood in the doorway as Alfred prepared to leave. He and Beckett had enjoyed their morning together, and she had enjoyed watching them reunited. They were like brothers, and it warmed her heart to see her husband so happy.

"Well, I'm off." Alfred adjusted his hat so that it sat at precisely the perfect angle upon his head. "Now, you must promise to come for a visit. Great Aunt Withypoll is up from Chilton and she is driving me 'round the bend. Say you'll come. I am not averse to begging, you know."

Beckett chuckled and patted his friend on the back. "Don't worry, Alfred. We would be overjoyed to see the dear lady. I think she and Isobel will get along famously. Tomorrow evening, then."

"Splendid!" Alfred said, beaming. He bent to kiss Isobel's hand. "Until tomorrow, madam."

"Goodbye, Alfred."

"Take care of her, Beckett." Alfred winked at his friend. "Your mysterious bride is quite a treasure, you know."

"I know, Alfred."

"I say, Beckett—since you had such luck finding a bride in a rubbish heap, I thought to try to find one for myself in the same fashion. What do you say? Perhaps I shall start looking directly. Yes, that is exactly what I shall do!"

The door closed behind Alfred, leaving Beckett and Isobel alone. For a moment silence hung heavily between them, and they looked at each other as if not knowing what to say. An uneasiness gnawed at Isobel's heart and she knew she couldn't ignore it.

As they walked back into the salon, she took a deep breath and said, "You asked me to remind you . . . you had something you wanted to tell me." *It is probably nothing,* she told herself.

"Oh, yes . . . that. I'm glad you reminded me." Beckett steered her toward the sofa. "It is quite an important matter, you see. I am convinced it will have a profound effect on our future as husband and wife."

They sat down. Isobel stared at her hands folded in her lap and braced herself.

Dear Lord, was he going to tell her he wanted to live apart? After all they'd been through?

She would be strong. She had to prepare herself for such a thing. If that was what Beckett wanted, she would go back to Hampton Park and live out her days alone.

"Isobel—" Beckett gently lifted her chin up so that she looked into his eyes.

*Oh, how could she bear it?*

"What I want to say is . . . well, I have been try-

307

ing to make something plain to you for quite some time, now. I tried to tell you when you came to my cell on the ship, but I was a bloody coward and I couldn't say it properly. Then I tried to say it on the deck just before they were to hang me, but as you know, I was very rudely interrupted. But it is important, and though it is difficult to say—"

"Oh, don't say it, please," she whispered, closing her eyes. As if that would do any good at all. It would be better to close her ears.

"*Don't* say it?" Beckett said, sounding perplexed. "But I really feel that I must, my dear."

"Oh, please, *please*, I beg you not to. For *my* sake."

"For *your* sake? But it is for your sake that I want to say it. And for my sake that I must. I assure you, this is much more difficult for me than it is for you, Isobel."

"I doubt it," she whispered.

Beckett grabbed her shoulders. Reluctantly she faced him, looking into the depths of his eyes as he shook her slightly.

"Isobel . . . you are making it increasingly impossible to tell you that I love you."

She stared at him in shock.

"You *what* me?"

"No, I don't *what* you, my dear. I *love* you. That is what I've been trying to say. I love you! Irrefutably, indisputably, and most conclusively. There. What do you have to say to that?"

Isobel didn't bother trying to hold back the tears that filled her eyes. They were tears of love.

Irrefutably, and indisputably.

"Oh, Beckett!" She threw her arms around his neck and laughed and cried and hugged him tightly as he hugged her. "I love you, too."

"I must say that I had my suspicions."

She pulled away and whacked his arm, but they were both laughing. Then, he touched his lips to hers in a kiss that echoed his words, and she felt both of them flowing into it—sharing their love with open hearts.

Beckett broke the kiss and stroked her face. His eyes glowed warm and clear like the Bajan sea. "I have loved you far longer than I knew, Isobel. I was simply too afraid of feeling anything so deep . . . so frighteningly pure. I'd been burnt by the flame of love with Cordelia. It seemed foolish to play with fire after that.

"But when I was in that cell, I had an epiphany. I realized that I had been fighting a losing battle with my heart. That was why it ached so unbearably when I thought of losing you. I realized true love is a prize reserved for those willing to give themselves up to it with an open heart. And I speak from experience."

Isobel sniffed and wiped her nose with Beckett's handkerchief. "I believe I was fighting the same battle myself—knowing that I loved you more than life, and trying to convince my heart to change its mind about the matter. As you discovered, it was a fruitless attempt."

Beckett smiled and pulled her close in his arms. "Well, I, for one, am glad."

"Oh, Beckett . . . I'm the happiest woman on Earth!"

"Well, that's good, because I am the happiest man on earth. And it is only fitting that the happiest man and the happiest woman should be married to each other." He kissed her nose. "Now, let me take you to bed, and show you *exactly* how much I love you."

Isobel smiled at his devilish grin and sparkling eyes. "Beckett—it's the middle of the afternoon!"

He stood up and swept her up into his arms, and she squealed and kicked half-heartedly.

"I know what time it is, my dear. And by my calculations, we can make love for close to three hours before Martha rings the bell for tea." Beckett bent his head and kissed her divinely. "Unless, of course, you'd prefer that carriage ride around Hyde Park. . . ."

# JAGUAR EYES

# Casey Claybourne

Daniel Heywood ventures into the wilds of the Amazon, determined to leave his mark on science. Wounded by Indians shortly into his journey, he is rescued by a beautiful woman with the longest legs he's ever seen. As she nurses him back to health, Daniel realizes he has stumbled upon an undiscovered civilization. But he cannot explain the way his heart skips a beat when he looks into the captivating beauty's gold-green eyes. When she returns with him to England, she wonders if she is really the object of his affections—or a subject in his experiment. The answer lies in Daniel's willingness to leave convention behind for a love as lush as the Amazon jungle.

___52284-5                                    $5.50 US/$6.50 CAN

# The Sword and the Flame

## Patricia Phillips

The fire that rages in Adele St. Clare is unquenchable. The feisty redhead burns with anger when King John decrees she marry against her will. Then her bridal escort arrives—Rafe De Montford—and the handsome swordsman ignites something hotter. But Rafe has been ordered to deliver her unto a betrothed she cannot even respect—let alone love. But Rafe's smoldering glances capture her heart, and with one of his fiery kisses, Adele knows that from these sparks of desire will leap the flame of a love everlasting.

## Lair of the Wolf

Also includes the seventh installment of *Lair of the Wolf*, a serialized romance set in medieval Wales. Be sure to look for future chapters of this exciting story featured in Leisure books and written by the industry's top authors.

# In Trouble's Arms
## Ronda Thompson

Loreen Matland is very clear. If the man who answers her ad for a husband is ugly as a mud fence, she'll keep him. If not, she'll fill his hide full of buckshot. Unfortunately, Jake Winslow is handsome. Lori knows that good-looking men are trouble, and Jake proves no exception. Of course, she hasn't been entirely honest with him, either. She has difficulties enough to make his flight from the law seem like a ride through the prairie. But the Texas Matlands don't give up, even to dangerous men with whiskey-smooth voices. And yet, in Jake's warm strong arms, Lori knows he is just what she needs—for her farm, her family, and her heart.

# Lair of the Wolf

Also includes the sixth installment of *Lair of the Wolf*, a serialized romance set in medieval Wales. Be sure to look for future chapters of this exciting story featured in Leisure books and written by the industry's top authors.

___4716-0                                    $5.99 US/$6.99 CAN

# LOVING CHARITY — CATHERINE ARCHIBALD

Vengeance is Jason Wade's only purpose; the Boston lawyer has sworn to avenge his wife's death. Tracking her suspected killer to Wisconsin, he knows that to entertain a flirtation with the lovely Charity Applegate is to court disaster. But her smile weakens his resolve and her honesty breaks down his defenses until Jason wonders if the path to salvation lies not in retribution, but in loving Charity.

On the eve of the Civil War, Charity Applegate accepts the risks involved in following one's heart. Her Quaker family aids the underground railroad, and the arrival of Jason Wade could expose them all. But caught in his passionate embrace, Charity realizes he challenges the strength of her courage even further—by daring her to trust him. And she knows she will have to make a great leap of faith for the best reward for all: love.

___4704-7                                          $4.99 US/$5.99 CAN

**Dorchester Publishing Co., Inc.**
**P.O. Box 6640**
**Wayne, PA 19087-8640**

Please add $1.75 for shipping and handling for the first book and $.50 for each book thereafter. NY, NYC, and PA residents, please add appropriate sales tax. No cash, stamps, or C.O.D.s. All orders shipped within 6 weeks via postal service book rate. Canadian orders require $2.00 extra postage and must be paid in U.S. dollars through a U.S. banking facility.

Name_____
Address_____
City_____ State_____ Zip_____
I have enclosed $_____ in payment for the checked book(s).
Payment <u>must</u> accompany all orders. ❏ Please send a free catalog.

# THE GENTLE SEASON

## DIA HUNTER

Nicodemus Turner is in a bind. Not only has the handsome gambler just found out that he has a daughter he's never met, but in order to get custody he has six months to become a proper father and marry. And while Nick is head-over-heels in love with his best friend Alewine Jones, the stubborn lady freighter doesn't take kindly to the notion of a wedding. The solution: a poker game where the prize will be a full house. Nick is Aly's closest companion, her best fishing partner, and he can make her insides go mushy with one lingering glance. That still doesn't mean she will up and marry him. But that mushy feeling comes back every time she looks into Nick's eyes. Suddenly Aly realizes that Nick has won more than her hand, he's won her heart.

___4705-5 $4.99 US/$5.99 CAN

**Dorchester Publishing Co., Inc.**
**P.O. Box 6640**
**Wayne, PA 19087-8640**

# Taming Angelica

## Alice Chambers

What is the point in having beauty and wealth if one can't do what one wants because of one's gender? Angelica doesn't know, but she plans on overcoming it. Suffragette and debutante, Angelica has nothing if not will. Lord William Claridge has a wont to gamble and enjoys training Thoroughbreds, but his older brother has tightened the family's purse strings. Strapped for cash, the handsome rake decides to resort to the unthinkable: Marry. For money. But when his mark turns out to be a more spirited filly than he has ever before saddled, he feels his heart bucking wildly. Suddenly, much more is on the line than his pocketbook. And the answer still comes down to . . . taming Angelica.

\_\_\_4682-2                    $4.99 US/$5.99 CAN

# GABRIEL'S FIRE

## GLORIA PEDERSEN

The War of 1812 rages. Nantucket has English soldiers garrisoned on its shores. Yet one woman risks the wrath of the British authorities to save an American captain. Serenity Penn knows her actions threaten the peace of her island, but as Gabriel Harrowe's gray eyes flash with summer lightning, she knows there is nothing neutral about the burning need the sailor arouses in her. Gabriel has vowed never to trust a pair of beguiling eyes again. But as the lovely Quaker woman nurses him back to health, his traitorous body threatens mutiny. Gazing into her blazing blue eyes, he longs to swear allegiance to the innocent beauty. The American privateer has found a woman worthy of his loyalty, and with the redcoats in pursuit, he knows their union will be his salvation.

___4669-5                                          $4.99 US/$5.99 CAN

**Dorchester Publishing Co., Inc.**
**P.O. Box 6640**
**Wayne, PA 19087-8640**

Please add $1.75 for shipping and handling for the first book and $.50 for each book thereafter. NY, NYC, and PA residents, please add appropriate sales tax. No cash, stamps, or C.O.D.s. All orders shipped within 6 weeks via postal service book rate. Canadian orders require $2.00 extra postage and must be paid in U.S. dollars through a U.S. banking facility.

Name_____
Address_____
City_____State_____Zip_____
I have enclosed $_____ in payment for the checked book(s).
Payment <u>must</u> accompany all orders. ❏ Please send a free catalog.
    CHECK OUT OUR WEBSITE! www.dorchesterpub.com

# Upon a Moon-Dark Moor

# Rebecca Brandewyne

From the day Draco sweeps into Highclyffe Hall, Maggie knows he is her soulmate; the two are kindred spirits, both as mysterious and untamable as the wild moors of the rocky Cornish coast. Inexplicably drawn to this son of a Gypsy girl and an English ne'er-do-well, Maggie surrenders herself to his embrace. Hand in hand, they explore the unfathomable depths of their passion. But as the seeds of their desire grow into an irrefutable love, its consequences threaten to destroy their union. Only together can Maggie and Draco overcome the whispered scandals that haunt them and carve a future for their love.

___52336-1                                     $5.50 US/$6.50 CAN

# Bewitching the Baron

## Lisa Cach

Valerian has always known before that she will never marry. While the townsfolk of her Yorkshire village are grateful for her abilities, the price of her gift is solitude. But it never bothered her until now. Nathaniel Warrington is the new baron of Ravenall, and he has never wanted anything the way he desires his people's enigmatic healer. Her exotic beauty fans flames in him that feel unnaturally fierce. Their first kiss flares hotter still. Opposed by those who seek to destroy her, compelled by a love that will never die, Nathaniel fights to earn the lone beauty's trust. And Valerian will learn the only thing more dangerous—or heavenly—than bewitching a baron, is being bewitched by one.

\_\_52368-X                                      $5.50 US/$6.50 CAN